Margins

DAVID KRANES

 Margins

Alfred A. Knopf   NEW YORK   1972

THIS IS A BORZOI BOOK
PUBLISHED BY ALFRED A. KNOPF, INC.

Copyright © 1972 by David Kranes
All rights reserved under International and Pan-American
Copyright Conventions. Published in the United States
by Alfred A. Knopf, Inc., New York, and simultaneously in
Canada by Random House of Canada Limited, Toronto.
Distributed by Random House, Inc., New York.

Library of Congress Cataloging in Publication Data
Kranes, David. Margins.
I. Title.
PZ4.K89628Mar [PS3561.R26] 813'.5'4 72–2240
ISBN *0–394–47920–3*

Manufactured in the United States of America

FIRST EDITION

for CAROL

Margins

i

The river smelled like hair. Mark thought that. It smelled like wet feathers and a woman's hair. He watched some gulls, scarcely shapes yet, overglide it, and thought of Jan. Her back had looked like cookie batter when he'd woken beside her. Why was he waking earlier now every morning? He looked down at the shadows on his wrists, then almost into them. He saw the corners of Jan's bedroom walls. His mind swagged. Jan had stapled a note to his T-shirt before she'd come to sleep, and he'd heard himself crinkle when he'd first stretched and roused. It had said, "Love: I worry about danger. J." And of course she was right. Mark felt the early trucks on the West Side Drive shake the crushed glass under the tar, then buzz the trunk of his spine.

He backed slightly away and squatted. Somehow, he hoped, if he were nearer the ground, there would be quicker light. Or more warmth. A piece of paper just in front of him looked slightly phosphorous—like a bulb—and he stretched, reached out and took it. All the print except a lower Broadway address near Twelfth Street had been bled off. Mark wadded the paper into a ball and pressed it between his hands. It felt like cartilage: like kelp or a small crab's shell. He smelled sand. Maybe he would go to where the address was. Maybe he would meet someone new. Maybe someone would discover him—for something. Maybe the wife and daughter he had not seen for fifteen years would be there selling fishnets or machine parts or Greek pastries or leather goods. Maybe . . . He stood up.

There was a sound in the dark above him: faint, toylike, but whirring, like a helicopter. Mark stayed and listened until it went. Then he turned in. He crossed the grass toward the city, jogged across the West Side Drive and moved into Riverside Park. He walked quietly. He heard his shoes breaking bottleglass and seedpods on the walk and imagined shapes not far from him, perhaps under shrubbery, shooting up. He passed an old man under a bush. The man wore thick black glasses and slept. Or was dead. Had he sold his eyes to get drink? Mark looked back toward the river. He looked up the park hill. Everything where he stood now, here on the edges, appeared hammered to him, whipped and frayed.

He had an image of ragshapes shaking in a wind the color of cold broth. When he checked the skyline, the city seemed all torn; its walls temporary and makeshift. And all the grass appeared patched. And the traffic shook. And even the river, that part of it which he carried in his head, repeated itself only in flat slaps.

Beyond the border, though, inside and beyond, behind, all seemed stable and to have place. No perimetrical wildness. Things were calm. There was gravity. There were whole blocks of stone. On Fifth Avenue, fountains climbed, stopped, returned. They were balanced; they were designed. And where the air here on the river fringes smelled like weeds, the inside air smelled prepared, like imitation leather gloves on the glove counter at Ohrbach's. Mark rolled the neck up on his Irish knit and moved on up the hillside and stairs; then in.

Inside he wandered. The day was free; he had no shooting to do. And October. Fall. Free fall. He smiled; he saw himself dropping past pretzel stands and umbrella salesmen, through street sprinklers and elevator shafts, and smiled again. He watched some Spanish children playing games of tetherball. From somewhere—the subway—rose a piano roll. He passed the Guggenheim and felt giddy. The city slipped and filled with strange eddyings. On the East Side, everyone seemed moving west. He taxied across the park. On the West Side, everyone moved east. Traveling up Broadway toward Columbia, he seemed to go against the general traffic, which was going down. On the campus, a strange fraction wind scattered fountain water like damp confetti over the stairs. Mark took a local subway downtown, which filled, stop by stop, to packing until Forty-second Street, where it emptied and he was left almost alone. He rode to West Fourth Street, where he got out and wandered east. Scraps—paper again and celluloid cigar tubes—swirled everywhere on the walks, tracing larger and larger circles, spiraling out. It seemed to Mark that his blood too moved out, that it was unusually close to the surface of his skin, winding up and down his frame through some vascular system of gradually expanding coils. He wanted coffee.

He bought a copy of the *Village Voice*. There was a counter, large enough only for the window to contain "Lunch" in white paint, and he went in. There was a very young girl at a miniature sink behind the counter rinsing white mugs, all of which seemed webbed with hairline cracks which showed up with the water on them. Mark ordered.

"You want a pastry or anything?"

"Just the coffee."

A blind man with a harnessed dog, four seats away, ate lime- and squash-colored melon balls with a spoon. Mark watched him while the coffee cooled, then read the "Public Notice" ads in the *Voice*: "Terry. There are Buddhist gardens hidden in this city. Can you find them? Love, Sheila." One even was addressed to him: "Mark. Please! Becky." *Becky*? Yes, that was possible. Someone named Becky might. *Rebecca*. Like *Rachel*. Like the daughter he had known only eighteen months, then not seen for nearly that many years—well, fifteen: Rachel. Rachel and Rebecca: they would be friends. They would be dark, have dark hair, like Rachel's mother, like Heidi, dark hair and long—long and with the smell somewhere in it of clove. Well.

The man with the dog got up and left. A melon ball dropped, like a soft orange eye, from his lap.

"Do you know who he is?" The counter girl approached him with a stained damp towel and a cup.

"The blind fellow?" Mark asked.

"He used to be famous," she said.

"For what?" Mark could see thin gray shoulderblades under her open blue uniform.

"I don't know," she said. "For basketball or something, people say he played. But they don't say what. They just say he was famous—and he played." She looked at him.

"What hours do you work?" Mark asked her.

"What do you mean?"

He paused. The coffee had a tinted green slick cooled on its surface.

"Why do you want to find out?"

". . . I don't know." He paid for his coffee and started away.

"Hey—look—it's all right. Look, I didn't mean to be rude or anything. Two-thirty! I get off at two-thirty! Did you want to take me somewhere? I had one thing on—well, possibly, but . . ."

Mark had no idea why he'd asked her. She couldn't have been more than nineteen. What was Jan's word? *Danger.* The random, the accidental, the strange; that old need surfaced for the first time since his divorce—*danger*, as good a word as any. He walked around the corner. Maybe at 2:30 he'd come back. The famous blind man was there, talking to himself on the other side of the street, his hands moving like mice, climbing the air, miming what for some reason seemed to Mark an acceptance speech. Mark remembered the paper.

He rechecked the Broadway address. It was close. He had wandered near somehow. He looked at the paper in his hand, studied the boxes which the folds made, gathered it again into a packet, slipped it into his pants. He remembered the scrap's performance above the river's frayed scum. He remembered Jan's note and words. He remembered an apartment on West End Avenue where he had once lived and where the formica in the kitchenette smelled like colored construction paper and flour paste, where murky pigeons mimicked all inside conversations from their ledges. Then he moved.

He had guessed an antique store, and he was close; it was the Strand, a secondhand bookstore he had seen, even browsed, before. Inside it smelled like an enormous train terminal in a foreign country, like that and old bindery threads. Everything had a washed finish, even sounds. It was cavernous, full of the pale unreal. Book piles rose and slanted against gravity. Browsers seemed impossible distances away. Blades of sun jackknifed, shifting position suddenly on what appeared a succession of dust-sheer draperies in air. Mark moved to a counter and began to pick up and scan books. He felt no actual objective or intent, only that he should. Words like tobacco scents drifted up, sensory only, without text—books on puppet making, Chinese wars, electrical circuiting in incubator designs: words like "clevis" or "snook" or "intrados." If they meant anything, they all seemed sexual to him somehow, like the weight of a dictionary to a child. He picked up an uncovered dull-maroon volume of Camus's *1942–1951 Notebooks* and began to shuffle it in the same way. Something like splinters or jots flew up and slowed him down, brought him open on a single page.

His senses localized, caught. He saw a woman's handwriting: marks, blue words in the margins, scratched there in good ink and always slanted. They formed wedges beside the print, blades pulling him in. Mark thought at first they were shorthand, rushed stenography. There seemed an almost violent motion in the pen, as if it had had to move at unnatural and impulsive speeds to keep the ink and the responses from pooling, from making ink bogs which swallowed up all the words. Yet they were there, even with such assaulting energy: messages, words, fragments, on almost every page, fragments unquestionably in a woman's hand. Mark could almost catch a brailled network of veins over the thin bones at her wrist: "I have never met a man who could take me with him," she had set down in response to something by Camus. Mark shut the book.

He saw a crater inside his head. He saw small liquid fires there, unwinding strange heat, throwing up febrile shapes against the walls. There was a sudden vacating of time. A score, nearly, of years caught in an updraft and were gone, mechanisms gone with them. Though he had never seen the book before, Mark felt his chest muscles tighten. Though he had no idea who the woman was or might be, he felt his temples warm like two electrical points. It became hard to breathe. He felt the grain of the Camus book with both thumbs. He squeezed the cover and felt the pressure of his touch travel along his tendons to his forearms. His hair seemed to gain weight, to grow more wiry at its ends, particularly behind his head. He tried to open up the book again.

Without looking either down or directly at it, he pressed a forefinger against the text. The pages felt like sharp strings. They were instrument wires, hard and ungiving. One cut him. He sucked his finger and tried again. The book opened but then shut. He worried that he might have left a pinprick of blood somewhere on her words, but he had no idea of the page. It was absurd: marginalia. There suddenly was marginalia as alive to him as a girl named Cynthia, whom he had, one summer when he was fourteen, once groped toward in a stifling and spidery boathouse where she waited for him in the dark without her bathing top, stretched out on half-inflated plastic seahorses. It made no sense. Still—still, maybe there was a bookplate glued to the cover; a name, an address inside, some number.

"Can I help you, sir?"

"What?"

"Would you like that book?"

"Oh, no. . . . No. . . . Thanks."

The bookman in his ashgreen cardigan shuttled away. He stopped and redistributed books, some onto tables, others onto a wheeled cart. He whistled Schubert or Schumann or something like that, a very cool, practiced control of notes, music which, whatever time of day, would always seem like late afternoon. Had he read all these books? Mark wondered. Had he read her words? A water main on the street outside broke and the water danced there in the sun.

Mark became rigid; his eyes clouded. What was he doing here—following accidental winds, taped scraps? What were all these drifts of fading glue and dust? Couldn't he just check inside the cover for a name and, if he found one, buy the book, put it in a plain paper bag, not even meet her, just *mail* it? Was that unmanageable? But he had tears in his eyes. His mind screamed, cursed at itself: *Stupid ass, nostalgic playacting bastard—stop!* But his fingertips, quiet on the coverprint of the book, swore they felt her. The outer nerves *said* that she was there, moving, under: Cynthia on the boathouse seahorses saying his name, "Mark, Mark," as if it were a magic question in the dark; Carmen Mendez when he was seventeen—a whore ("Carmen Mendez, Apt. 7-G, 206 W. 47th St.") who had buzzed him in but never seen him, because he waited nearly two hours frozen in the lobby imagining her moving in her bed seven floors above until everything happened in his mind and he went: those senses drowned his pores. He pushed the book back toward the table, felt it touch, felt his fingers leave it, turned and left.

He hurried; he got away. In the subway vibrating down to Canal Street, he sat alone in the end car, measuring the length of walls and seats, thinking about the book. He found himself in an overhead ad toward the other end. He was wearing a white tennis sweater, smiling, smoking. Mark remembered the sweater, but had forgotten the ad; too many, too many ads and commercials these last years. Then under him, under his ad, in bold graffiti, was a giant cleaver, with "Butchers" magic-marked along its handle and the members' signatures in a fat column down its blade—one girl, "Benita," announcing herself in lipstick at the bottom of the list. Mark imagined her, what it must be like to be had by seven guys calling themselves "Butchers." The car smelled suddenly like animal hide, then, off and on, of newsprint and of tar. There were the entrails of morning papers along the floor and benches.

From Canal Street, he walked to Mott and then to a favorite place called Hong Fat's: "Famous Noodles." Around him were the sounds of what seemed dislocated tropical birds and church carillons playing what he took to be Chinese hymns. Far away, down by the Bowery, a policeman sat quietly on his horse. Mark thought he could see fish scales on the street.

Hong Fat's was full. The man whom Mark had always taken to be Hong Fat himself seated him at a table with an old, nearly bald, freckle-headed Chinese and a younger Caucasian woman, who kept licking her fingers, brushing scallion flecks from her lap and taking refuge in her napkin. Mark, diagonally across from her and beside the Chinese, ordered a large bowl of duck won ton, took out a ballpoint pen and began to make angled lines on his napkin while he waited. He drew a frame there, made margins.

The Chinese got up and left without paying, and the woman seemed to relax. She was eating her lo-mein noodles with a fork, losing pieces of bean sprout and scallion onto the table and her lap. Mark's won ton arrived, and he ladled some from the big bowl to the small, sensing the woman watching him. He looked up.

"It always makes me nervous to eat with a Chinese," she said to him, wiping the corners of her mouth with her napkin.

"It's been really rough lately," she started in again. "This guy's been giving me a time. You wouldn't believe it. It's incredible. He's married. Yeah, and you can bet it was four months before I found that out. Two kids. You know, the usual thing. So—the usual thing—he says he's going to leave her, says it's all over, no future. He gets his piece, then goes home. I don't know what to believe any more, you know. I just don't. The one guy I was really in love with eight years ago got sent up for life. And now that's all over. This guy now's about the sixth one. I don't know. I come down here and eat Chinese food because if I ate somewhere else I'd get really fat and I can't afford it. But it really scares me eating with a Chinese."

Mark nodded. He cut a won ton with the edge of his spoon. He would like to bring the girl in the margins here sometime when he knew it wasn't crowded. He would like to order special things for her; she was the type, he bet, that would appreciate it: snails, abalone, and then, then afterward, take her for dessert to his favorite pastry shop, buy her egg custard.

"Did you hear what I said?" She was staring at him.

Mark looked up. "Yes, yes, I did," he said.

— *12* —

She looked straight at him, resentfully. She looked as if she were about to challenge him. Instead she wiped her mouth, dipped her head and took another forkful of noodles. Mark turned back to his soup. Then suddenly she was gagging, choking there across from him, strands of noodle barked out on the table in front of her. She seemed unable to get air. Her eyes were blown, tearful; her face seemed alternately to swell with redness, then grow pale. She started slamming her fork against the table, but Mark somehow could only sit and watch, could only pace the rhythm of her fork hammering against the aluminum edge.

Everyone stared. She stood. She started staggering around the small room, bumping from table to table, silverware clutched hard, prongs up, in her fist, but no one moved. Mark began to rise. Then someone shouted something in Chinese and Hong Fat arrived from the kitchen to grab and hold her before she stabbed someone with her fork.

Mark, up at his place now, saw her eyes. He saw her watch Hong Fat coming to station her. He saw an unheard scream spiral wildly around her whites, saw the tear ducts suddenly gorge, tears drain from them down her cheeks, some kind of plea bubbling through all the wash, hurled almost directly at him. Hong Fat had her now, had her clamped hard. Then he was forcing tea into her mouth, another waiter holding her arms. She went limp. Her eyes shut. Whatever had been choking her somehow washed out and she was breathing again. But she would not open her eyes for Mark or Hong Fat, or his waiter, or anyone. Only outside sounds and the crisp occasional static of frying from the kitchen broke. Everybody was waiting.

"O.K., *eat*," Hong Fat announced, and then delivered her to Mark—because he was there, poised. He wanted to protest, but he took her shoulders anyway, and seated her. The shoulders felt soft, irregular, lumpy, like small overripe gourds, and before he released her, she crossed a damp hand up across her flattish chest and clamped him there. He remained a moment, then withdrew, took his hand away. She ate the rest of the meal with her eyes shut, never spilling a sprout. Neither Mark nor the woman talked. Finally she rose, with her eyes still blank, set two dollar bills on the table and left.

Mark watched the diced pieces of scallion agitate slightly in the small steam of his soup. He pushed some under with his white porcelain spoon, removed the spoon and watched them rise. He pushed a fat pocky won-ton noodle around the circle of his bowl, drawn by the changing patterns of the steam. He picked a piece of duck up on his spoon and stared at it, fixed on the wrenched gristle by the bone. He lowered the duckmeat back into the broth, carefully setting it on a large leaf of watercress. He mused that perhaps if he was gentle, the watercress would bloom or the duckmeat croak at him. Mark waking up in the middle of the night once before they were married to find Heidi sitting up beside him, quietly crying: watery sounds which she said he would not understand but were joy. He set two more bills very gently on the woman's money already on the table before he caught a cab back to Twelfth Street and the Strand.

The book was gone. Mark assumed it had been covered up, other browsers, and began to check each book, stacking them systematically to not repeat. He checked two nearby tables the same way. Nothing: no Camus, no woman wedging herself there in blue beside Camus. She had left. *They* had left. She had taken Camus with her. They were living on the coast of Algeria somewhere, and she was making him incredibly happy. Sometimes they were brutal to one another, but . . . Mark was in the boathouse again, trembling. He was clutching ebony in a phonebooth. He saw women's shapes falling irretrievably from sight through years of sea-horse rings: waitresses, wives, infants. He found the green-cardiganed man.

"There was this book," Mark found himself almost pleading. "It was by Camus."

"Which one?"

"Which—his notebook!"

"Years?"

"I don't . . . maroon!"

The man sneered at him.

"It was maroon! The cover! Maroon. Maroon cover and writing! Notes. Notation. All in the margins. It was . . ."

"Let's see. . . ." The man dealt books off like cards. "Maroon. Maroon cover—*'42-'51 Notebooks.* Camus. That was right around . . ." There was something sleight-of-hand about the way he checked, turned the titles over. "Camus . . ." He moved counterclockwise around the table, whis-tling again, afternoon music. Mark was sure he could produce the book, positive. "Well," the man said with unquestion-able definition, "it appears to have been bought!"

"What?"

"It appears—"

"But it was on this table."

"Yes. Nevertheless, it appears—"

"Two hours ago! Less!"

"It appears to have been bought!"

The man turned and moved away, back toward the front counter. Mark watched him. He sailed; he crossed the dust patterns like water, bobbing, tilting, afloat, rounding cor-ner markers, tacking the counters like buoys. Mark felt himself almost being blown backward and away. The man seemed as weightless as frayed thread, light as dust. Mark pushed himself forward.

"Well, then, do you have records?" The man's back was to him. He moved through a hinged counterspace and brought the counter down between them before he turned.

"No; just books."

"No; I mean *of*. Records *of*. Of who might have bought the book."

"Sir"—the bookman's breath smelled like mildew. " . . . Sir, I'd suggest that if the book was so important to you, that you should have bought it two hours ago. When you were here first." He begin to catalogue. Mark's fists clenched. He held his breath and chewed lightly on the inside of his cheek. The man kept turning over volumes, stamping something inside them, writing figures under the stamp in soft pencil. His brow was moist; his nose red.

"Look . . ." Mark couldn't seem to control his own pressing.

"Look, yourself! Why don't you just leave?"

Mark turned and walked away to avoid striking out or shouting. He walked to a clifflike corner of books and faced into it, breathing hard, both hands up over his eyes. He worked to regulate his breath; he lowered his hands gradually, made his tension an exercise. Titles scurried in front of him, scribbling without sense. As a child, he had used letter blocks that way, jumbling them again and again to work out an anger, just using the blocks and the letters, never making words. He could do that. He could fasten himself that way: use letters as nails, words as staples.

Finally he took a single book in. It was a fat, falling-apart, badly bound history of theatrical costuming. He slipped it from the shelf and began to thumb. He studied the plates: pictures fifth century B.C., Greek pottery, low-comedy phalluses and masks. The book chaptered itself by types. Mark looked over the centuries of "Hero Costumes," "Buffoon Costumes," "Lover Costumes," "Lunatics." The final plate in the book was ripped, its description torn off. There was no way of knowing what it was an example of. Shown only was a photo of what appeared to be a New York store window filled with clothed mannequins. Mark guessed that the picture had been taken in the early 1930's, shortly after the year of his birth.

He set the costume book back and took a breath. He turned. From his corner, he could look out across the granulated sun-supports to the front desk where the bookman thumped his stamp into covers, as regular as a heartbeat. Mark's mind set out bold labels in a sequence: "Faggot," "Prick," "Pimp," but they all curled and dusted in the space. There seemed, somehow, to be absolutely no moisture in the store. Even his teeth felt dry. He had an image of himself never leaving this corner, becoming as squeezed as everything else, vestigial, secondhand. He saw others coming to him there, taking hold of a finger, his hand, his hair, having it come off into theirs—like some loose page in a book. It was possible, he thought, for him never again to move, for him to simply, day-by-day, desiccate, be consumed slowly by flanks of silverfish.

Then, from his binding, Mark saw someone a half-dozen tables away, someone holding what appeared, in the dusty intervening light, to be a maroon-covered book. He moved forward. His throat felt talcumed, his lips chapped. The man with the book was small, dwarfish nearly. He wore absolutely clear wire-rimmed glasses and his hair, weightless and white as milkweed, seemed to float, air-supported, around his head. He wore a frayed Chesterfield coat which seemed, in fit and size, as if it could never have been his own.

Mark approached, and the maroon grew sure. And there were letters in blue, a title, the right words. The man turned pages forward, then back. His brow wrinkled. He rubbed his ears. Mark played at considering books on the tabletop between them, trying to catch, in the man's expressions or stance, how intent he seemed. But there was no pattern to the way he studied the book. He would look ahead, then turn back, then stare off across the dust, his eyes turned in. The word "henchman" floated up into Mark's mind. It was a silly word, but Mark would not let the man have the book.

He thought of just asking: "Oh, could I see that book? Are you through with it? Could I have it, please?" but that might make the book seem more than personally valuable. The man might never, then, give it up. He considered staging an accident: bumping into the little man, knocking him down, dislodging the book, snatching the book and running off. But the man looked so frail. Mark would have dreams of dead moths wearing Chesterfields.

So, instead, Mark picked up a random title and started thumbing it. He played it quietly: stop at a page, head forward into words, pause, sounds, almost mute groans of intense interest and surprise, sounds unattached to words. Soon the man began to glance across at him.

"Jesus!" Mark muttered, then turned a page, feigning disbelief. He could just barely see the man study him. Mark shook his head from side to side, telegraphing private incredulity. "Incredible!" he said, making sure it seemed private; then, after a pause of three or four seconds, he repeated, "Incredible!"

"What?" The man rolled small red eyes barely over his wire rims. "What is it?"

Mark pretended not to hear. He turned another page. "Christ!"

"What have you *got?*" the man asked him.

Mark paused, then jerked his head from its attention in the book. He played distraction. "Excuse me?"

"What did you find?"

"Where?"

"In the book." With a forefinger, he pressed the glasses flat against the first rising of his nose.

"Oh . . ." Mark shook his head. "Nothing . . .. nothing." He turned his body forty-five degrees away and read on— doing it all with eyes and brow now, giving the appearance of taking great care not to utter a word or sound. He made his brow contract, then expand; he exploded his eyes, wrenched his lashes and brows.

The man cleared his throat, an amazing huskiness for his size. "Could I see that when you're through?" he asked.

"Excuse me?" Mark raised his eyes again, but did not move his head.

"I'd apperciate seeing that book when you're through with it," the man said.

"Oh . . ." Mark lowered his eyes again. ". . . Sure." He could feel the man swaying. Mark timed it out. Suddenly he dropped his jaw, then shot a hand to his open mouth to cover it. He worried suddenly that he might be pushing the act too far. Slowly he closed the book, bringing his thumbs together, leaving them there in precise line so that the book remained open just a crack. He drew all expression inward, tried to make every muscle slack. As through gauze curtains, he could see that the man across from him had stopped reading the Camus. He too had shut his book and held it with two hands.

Mark kept the moment, played it out. He considered a slow turn to the man, a look directly at him, saying something like, "Trade?"—but no, too obvious. Mark lowered his book very slowly to the tabletop, then almost imperceptibly let it go. Immediately the man snatched it up, simultaneously tucking the Camus tightly under his arm. Mark coughed, but he held his pose, modulated out of it, then drifted away.

He stood with his back turned, sweating. He heard movement, shifted and saw the Chesterfield coat heading across toward the front desk. Mark knew the bookman would never honor a first claim, so he slipped, as swiftly and cautiously as possible, directly forward from where he stood and out through the front door.

Even in his cabled turtleneck, he could feel the wind change. There was more scratch and rattle of rubbish scraps in the air. There was a shift of street smell too. Mark would have liked a shot of Cointreau or Benedictine but he gladly backed into a thin storefront and held on. Moments later, the man exited from the store, drew a scarf from his coat pocket and wound it tightly around his neck. He headed crosstown into the wind.

Mark kept a good distance behind: waiting interminably outside a coffee shop while the man had what must have been lunch, following him next to a bench in Washington Square Park, where the man sat, unbagged his books and read. On the far side of the fountain, there were guitars. Their songs were misty. He thought he heard a woman's voice in the spray; he tried to read the lips of every woman that went past. He was panhandled twice before the small white-haired man stood and started off again.

They walked toward Sixth Avenue, Mark staying about a halfblock behind. The man bought something at a green news shelter, stuffing it deep into the pocket of his worn coat, then stood pensively in the gutter at the corner of Eleventh Street. Mark worried that the man would hail a cab and evade him, but instead he turned uptown again, taking short precise strides. At Fourteenth Street, he went underground to catch an uptown express—Mark, with as much caution as he dared, fastened dangerously near. But it seemed that the man was lost to the outside; his fingers moved quietly in his lap, monologous, mute.

At Times Square, they got out and rose with the smell of marijuana and overcoats to the street. The man went to a Mr. Tie shop and bought a tie, then to a pornographic bookstore. Mark became angry: Christ, was he going to try to *sell* the book? Did he think it was obscene? But through the window he saw the man thumbing magazine pages and was relieved. He watched. He saw the man close the magazine cover, pinch his lips, scan the novelty items on the wall. Mark tasted his own saliva, felt it go thick, go sour. The man left and he tracked him to a cheap all-night theatre where, fifteen minutes later, in a slant-walled men's room under *Sexual Freedom in Denmark*, Mark got his book, snatching it from under the man's stall, shattering some sad gratification, crashing out through the door, sprinting the stairs, tearing down the short lobby ramp and out.

He met the street air like a mad flankerback, energized. He looked for openings, looked for slots. He heard half a stadium of cheers rising up around him as he wove, dodged, side-stepped, angled on. He had a fantasy of straight-armed shoppers in a wake behind him and felt bad. But the cheer was there, and he ran it, charged, went for the blue, and he had the ball, *book*, Jesus! Jesus, he was in motion again; he was alive. He loved it. Finally, after so many years, finally, the wind felt good. He loved the crosswalks; he loved the signal lights; he loved the engines of cars. Even the neon felt intimate around him. He could . . . he could own New York. It was his city. The bad knishes and the greasy kraut, even the monoxide air—all tasted beautiful.

For years now, and without clear purpose, Mark had wanted to possess a chainsaw. He found the nearest dealer of Craftsman saws in the Manhattan yellow pages, jogged the necessary blocks and bought one. It was called "The Trimmer" and was painted metallic red. The chain was oiled and prepared; it was all fueled, and the blade—like an airplane's wing—was silver. With it and with an amazing woman waiting for him in the margins, Mark headed off for the New York Public Library, where he stretched himself in a large chair and streaked through an entire afternoon.

ii

The lights had been on for at least two hours, and with an
October wind sweeping the city air, Times Square became
a meadow of rustling neons, sharp and crisp—in their absence—as autumn leaves. There was a sense of season remarkable for New York. All the acres of Naugahyde
smelled like wood; the streets like ponds.

Mark sat spread out in Tad's, cutting his overtenderized
steak. To his left lay a looted Manhattan telephone directory open to "Weiss." Not quite out of reach, across
the table, sat the chainsaw. And to his right, open as well,
lay the book. There had been a name—on the upper right-
hand inside-cover corner: "Weiss," followed by the initial

"S." It had seemed, even though penciled and printed, to be the same hand which followed, so remarkably, after, filling the blank front pages and the margins with a woman's ink. Her name was Weiss, then: S. Weiss. *Sandra? Sarah? Susan? Shawn?* Mark checked the "S. Weiss"'s in the directory, trying to find an address that most seemed to fit.

There were, in all, thirty-seven possible listings, either "S" alone, or women's names which began with "S." Mark copied them exactingly onto a small memo pad, making a list. Of the thirty-seven addresses, only eleven seemed reasonable for her, Mark's sense of all she should be. The other twelve were addresses like East Forty-eighth Street, places not near the river.

Of the eleven checked as likely, Mark underlined four, all a strong and direct impulse. The possibility of proceeding entirely on impulse and making pure and initial connection was exciting. He volleyed his eyes, swung them between her inside-cover words and his list. There was a fine mystery in it, a sort of trance. Her words moved and eddied. Mark thought perhaps the right name and a phrase would swim together like two small mating fish.

"I went to an apartment. . . ." Her first marginal voice began in an admission that seemed to Mark both compelling and strange. He wondered what had brought her to write this account in a book cover. And why this *particular* book? Why even before the book had begun; what was it in response to? He read the entry a fourth time, hoping that the right name would break away from his list and join it. Around him, in the aisles, eaters moved in a general impression of steak sauce and garlic bread.

"I went to the apartment," she admitted, "in response to an ad. It was in no way habit. Someone, though, had paid

— 24 —

to insert 'Exceptional People' with a Riverside Drive apartment number, time and address. And I felt I should go. Oh, yes, I know—how pathetic I really am. How sad. How unnatural and absurd. Still . . . yes, why not 'exceptional'?" Mark smiled. Indeed exceptional. And with choice quiet irony. He moved on, never let her really go.

"Along Sixth Avenue, strolling Madison, outstaring the Columbia fountain, why not—given this grimed, fatuous shell—'exceptional'?" Mark smiled again, nodded, pushed his plate with its dry potato case and meat-fat strips out of sight and drew himself closer. "People look at me. Fair to say, they stare." Mark imagined it. "I used to think—and still do more often than not—it was because I was so, *am* so, hideously unattractive; gaunt and mad-looking. But it becomes even more possible that I am just, after all, 'exceptional.' " Mark's hand moved quietly to the corner of his mouth.

"The modeling that I did—that I've laughed about. Also wept. *H. Bazaar!* My God! What did they think I would project? To be stopped on the street by a man and to assume that he wanted me for filth. Then to discover . . . 'fashion.' And 'high,' at that! What an exquisite play for me with those words." Mark paused, to replay *her* play, gauge her delight: all fine; all wonderful; rich as dragonfly wings just before dark. How incredibly clear she still became and was to him!

"How did they assume I would 'read' gowned in that way? I have always thought of myself, my image, in terms of '30's breadlines." Mark took a long drink of his now very lukewarm coffee. He knew what was ahead. For a fourth time, he prepared to be unsettled by the openness, there in the margins, of her pain, the self-inflicting of her irony.

Mark wondered at that kind of vulnerability. He had watched butterflies chase and mate once in an open field and felt the fact was nearly beyond his belief.

She described her answering of the ad; her arrival, the room, the five others, the pretentious silence which they all kept. Again, he was struck by what she noted. "One man," she said, "had large hands which gripped together often in the sun." Another, older man, "must," she'd decided, "have been either a musician or an anthropologist." The apartment itself was "an Edward Hopper with a light flurry of Villa-Lobos."

As he read, Mark felt the tips of his fingers again grow moist, his eyes, once more, tighten and pinch. A thin mute-faced boy in bloody whites slid Mark's thick dishes off the table and tossed them into an ambulatory steel bin. But Mark moved on reading. "Still, no one seemed . . ." She went on, she described isolating herself with a glass of Dubonnet at the apartment window, simply staring, finally, across the river at the lights of Palisades Park. It was uncanny, in a way, but Mark could see her. He could sense the visual depth of the scene, moving out from her skin in the foreground to some vanishing point of bulbs. He rose—and, still carrying the book, moved off to get more coffee. His mouth seemed stale and blistery without it.

"*I have always looked for strength*"; she had underlined this, and he reread it, standing, waiting, trying, as precisely as possible, to make her final word, "strength," tactile inside his mind. She described the fabric of strength and weakness in her own short marriage, strength's ultimate surfacing—"at which point I became useless," she summed up. Mark felt the weight of the filling coffee cup in his hand. "Why had I come there to that room; to be 'exceptional'? Was it strength? Did I stand there, back to the others, eyes nailed to the insect lights of the park, hot from some cue in the noonday news, so that I could feel that I was 'strong' and 'exceptional'—*as long as it was by myself?*"

Mark carried the book and new cup back unsteadily to his table. He set them down and sat there, drawing the steam in through his eyes awhile, feeling it float her words, letting it warm and release his mind. She was like him, perhaps too much. It was his practice too, he knew it, to surmount his life with lights at windows. How often now with Jan, when she might need something, had he stood, looking down, invulnerable, 'strong,' 'exceptional,' watching the signals on Second Avenue measure red to green, green to red, red to green.

Mark let their similarity drift, diffuse, not exactly fade. Then, suddenly, he broke it with what her words had moved toward for nearly two and a half cover leaves. But the words broke too, moving out of a preface in the past, becoming determinedly and immediately present. He felt the tense demand "now" effect; "And so I turn"—she became almost unbearably present and close—"I turn from the window and ask. I ask the younger man with the strong suncolored hands to come with me. And he comes. And we live together nearly two weeks. And I struggle as I have never struggled in my life to be strong *in* another. I swear I do. And perhaps it is a wrong choice. We seldom talk. We touch. We hit. He leaves. And . . . and what? I remember the way he peeled oranges. That's it; that's all—the hands and rinds.

"But I *did* try. Honest to God, that *is* so. I tried. . . . I listen to churchbells . . . and to dogs barking . . . they are the same sounds." The last thirteen words she had then rearranged twice, two versions of a four-line free-verse poem, below; "I listen to church/bells. I . . ." etc.

Mark drew a star beside one of the four underlined names on his list, "Serita Weiss, 318 W. 98th St., UN 2-4579." He left the telephone book on the table, picked up her Camus and his chainsaw and crossed to a panel of enclosed telephone booths along the far wall. He entered one and swung the double-hinged door closed behind him. He felt overclothed and hot. He wondered about the wattage on the overhead bulb; did electric bulbs draw oxygen? The air inside the booth seemed so heavy and used, so hard to inhale. Mark thought of first-football-practice field houses where he'd been at that age, of buses taking him where he'd never been. What was he after? He stared at her name and number on the list. He had a picture of her in the room; she wore a knit dress. Mark lifted the phone from the hook and dropped his dime; he listened to the dial tone, swept his eyes over the graffiti and numbers on the wall. Somebody had recently written, in stark red ballpoint, "She would not come," and a number.

He dialed. A man answered. Mark hung up. In the holding of tight breath, for close to forty seconds, he heard the man's gritty inflection echo. Could it be that the man with the tanned hands, the one that had peeled oranges, had come back? Mark dropped in another dime and dialed, but after the same voice answered and he'd again hung up, he placed an "X" boldly to the right of Serita Weiss's name. He'd been wrong. It disappointed him. He had wanted very badly to find her—cleanly, amazingly—right at the first.

And now he worried about Jan. There was a fairly good chance that she was home and had cooked something for them, made a dinner. And so he called.

"Hello? . . ."

Mark pressed his finger against the cutoff lever and held

it down, trying to clear an overflow of shapes from his mind. He had probably scared her. She hated that, empty, unvoiced calls, even wrong numbers; her shoulderblades would begin to rash. She'd be checking the shades and window locks now, double-fastening the door. Mark saw her, sitting in the dark bathroom, waiting, pinching the palm of her hand. He let the lever ride up again, set in another dime and called.

She was refusing to answer, afraid, so he outwaited her, let it ring.

"Hello?" Her voice shook, had a dim buzz, but it was also struggling, as she always so nicely did, to be strong.

"Hi."

"Did you just call?"

"Yeah. Something broke it."

"I was scared."

"I figured."

"I double-checked all the windows."

"How about the door?"

"Yes. And my shoulders began to itch."

"I can't believe you're actually *from* this city."

"Are you coming home?"

"Home?"

"*Up*? I have something. Special. It's been waiting."

Mark had no desire to go. What he wanted was to sit with five dollars' worth of dimes, calling, sampling voices until he found S. Weiss. But he'd scared Jan. She was alone, uncertain, with something that she hoped he would like. So he told her he'd be right along.

"Mark?"

"Yeah?"

"You're a very nice man."

"Sometimes."

"To me."

"Don't leap to conclusions too rashly."

"You *are*."

"Mmm."

"Bye, nice man."

"Bye."

She laughed. They both hung up, and Mark sat.

Through the cell-like divisions of the mesh-and-glass booth door he could see the interior of Tad's. It was all flaccid and dumb, a space somehow perpetually phantom. People in dark weathered coats sat by themselves gutting husks of huge potatoes, bandaging their mouths and eyes with garlic bread. The Muzak seemed distant, miniature, almost trapped in the wire hexagons of the door. Mark had a vision of the whole place filled with enormous and furry bees. He had an impulse to start his chainsaw where he was, but he wasn't sure that it would actually drown anything out.

He tried to pinpoint a word for his precise relationship with Jan. "Fond?" No. "Casual?" Partly, but not; too sweeping. He couldn't really discover one; no exact word framed. All he could do was catch the rough shape of—if not their word, then their prose, their print: himself and Jan on the ferry, having a breakfast of cinnamon pears, cutting across the park; but there were always washed and indefinite edges, like pictures ripped hurriedly from *The New Yorker*, nothing hard.

Mark pocketed his book and list, picked up his chainsaw and moved out. Without the intercepting glass he was struck suddenly with another, very different sight: fields of configured brass. From the borders of the red mock-leather upholstery on the lower walls and chairs, he caught arrangements of decorative brads. He had a sense of hammered brass everywhere, constellations. Was there some hidden, petrified cosmology here in Tad's? If he studied it patiently enough, could he predict? In a light, somewhat bizarre mood, he left and rode the I.R.T. uptown, shutting his eyes, letting the train gently rumble him, tilting his head back, letting his mind field skies of glimmering tacks. He was star-crossed, nail-crossed. Who was he to interfere with Cosmic—or, at least, Manhattan—Destiny? *S. Weiss, whoever you are, I drift toward you through the night!* The heavens! An older couple, directly across from Mark, watched him a full five minutes: his blind smiles, his head-drifts. They were more than apprehensive; they were scared.

On Sixty-eighth Street, where he rose to the street, the wind was fine. Mark held his face to it and stood feeling a new kind of energy, not exactly young. Maybe he would just stay briefly with Jan, make some excuse, leave and begin to call. If he could locate S. Weiss tonight, then he could be outside her apartment house at dawn, wait until she came out and follow her through the city for days. Mark felt the chainsaw heavy against his thigh, turned and walked east toward Jan's.

He could see her windows from a halfblock away. She'd woven the curtains herself, purples and blues, and they were all pulled closed, the overglare of lights behind them giving the casement openings the appearance of electric burlap or electric gauze. Mark stopped underneath, in the fall of her light and the street's light. He considered not going up, finding a phone instead, calling, excusing himself, but then he saw her step into her own weave, and he took his key, opened the foyer door and climbed the seven flights to her floor. He caught his breath; the climbing had felt good. He had a perverse impulse to scratch suggestively on the door to frighten her, but he checked himself, took out his key. Jan was in the bathroom.

"Mark?" She heard and called to him.

"Yo!" He set his chainsaw down, went to mix himself a drink. That was the one thing he regularly did, keep her bar supplied.

"Is that you?"

He could hear, off and on, water running.

"No!" He smiled, dropped two cubes in a glass.

"Are you on your way?"

"I just bought my token for the subway."

"Will you be here soon?"

"Soon!" He poured Jim Beam over the ice.

"Well, who just came in, then? A monster?"

"Yes. I think so."

"What should I do?"

"Well, he's mixed himself a drink. And so I think if you just stay in the bathroom till I arrive, you'll be all right." He sat down, spread out, on the couch.

"What will you do?" She sounded muffled, as through a towel.

"When?"

"When you get here."

"What do you mean?"

"To the monster?"

"Get him to give me his drink."

"Then what?"

"Tell him to fuck off."

"What if he doesn't?"

"Well . . ."

"I'm scared."

"No sweat."

"What if he doesn't fuck off?"

"If he doesn't fuck off, I'll fuck him off!"

"Oh, you're so brave. . . . Are you here yet?"

"Walking up the street."

"Should I just stay here?"

"Yeah—and shut up, because the monster's beginning to hear you."

Mark heard the water tap turn off, then listened to the silence. Quietly and to himself, he laughed. Then he began, in a low and throaty rasp, to growl. Jan whimpered appropriately from behind the bathroom door.

"Are you here?"

"Key's in the lock!" Mark slammed one foot down to simulate the effect of a door banging. He feigned a hero voice: "Hey, what are you doing here?" Then shifted to something more guttural and coarse: "I'm a monster drinking bourbon. . . . Yeah? . . . Yeah! . . . Well, haul ass, monster! . . . Haul ass yo'self, man; I'm not moving a goddam inch! . . . O.K.! Well, then, take *that*! . . . All right, you asked for it, mother!" Mark made sounds of fierce physical battle, slamming himself on the chest, forcing deep visceral groans. Jan stayed behind the door inserting princesslike "ooh"s and "ahhh"s. Mark pushed over a small chair.

There was gasoline in his chainsaw, and Mark picked the instrument up as he continued simulating struggle in a strange stomping dance with his feet. "O.K.!" he said again, his hand on the saw's pull string, "I'm afraid I'll have to use this!"

Mark pulled hard and the saw started up its growl. But in the imbalance of his clowning, the blade swung around freer than it should and brushed against the back of his left hand.

"*Owww! Shit! Fuck! Piss!*" Mark screamed, dropping the saw to the floor. "*Fuck! Shit! Jan, help! Shit!*" A suffusion of blood washed the back of his hand and streamed down his arm. Jan was still behind the bathroom door sighing out "ooh" and "ahhh."

"JAN, COME HERE QUICK!"

She entered and screamed. Mark's blood was dripping onto the parquet veneer of the floor.

"Mark!"

"Get a towel! Bring me a towel, quick! *Shit!*"

Jan rushed back into the bathroom, and returned running, with a large toweled wad.

"Goddam, fuck, shit, sonofabitch, bastard!" Mark streamed as he wrapped himself. "Stupid cock!"

Jan stood with one hand over her mouth, the other bunching her blouse. "*What happened?*" Mark's face was twisted, pained. "Mark, what happened, *please!*"

"I was stupid!"

"What do you mean?"

"Jan, will you just let me get this under control first? See if I lost any fingers or anything? *I can't even think!*"

"But I don't understand what . . . " She clamped her hand over her mouth again.

"Run the water in the sink! Just barely warm."

"Yes." She ran off.

"Got it?" Mark was pacing, short strides, back and forth. "Got it? Is it warm?"

"Yes."

He moved in to her. "I think it looks much worse than it is. But let's take a look."

"What happened?"

"Jan!"

"Yes. I'm sorry. O.K."

Mark unwrapped the towel from his hand. It had soaked up considerable blood. Jan stood by, both hands to her mouth, alternately looking and turning away. Suddenly she bolted, fell to kneeling by the toilet and retched.

"One of us isn't bad enough!"

"It's called empathy."

"It's called puking at the sight of blood."

"Yes. And I'm going to do it again."

She did. And Mark kept the last wrap of toweling around his left hand, reaching across with his right to flush. Then he rubbed her back.

"I'm supposed to be helping *you*." she said, sniffling, partly through tears.

"You are. Through distraction."

"Glad I could be of aid."

"Yeah. Me too."

"How's the hand?"

"Just a minute and I'll tell you for sure."

Mark gave Jan's shoulders a final press and squeeze, brought his hand over and undid the towel for its final turn.

"What?" She was sitting on the floor, wiping her mouth with toilet paper.

"You like your steak rare?" Mark asked.

"*Tell* me."

"The skin between the thumb and forefinger is chewed up. But it's not very deep. The blood's just seeping now. Just very light. Have you got any alcohol?"

"Just that bourbon and shit that the monster was drinking." She was kneeling now, hugging his legs.

"Look . . ." Mark rinsed and dabbed his hand. "Go on out. . . . Go on out and get me some gauze bandages and alcohol and stuff. Take my wallet. It's in that pocket." He nodded back toward his right hip.

"O.K."

"Thanks."

She took the wallet and kissed him. He watched as she fluttered into her coat and moved toward the front door. "What are you *do*ing with that, anyway?" she asked, looking down at the saw. "God, it's awful!"

"I've always wanted one," he called.

"Since when?"

"Since my first tooth. I love cutting."

"I *hate* it."

"Go get the fucking bandages, please."

"Yes, sir."

She left and Mark sat down on the gray-white tiles of the bathroom floor, feet against one wall, knees bent, back against the small squarish tub. His eyes blurred. He began to feel the hand ache now. Why hadn't he thought to ask her to get something for that? Never mind, there was enough booze.

He began to laugh. He caught a picture of himself—two-voiced, saw in hand, jumping around, presenting some weird children's theatre for Jan, unseen and mock-involved behind the bathroom door. What the devil *led* him into things like that? His work? Modeling those ads, those fantasy images with cigarettes, aftershave lotions, gin? Was it all finally curling his brain? And why did he want a chain-saw anyhow? Were his lobes scalloping quietly inside his head?

His hand throbbed. He rose, ran cold water over it, wrapped it in a clean towel and wandered, less than steadily, back into the central room. He poured some more bourbon, this time without the ice, and forced nearly a whole Old Fashioned glass down. He poured some more over the fisted towel, let it soak, refilled his glass and sat down, still clenching the bottle, on the wood floor. He stared at the saw. He smiled. He smiled with a backglance at the whole day which now seemed to him, warm and giddy with the bourbon, absolutely phenomenal and new. He felt "heroic"; the word came to him totally uninvited and wouldn't leave, even when he laughed at it. "Heroic." It was nice. For the first time in uncounted years, Mark could trace the blood and body chemistry of his getting drunk. The bourbon tasting, drink after drink, like bourbon, having temperature. He could feel it move and when it moved far enough he could feel his blood. And he could feel the texture of his raw flesh even wrapped; he could feel his body working there. He was—that was it—aware again that he had a body. The hard floor under him became a specific point of contact which he knew as clearly as he knew the texture of thick glass in his right hand. He could actually feel the notes of Ian and Sylvia on the tape physically approach through the air, enter his lobe, move along his nerves to join the bourbon in his blood. He could smell, *taste*, Jan's surprise, what she had alluded to on the telephone, with the nerve endings of his tongue; shrimp with lobster sauce and fried rice warming in tapered boxes in the kitchenette. And when he concentrated, he could . . . *yes!*—yes, he could actually locate his anatomy, *feel* his bones. Mark smelled the bourbon rising from his glass, felt it cling to the moisture gathered at the corners of his eyes. Once, years ago, he had watched a daughter born and something today was like that.

Sometime in the middle of the night, Mark became aware that Jan was no longer close to him. He felt, opened his eyes and checked, but she was not in the room. He pushed himself up and sat. He heard Mahler playing almost secretly beyond, and knew instantly where she was, what it meant. He sat listening, strangely confident and warm. None of the precision of his senses had passed. He could smell the unwashed dishes in the sink, the bloody towel in the bathroom hamper slowly drying. He could feel the white cells converging there on his wound. If snow had begun, four hundred feet above, to form, he would have heard it crystallize. Mark swung out of bed, lifted the unfinished drink from the bedside table and moved very quietly out through the bedroom door.

She was sitting, as he knew she would be, on the floor, in the near-middle of the room, her nightie on, listening, turned away. There was some uneven light from outside, patches, some of which moved like fish on the ceiling and walls. Her skin seemed ghostly, nodular and tight.

"What is it?" He waited her out. She didn't turn.

". . . I woke up."

". . . I see."

Mark moved further into the room and sat, also on the floor, within her sight.

"You're naked."

"Yes, I am."

"How's your hand?"

"Oh—that's not naked. It's wrapped."

"I meant—feel?"

"Healing."

"I'm glad."

There was a silence. Mark heard every sound outside. He looked directly at Jan. She stared just in front of her at the floor, then shook her hair and looked up and stared at him. He noticed especially the clenching of her neck and jaw.

"You're upset," he said.

"Of course."

"Why 'of course'?"

"You've found someone else."

"What do you mean?" He kept eye contact.

"You've found someone else." Her voice gained an edge. "That's not ambiguous. You're seeing someone else."

"That's wrong."

"O.K." She looked down, brought both hands up briefly and covered her eyes. Then she set both hands back on her bare legs again, grew inward, rose to make herself another drink.

"That's wrong!" Mark let his words follow her.

"O.K., that's wrong!"

"It *is*."

"That's a lie."

"That's not a lie. I am not *seeing* someone else."

"But you *are*." She turned back, glass in hand and abruptly.

"O.K.—tell me about it." He took a drink and watched her begin to pace.

"It doesn't matter."

"No! What makes you so sure? If we're going to hassle this, tell me about it; get it out."

"It doesn't matter! Just don't lie, Mark. That's all; just don't lie to me. I *hate* that."

"Jan, this is beginning to piss me off! I am not *seeing* anyone else." Mark fought exactingly for the letter of his words. She did not answer him. She just cried. "Look . . . look, Jan, Christ! This is insane. What the hell's happened all of a sudden? What have you latched on to?"

"*Serita Weiss!*" she screamed at him. "*Serita Weiss! Serita! Weiss!*"

The room resumed its background of sounds: cars, Mahler, thought. Mark felt his chest and stomach stretch.

He took a breath. He heard her repeating the name in a teared, whispered chant to herself. He finished most of the rest of his glass and stood. By her, he lifted and took her, crying, with an awkward thud against his chest. He kissed her just above the ear.

"What's she like?" Her lips moved—muffled; like moths —against his skin to ask.

"You found a notebook." It was his cornerstone of reassurance and release.

"Yes."

"With a list of names."

"Yes."

"It was inside my wallet."

"Yes."

"And were all the names different?"

"No."

"Do you mean they were all the same?"

"Yes."

"They were all 'Weiss'?"

"Yes."

"Isn't that a bit strange?"

"It's the one part I couldn't figure."

Mark saw his way. "Would you like it to be explained?"

"I would like that. Yes. Please." She nuzzled, played little girl.

"I have to do an English Leather ad."

"Another?"

"Yeah—they like me."

"So do I."

"Thanks."

"When?"

"This week."

"And?"

"And I get a voice in the girl I work with."

"You must be important."

"O.K., I am."

"And?"

Jan kept rolling out the carpet. "And I remembered working once—a Yardley thing—with this girl named Weiss, who, as the ad's been outlined to me, would be just right."

"But you couldn't remember her name."

"But I couldn't remember her first name. That's right."

"And so you went to the phone book."

"Yes—and so; et cetera—yes."

"And made a list."

"True."

"Of the girls named Weiss."

"Of the girls named Weiss."

"And decided it was Serita."

"Good. Very bright."

"And so now you won't need the list." She looked up at him elfishly and smiled.

"Sure—except that it wasn't Serita." Mark handled it without a gap.

There was a pause. Jan's jaw trembled slightly—although she was trying very hard to maintain. "Who was it, then?"

"I don't know. I still have to check."

"That's a lot of shit."

Mark let her go, turned roughly, strode back into the bedroom and snatched up his clothes.

"Mark!"

He checked his pants pocket and it was there. She had returned it with the wallet when she'd come back. She hadn't quite the nerve of action that she had of word. He slipped his shorts on and his pants almost in a single gesture.

Jan arrived, looking scared and diminished; she stood in the shadowed door.

"What are you doing?" Her voice was hidden and unsure.

For the first time in hours, Mark felt his hand ache. He tucked in his shirt. He sat down, threw on his socks, loosened his shoes.

"Mark, don't, please. I . . ."

Anger came—as much as Mark had wanted it clenched within. "Fuck this," he said tight-jawed to her. "Fuck this whole scene."

"Mark . . ."

He made bad knots in his shoes, stood. "Jan, I'm forty-one years old. You're twenty-two. That makes our relationship almost a cliché."

"No!"

"I'm almost twice your age!"

"Don't!" She was hugging the doorframe, drumming one fist dully against it, biting a knuckle of the other.

"I mean, what do you think is going to happen, anyway? You have some vision of a church wedding and children? A hundred friends of your family's and a hundred friends of mine?"

"No!"

"You thinking in terms of a honeymoon next spring in Bermuda? Coming back; buying all kinds of 'neat' things for the apartment at Georg Jensen? You just crazy to run 'barefoot in the park'?"

"No!"

"Shit, lady; I am forty-one years old! Four decades and a year! This is not a relationship to be thought of with futurity. Christ! God! O.K.! O.K.! Let's just, for the sake of argument, say I'm fucking every one of the Weisses on that list. Let's say I have a Weiss fetish. Jan, baby, I'm a consenting adult! I get to *do* all that stuff! 'Free and the brave' and all that! Bill of Rights! Listen—you want to know the truth? I'm making a porno movie in which twenty-three Weiss girls, *led* by Serita, perform abortions on each other simultaneously. I mean, what the—!" He slipped his jacket on toughly, tearing it in the lining. "Oh . . . *shit!*" Jan began to laugh.

Mark slipped his jacket off again, held it up to inspect the tear.

"Gee, Bronson, I guess if you have to leave . . ." Jan said, biting hard on her hand.

Mark tried to explode. He set his jaw, clamped his teeth, bushed his already heavy brows, took in more breath than he could manage and choked. His eyes leapt. His skin, with violent instancy, became almost blistery, watery and red. He tried to curse Jan. His voice ground like a key turned in an ignition too long. There was phlegm on his mouth. The wax on his ears seemed to illuminate. Jan fell to the floor convulsed. Mark watched her kneeling there, rocking, holding her sides, moaning, shaking her head. Her voice was weak.

"There's some spit on your eyelash."

"There is not!"

"There is!"

Mark wiped it off, then broke himself. Jan was beating her shoulder against the floor, contracting almost breath-less, and Mark's eyes started to run. He fell back against the wall, slid following it down, tipped finally, off-balance, over on his own side. Their laughter roiled like tidewater around the room: booming, spilling, without real course.

Finally they slowed, quieted to a chorus of small spoken vowels: "Oh," "ah," "ee," a silly counterpoint. Then, almost on cue, they crawled across the space between them and made quiet and childish love.

Mark knew Jan would never mention the list again.

iii

Mark woke even earlier in a dark that felt very much to him like light. It was clear. There was a warmth about it thrown back to September. It smelled distilled. He had a sense of all the city's air conditioners having been silently turned on, miles of brownstone having been washed or scrubbed. He wondered if it had rained, and sat listening, trying for any sound of spatter against the stone building walls outside him, just beyond. There were engine sounds. There was someone whistling down on the street. Two dogs somewhere in Queens answered one another. But there was no rain. He looked at Jan. One buttock was pressed against his left thigh, and as he drew carefully away he heard a slight, quietly adhesive sound. He paused. He did not really like to leave her unconscious in the bed. But when they had tried early lovemaking, months ago, the contact had been only vague.

Mark felt his bandaged hand. It felt drunk. It buzzed under the gauze like a cheap travel clock. He tried to slip away and leave it, leave the bad hand somehow in the bed, but it came with him and he accepted it, dressed in the dark and left. Outside, he stood mouthing the word "Weiss" in the uncarpeted hall: "Weiss, Weiss . . ." It felt soft underfoot. Then he shadowboxed in the elevator, walked across the lobby and out, jogging instead of taxiing down to Grand Central.

Inside the station, he stood excitedly. He faced his lockers. He hummed some trumpet voluntary that he could not precisely name. There was a very fine edge on everything that he touched. The texture of clothes, the choice of clothes, something that trivial, he knew would today give him near-boyish pleasure. Time slipped its own tumblers and allowed that. Where was he? Amherst again? Why not! Why not—it was Saturday, Saturday morning, sure, and he was dressing, dressing to meet a train which would arrive in an hour, a bit less, and on which would be a weekend date from . . . where? Connecticut College, Holyoke, *Wellesley.* Yes. And ahead, ahead somewhere with her in the day—of course; he could even smell it—was that really finely sharpened pleasure of walking through ponds of fallen leaves, slightly drunk, sun going down or down, papercup in hand, jazz bands playing from wide-porched fraternity houses across lawns.

It was a system. Here, in the cornered ribs of Grand Central, he had a very complete system all worked out. He kept his coats, pants, and sweaters in one locker; underwear, toiletries, accessories, and shirts in the next; ties, socks, suits, and shoes in a third and his dirty-clothes drawstring laundry bag and more pants in the last. It came to two dollars' rent a day, fourteen dollars a week. With coin toilets, coin showers, coin shoeshines, coin sunlaps all in the station's enormous men's room, and with some tips to attendants, Mark figured rent close to $86.50 a month. In Manhattan, if you were sleeping with some girl, it was much cheaper that way. The only real problem was the bagging of pants pockets, carrying enough quarters and dimes.

Mark rehung yesterday's jacket, slipped off and folded his cabled sweater, setting it also inside the first locker, on the sweater stack. He considered his coats. There was a new pleated Norfolk he had recently bought, but it was not precisely right; it was style, and style was distance, and distance was something which today he did not want. Instead, he took a tan suit, corduroy, that and a darkbrown tapered shirt, a wool tie and soft, low, leather boots: clothes for a fall Saturday football game.

In the men's room, his doubleblade electric razor sounded first like a street leaf-mulcher, then like his saw. His bandaged hand twinged. Diagonally behind him at some distance in the mirror, he could see another man, younger, but with an older face, watching. Others jostled around him, but the far man stayed, seeming to center Mark in his vision. Mark checked his change of clothes hung directly beside the sink. He switched the razor and grabbed the near sleeve with his free hand. The man, when he checked him again, was still at the periphery of Mark's reflected sight, still staring.

When he paid for his shower, he gave the attendant an extra dollar to carefully watch his clothes. "I think somebody wants them," he said. The black attendant nodded and said he would do his best, that he was sure nothing would happen, but that if it did, he wouldn't finally be much help because he could never grab for or touch the suit.

"Why not?"

"I'm allergic to corduroy."

Mark slipped into his stall, wondering if that was possible: allergic to corduroy—it seemed almost a guise. He showered, soaping himself rapidly and hard, feeling the vibrations, the new life in his skin. Even his injured hand seemed, under the water and now sick, dangling bandage, to, on the moment, heal. Can they give you new skin, Mark wondered suddenly in a warm barrage of water, not just a simple graft but *new skin*, a whole system? A pore transplant? At one point in the shower-brilliance of his musings, once when he bent to pick up the soap, he thought he saw a pair of black wingtipped shoes just under the stall door. But when he'd finished, dried himself and exited, he saw only the brown shoes of the attendant.

"Any trouble?" Mark asked.

"No—except that I've started to itch."

Mark tipped him another dollar and moved off. As he dressed, the corduroy felt good, right. It looked good too, he thought, checking himself in the mirror. He had quiet taste. He pressed the button for the warm-air hand dryer, listened to it whirr on and placed his hair down close to dry. At one point, with the warm air churning past both his ears, he sensed someone standing behind him, but when he turned to check, there was no one there.

The dryer moaned off, and the whole enormous underground world of pipes and basins switched quiet. Mark became aware of tiles, tiles and sinks, white porcelain squares all around him, close and at distances, as if they were somehow announcing themselves, shutting off, freezing. The color white reiterated in a glazed and very scrubbed precision. Men seemed to hold their positions, breathlessly, inclined toward mirrors, bent forward over sinks. The shoeshine stools stood empty, appeared almost amputated. No one moved from the urinals. Only the wheeled canvas bin filled with blue-lettered white towels near him seemed alive, some kind of strange logy animal. There were distinct aromas of bacon, toast, coffee, eggs from a restaurant far, perhaps miles, above. He punched the warm-air button again. The machine respired. Everything pulsed, fleshed and resumed.

Mark knotted his tie, transferred his wallet, the Camus, his change and keys. He put a quarter in the coin sunlamp. He could taste its warming, the smell of the ultraviolet rays on his tongue, feel the wide band of heat wrap his face. He wondered about the wedding of invigoration and fear. Why were there peripheral thieves today? Why black, threatening, under-the-showerstall wingtip shoes. Why did all the porcelain become sinister when he was just coming, in so many ways, again to life? Was there some secret information coded in the margins of his book? Had he accidentally bonded himself to an underworld?

He felt his face glow, felt the skin color and tighten. Somewhere he'd read that he would get cancer this way, using these damn machines, flaking regenerated layer of skin after layer away. He worried more about blindness, though. Under his lids, the eyes seemed the only part of his body at all tremulous, objecting or scared. Mark dreamed, standing, that he was in a motel in Phoenix with S. Weiss. They were sunburned in bed together, laughing, doing celebrity impressions.

Later, everything returned and the lockers locked and the

keys all in his inside jacket pocket, he sat in a coffee-shop booth by himself, drinking his orange juice and coffee and trying to guess, within the hour, when he would find her today. He had time for about a dozen phone calls now. Then he would have to call his answering service and see if he had a job for the day. If so, he would probably have to break and pick up the calling sometime midafternoon. If not, he would have heard her voice, certainly, by nine. He smiled. All the lurking figures had vanished. He was on some incredible and acute wave of energy again. He paid his bill and got two dollars in dimes.

The seventh call, just before 8:15, sounded close. She was a quirky-voiced woman, a wonderful shifting texture in the sound. Two of the first six had not answered and the other four clearly were not right. One he pinpointed as a secretary in a questionable law office; another was too elegant and much too old; the third, after she had said hello and he had said nothing, kept asking, "Jerry? Is that you—Jerry? . . . Jerry, he's home. O.K.? He's home," and had hung up. The fourth had been someone *like* a student.

He sat calculating his second call to her. If he said nothing, she'd hang up and he wouldn't be any closer than he was now. He took the book from his pocket, opened it randomly, trying to hold the voice he had just heard and direct it with the marginal words. On a central page, Camus had set down, "In Russian *volia* means *both* will and freedom." And she had commented, "For Russians, it *can*." Mark set the four words to the voice toning inside his head. He heard her there repeating them, again, and again, "For Russians, it *can*," and sounding right.

He dropped a dime in and dialed. She answered again.

"Mrs. Weiss?" he asked.

"*Mrs.* Weiss?" He could almost touch the tightening of her voice.

"Is it *Miss* Weiss?" Booth, phone, building vanished in his attempt to concentrate, his need to hold her there long enough and in sufficient positions to be sure. Mark was photographing her through her voice and words, comparing the image to that caught in the blue ink of a woman's hand traveled through marginal space.

"Who was it you wanted?" she asked, her voice moving like brush strokes, almost playfully sure. "A Miss or Mrs. Weiss?"

"Well, I'm terribly sorry to bother you . . ."

"*Which?*" The question came with a kind of confident, protected pleasure.

"Well, you see, this is Mr. Appleby. . . ." The name just came neatly to him. "This is Mr. Appleby. . . ."

"Who?"

"At the Strand Bookstore."

"Go on."

"Down in the Village."

"Mmm."

It was almost as if she were mocking him: no, that was wrong—toying.

"And a woman named Weiss—I honestly thought it was *Mrs.*—has, on occasion, has occasionally sold us books. I thought that I was calling the right party."

"I see."

"*Have* you sold books to us?"

With each word, each pause, each inflection, Mark grew more sure. There was a fine sense of weave about it all, her voice at once tactile, graceful and very much—he could almost see it turn in margins of sky—in motion.

"Well, the . . . lady I had in mind, if I remember correctly, has sold us some of her hard-backed editions of certain contemporary French writers. Such as Sartre. And, of course . . ."

"Sartre?"

"Jean-Paul Sartre. And Camus."

There was a strange pause. The sense of some kind of adjustment being made, some question being turned over, weightlessly and without actual gravity, in space.

"Is it 'Mr. Appleby'?"

"Yes."

"Mr. Appleby, why do I get the feeling that all this is, somehow, code?"

It was her.

"I don't know."

"Well, I tell you, Mr. Appleby. . . ." Her voice had a certain moistness to it now. "I've given all my Sartre—all my Jean-Paul Sartre and my Albert Camus—if this doesn't all sound too much like a Simon and Garfunkel song—to friends."

"I see."

"But I don't think it's done any good."

"Well, we just had a request, and I thought . . ."

"Perhaps my friends sold you my books."

"Yes, perhaps."

"Why does this conversation still seem like code?"

Mark's throat seared. "I can't say."

"Mr. Appleby?"

"Yes?"

"Is that all?"

"Yes. Thank you."

"It's my pleasure." She hung up.

Mark had traced and retraced a large penciled box around

her address: 526 West 123rd Street. That was near the river, near the river and not too far from Grant's Tomb. It seemed to line up, even with old memories; it seemed right.

A moment later, when he checked, his answering service told him he had a job in a half hour. "Can you make it?" the girl asked. He told her yes, he could, hung up and sat for a moment in the booth. His skin felt gray, loose, as if it might slough. He could hear the blood beating in his head, uncertain blood, scared. Memories of being twenty and on the verge of something equally enormous pounded up. He thought of Heidi. In *felt* time, despite what he had drilled himself recently to believe, there was no deterioration with age. He left and bought a pair of high-power binoculars before he caught his cab.

It was a cigarette ad. Everyone and the equipment got packed into a helicopter and they all chopped out to Montauk to shoot. In flight, Manhattan seemed angry, smoked and vibrating beneath them. Mark, trying out his new binoculars, located Grant's Tomb, caught a general pattern of people moving near it. He had always wanted to make love there some warm July night. He had grown up in Vermont and the wonderful domed vault below somehow seemed, for this city, the ultimate cemetery. Mark shared that natural instinct for simultaneous love and death. He set his binoculars back into their case and noticed the girl he would be shooting with, a girl he had never seen or worked with before, watching him.

They set down on the beach, the copter descent matched by the dispersed ascent of gulls, the murderous flap of props dying away, gradually replaced by the near-soundless clutch of gull wings massaging wind. Mechanically they piled out. Mark and the girl stood with the director, listening, while the equipment got set up. Someone else stood waiting with two horses that had been brought to the beach. There was to be, they were told, "a California feeling" to the ad. The director moved away to pace off some distances, measure some light.

"You're Mark Eliot," the girl left standing beside him said. "Aren't you?"

"Right," Mark said, counting the waves as they rolled in, trying to let something about them unravel him, or him them.

"I've seen a lot of your work."

"Thanks." He was trying to become crystal. The waves were carrying him, buffing all worthless parts away, washing down, washing down, getting him to something he *was*, or he'd forgotten, or he should know, or realize. He didn't want anyone else near him. He wanted to listen, concentrate, watch. There was no way out now, he realized. With her, with Susan; Susan Weiss. No escape from finding, being with her. It was elemental and set. It was at the center of his life. But the waves. There was some secret to it all, something important, something he would have to know, which, if he could find it early, would help. He didn't want anyone interfering now. He only wanted to concentrate.

"I've just started, really."

Mark nodded. "Mmm."

"I started with fashion. Well, underwear, really. I have the right kind of thighs. That's what a number of people said. You know, panties and girdles. Something about my thighs, my stomach too, my crotch. You don't mind that, do you? 'Crotch?' I mean, the word?"

"No . . . no."

"Sometimes I'm talking to people. You know, just describing my work—and they get offended, but I just look on 'crotch' as a technical term."

It was obviously an apartment house near the tomb, Mark thought, but how would he get to see her, know who she was, without her seeing him? He felt he had to get at least to that point by night. Maybe waiting by the mailboxes would work, checking her that way. But the quarters would be close. She would most likely see him.

"The funny thing was, I never really understood what was all that great about my thighs and crotch."

"Yeah." What was that gull doing in those waves? What was he trying to get?

"Oh—and my navel: you can't believe how many ads I've done just for my navel. Strange, funny how you never think of any of those things as being important. You know, as you're maturing, growing up."

She almost certainly had black hair. Mark sensed that. Long, but probably done up mostly. She would have a small scar somewhere on her face—why did he think that?—but she would.

"Anyway, I'm glad to be finally doing ads like this. I'd much rather be used for my face. What are you looking for?"

"Huh? . . ."

"Out there. You're staring."

"Oh . . . right . . ."

"What?"

"Bird." They looked at each other. It was strange; she watched his eyes and mouth as if she expected, momentarily, for him to take and kiss her: that same attentive and somewhat uncertain hunger. Perhaps she was practicing for some leading part. "There was a bird," he said to settle it if he had possibly been vague, if there remained doubt.

She nodded. "Do you know what I think of you most as? From your work?"

"No," he said, "what?"

"Shoulders."

They gave him a sheepskin coat with canvas patch pockets and bone buttons, and he put it on. Two men with battery blowers worked on his hair trying to create what two hours' wind horseback riding on the beach would have. "That's too much; *too* much," the director said at one point. "Wind, not monsoon!"

They gave him color. They gave him gloves. They gave him a hat to wear in some shots, hold in others. They gave him a scarf. They gave him rings. They gave him longer sideburns and a mustache. They penciled more hair on the backs of his hands. They gave him a different pair of boots. All the while, about twenty feet away, they were working on the girl too.

They changed her. It looked from where Mark stood as if they were pulling the tendons out of her face and stuffing them back again. And, like him, she just stood. Her eyes might just as well have had threads on them, to be screwed in and out, interchanged at will. Mark thought he saw them take her hands away at one point, carry them off to the copter cab and return with new ones. And the hair—wig after wig—at twenty feet it began to seem as if they were taking the lid of her head off again and again, almost as if someone had misplaced it. Memories of the skulls of jack-o'-lanterns pushed back. Was it possible that all the wigs were notched? That they were trying to line the right notch up with some notch on her brow?

Mark had learned not to have any opinions in this work. They always clashed. "Trust," he had been told by nearly everyone at the first. "Trust the director. That's all. Just trust. And keep quiet." So he gave his body over—to trust. It was easier than acting every night; auditioning, always auditioning. And you never had to watch the faces as they read the ad, constantly check for response.

"O.K.!" the director yelled. And the shooting began.

There they were. In fall. On a California beach. They were real people. Vital. Alive. They loved the seasons. They loved the out-of-doors. They loved wild things, horses, animals. It touched the animal in them. The Man. The Woman. They moved with the cycling of earth. Moved close to it. In rhythm with it. They felt wind. They smelled sea. They heard tide, music of moon and water. Never ceasing. Eternal. They had felt their bodies move to the blood of an animal. They had moved together. One may have pulled ahead. And then the other. But when it was done, when it was finished and they had stopped to rest, dismounted onto the cooling-after sand, they knew. Each in his way knew. That they had moved together. In the wind. Along the earth. Beside the water. Blazed by the sun's fire. In air, earth, water and fire—they had moved, together. Laughed, thrilled and breathed life together. And now. Now quietly. Quietly they stood. The sea glistening beyond them. Their animals beside them. At rest. In harmony. At rest. Sharing the same cigarette. "SOMETHING TO SHARE," it would eventually read.

"Let's get this shit printed up," the director finally said, and they all repacked and left.

"Well, I guess I'll be seeing you," the girl said as they stood on the corner of Madison and Forty-eighth Street.

"Yeah," Mark said. "Good work." He put his hand up for a cab.

"Listen, if you want to drop by for a drink or something sometime, it's 1324 Second Avenue, Apartment 2-B."

One caught his signal and was slowing down. "Thanks," he said. "I'll give a call."

"*Or lunch*." She almost shouted as he opened the cab door.

"Take care." Mark smiled at her, then pulled away.

He did not want to get out right in front of her building, so he had the cabbie stop at the corner and, with his binoculars cased and slung over his shoulder, walked. It was a large stone building. There was wrought-iron grillwork on and near some of the windows. It fit. It was the right kind of building for her. It was appropriate that she should be living there. It had a sense of impenetrability about it: monument, hut and fort.

There was a doorman leaning against one marbled wall, just inside the door, on the wall just opposite the buzzers and mailboxes. Mark entered with the strides and gestures of specific business, moving precisely to the mailbox wall. And he found her: Susan Weiss, Apt. 3-C. She wasn't home, either. There was mail in her box.

"Can I help you?" The doorman stood at the center of the foyer. There was professional suspicion in his voice.

Mark turned to him brusquely, and with officious annoyance. "Excuse me?" he asked.

"Were you looking for somebody—sir? In particular?"

"I understood you had an apartment. Had one vacant. But they all seem to have tags."

"That's right." The man smirked.

"Why was I given the impression, then, that you had one vacant?"

"Who said that?"

— *58* —

"A friend who's quite familiar with this building."

"Someone living here?"

"A close friend of someone living here. They said it was one of the apartments with a view."

"*All* the apartments have windows—and views."

Fuck him, Mark thought. "I meant of the street"—Mark pointed to punctuate—"the street here. As opposed, say, to a view of an adjoining apartment-house wall. Or an alley. Or garbage cans. Or something like that." *Up his.* "I think it was apartment number 4-D."

"Couldn't have been." The man's voice was more apologetic now.

"Why is that?"

"Because the only apartments that face the street are B's and C's. The B's on this side"—he indicated left—"the C's over there."

"But to your knowledge none are or soon will be free?"

"No, sir."

"Thank you." Mark started to leave.

"You might try 329, just across. I think they've got a street apartment there."

"Oh," Mark said, freshly excited by the possibilities. "Oh, very good. Thank you."

"That's all right."

Three-C, Mark thought, moving out. *O.K.; it's on the right side.*

The building façade had been recently sandblasted. Mark stood checking it for a moment, then crossed, looking back, seeing primarily how the windows lined up. A third- or fourth-floor apartment anywhere on the street, he could see, would give sufficient line.

He went in and asked about the apartment. They had one on the fourth floor looking across the street. He followed a gray-haired, five-foot-six and extremely well-dressed miniature Lee Marvin into the elevator corridor and finally the apartment, walked to the windows, aligned them with hers and wrote a check out on the spot for security and the first month's rent.

"When do you expect you'll be moving in?" the man asked.

"What?" Mark could see that her shades were not drawn.

"Moving in. When should the men downstairs expect furniture?"

"A few weeks, at least," Mark said, turning and walking back to the center of the room, rotating there in vague study of the ceiling and walls. "But I'll be in and out. Trying to make some decisions about drapes and lights. May even haul a mattress in. This is quite convenient to my work."

"Haven't I seen you somewhere?" the man asked.

"Possibly," Mark said. "What did you mean?"

"I'm not sure," the man said, studying him. "We have a couple pretty well-known people with apartments here. And I just thought. . . . Do you know Travis Michaels?"

"Who?"

"Travis Michaels."

"No."

"He writes books."

"Never read one."

"Louis Stoltz?"

"Nope. Doesn't ring a bell."

"He paints."

"Well . . ."

"They both live here. . . . You've never been on the Johnny Carson show or anything?"

"No."

"Well . . . You just had that look."

"Lot of people mistake me . . . that way."

"For who?"

"Anyone . . . People they've seen, known somewhere."

"I'm that way myself."

"Well"—Mark grew cool—"that's the key, then?"

"Yes."

Mark held out his hand. The man delivered it.

"Thank you."

"Just give us a couple days' notice before the furniture comes."

"I'll do that."

"And if you need anything—just let me know. The name is George."

"Thanks, George."

George withdrew—backed, then seemed to atomize in a kind of camera-fade at the closing door. Mark moved quietly to the window and knelt. He peered down at her windows—shades up, drapes slightly parted—wondering whether, in the last half hour, she had returned. The outside light, he saw, shrank fast now, late-afternoon shadows moving steadily across the city, spreading dim frost down all the streets. Some frames across from him had lights behind them, but hers stayed, remained cool and absent.

Still kneeling, keeping his eyes on the space, he unfastened the catch on the binocular case, drawing the glasses out. They felt strange in his hand, like something fragile, something frail made out of coarse stone, twin sandstone eyes. Mark put them to his eyes. He focused. He checked to see that he had the right windows. In one he could see a bowl of fruit atop some kind of windowside cabinet. The drapes were grainy, an uncertain shade of gold. And beyond the drapes and modeling of clustered fruit was the filmy vagueness of an unlit room, no apparent life or movement yet there.

The other room, the one he judged the bedroom, had the same rough gold drapes. Had she, like Jan, woven her own? Was he drawn to girls who wove? Had Heidi? No; no, she'd just knit. Did his daughter, did Rachel weave? There was a lightly spread bed or sofa beside the window (he could see the far edge) and a simple (probably wood) chair beyond. And somewhere in the far or middle distance stood the shadowed anatomy of a rack, probably for clothes. It was all like a painting, the space stroked and generalized, having trick dimension and, like the other room, without life. Mark suddenly felt hungry, his knees sore. He sat, glasses lowered in his right hand, wondering how he could get food. He checked the street to see if anyone who looked right might be approaching. No one moving measured against the picture that he had.

If there'd been a telephone, he could have called out, had food brought in. He heard sounds, youngsters playing below. He raised his window and checked.

"Hey!" he called down to two kids who seemed somewhere close to twelve. They were well dressed and had probably been cautioned about *strangers*. "Hey! Hey, you fellas!" he called again.

They stopped playing and looked up. He kept one eye on her windows, alert to any sudden light across the way. "You calling us?" one of them asked.

"Yeah! Look—I'm working in my apartment. Painting. I don't want to take time to go out. I don't have a phone or I'd use that."

"We're not coming up!" one of them yelled.

"No. No, I know. I wouldn't ask you to. I'm just going

to drop a couple of bucks out the window. They're *yours*. If you just go around the corner and order some kind of sandwich. Any kind. It doesn't matter. And about four orders of coffee. Have them deliver it to this address, apartment 4—" *Christ,* he couldn't remember what the letter was. "Just a minute!" He got up, ran to his door, opened and checked it and returned. "To this address, apartment 4-C! Here! Here's another couple bucks for the food. And . . . and when it gets here, come back and I'll toss down another five."

The kids stretched up and caught the last two bills like slow ashes from the air. Something about the moment, watching it, seemed so like dance.

Nearly an hour later, the food arrived; two cheeseburgers, fries, and four containers of coffee. The kids had used every penny of the two and more. Mark dropped them five. "Thanks, Mister!" they both yelled and quickly disappeared, plans to spend it obviously made. Mark watched them again until he couldn't any more, something about them, the way they moved, jogged, sprang their bodies, grabbing at him. They took him with them: ahead, back. Perhaps it was just the smell of fries. He kneeled again, nibbling a cheeseburger, focusing and refocusing his binoculars until it finally occurred to him that the clouding, that the blur of focus, was in his eyes and not really in the glass.

iv

Mark dreamed beneath his binoculars, their long black strap looped down into his half-open hand. Across the street a light went on.

The glasses, aimed almost perfectly on their window ledge, seemed to pursue a detached intelligence; they adjusted focus and found her. She rose. Mark shifted a leg. He coughed. He mumbled something, threaded his brow, took a deep breath and let it out. She sat on the edge of the bed, sat there rocking slightly, rocking herself awake. Mark twisted slightly around his own spine. She was thin, slept without clothes, and had what looked like two large faded bruises; one just below her left shoulder, the other further down her back. Her hair was black, thick and long. Her neck was angular. Her teeth were small. In the almost perfect dark outside and between them, furnaces, trucks, street machines, converters kicked on, hacked and ignited, their action vibrating the window and lens glass with a diminished insectlike chord. Mark dreamed of water. The book lay pressed open under him to where Camus had noted, "There are at this moment distant harbors in which the water is pink in sunset," and she had replied, "Such is the pastel violence of even our best bacteria," and Mark himself, crowding in black ballpoint, had asked, "But what actually matters: *water* or *harbors*?"

The water in Mark's dream began to feel like a swollen hand. It had salmon-colored follicles, pores. The room smelled animal, meatlike, its air too uncirculated. Across the street, she brought her knees up, hugged them, tried to compress herself. She looked like a budded seed, head tucked low. She stood. She reversed herself, stretched out, legs apart, hands outstretched, head way back, shaking, hair shaking loose. Then she disappeared, presumably to a bathroom out of sight. Mark's eyelids vibrated like an alarm. He rolled. Bent now against the lower wall and window sill, he sniffled and yawned. The 5:30 sounds, humming at the windowpane, shook his hair, threatened the roots. His body fought. Eyes still shut, he lifted a hand, gestured almost in check of his face, searching whether it was still there. His hand groped the flesh awhile, slowly and disconnectedly, eyes, cheeks and lips. Then, suddenly, both hands shot to the face, prying the eyes open. Mark shook his head. He made some strange sounds in his chest and shook his head again, taking in the room, discovering himself, reflexing, locating, remembering.

He turned violently to the window and saw, across the

dark street, her light. He grabbed the glasses up, snatched them to his eyes, took them down, rubbed his eyes again to exercise and clear them, then set the glasses back. She was not there. He could not find her moving in the room. He checked the other dark window and could find nothing, a mute flickering, perhaps, of drapes. He swung the glasses back to the lit window, and, kneeling cleanly, kept his stance.

Was it possible that she had already risen and gone and left a lamp burning in the place? When had she come home? It had been sometime after 2:30 when he must have fallen off and she had not returned by then. It was just three hours later; was this the light of some return or leaving? Mark felt a chill. What if some seventy-year-old woman wavered into the light? Could he deal with that? Or should he just break the whole thing now, leave, walk out, give it up, forget? It was irrational anyway. The binoculars felt like sand and plastic in his hand.

She edged in. And he saw: a flesh almost in perfect dovetail with his vision, a woman so incredibly close to the *idea* of herself ripened out of less than forty-eight mind's hours that Mark felt himself, once again, shiver. With a single entrance, the blood and breath of each cursive stroke, each comma, each slant, each ungapped "a," each "i" dot, each blend of letters to sounds, words and sense, each hesitation or rush of hand fused, linked, became skeletal, became system, became *her*, woman, as he had sensed her almost from the first: bony, irregular, aslant, moist, finely strung, intense, shadowed. She paused, scratched herself lightly, almost unconsciously, just above an unself-consciously small breast. Then she moved left, once again breaking sight.

Mark tasted his mouth. There would be no ritual of Grand Central's men's room this morning, no half hour hygiene and lavation by machine. He could not break the bond. The best he could hope for was a clean shave, and he fumbled blindly for his suit jacket and, finding it, searched the pockets for his electric shaver. It was there, cord dangling after, a strange animal birth, cold, no-sound detached from outlet, like a petrified infant rodent—he could feel the teeth—still and dead.

He would not take his eyes from the frame, and so, again blind, he searched the baseboard, within the limits of vision, for sockets. There was one. He plugged the shaver in and began to raze. But when, just for an instant, now in underclothes, she came back into sight, he turned it off: as if the sound, as if the buzz of small bladed gears would somehow contaminate his eyes.

She looked tired. She looked sad. She had brushed out her hair and pinned it back, made up her eyes, lined them heavily, *blue*, so far as glasses could identify the color for him. She seemed in her late thirties—what he had expected, about five years younger than himself.

She moved out of vision again, and he flicked the razor back on. He could smell the machine, smell the fresh-cut hairs inside, feel the slight burn on his face. Several trucks shrugged by lumpishly along the street, their labels obscure in the wash of dark. Mark tried to set a strategy. He had four flights to the street; she had three. If he waited until she cut her light, she might be out and away before he could resight and follow her. It should be done gradually, not be rushed. When they met, at a point somewhere ahead, Mark wanted it to be without blemish, organic, fluid, natural. They would just move together, join, as if two lifetimes, the natural motion of them, were the only cause. She appeared again. He shut the razor off and groped for his comb.

It was her profile that the glasses now trapped: angling out at the brow, then in deeply at the eyes, cutting diagonally at the nose, then sharply in, then out again for a series of curves, soft at the lips, more rigid at the chin. Her thin, almost instrument-like hands were up behind her neck clasping a piece of jewelry that looked like jade strung on silver. She wore something purplish, knit and belted, a wide black belt, something textured and very soft, almost like velvet. For a moment, after the clasping at her neck, she stood and just stared ahead. Mark assumed a mirror which was out of sight. But she studied. And in the studying—in her eyes and the high bones of her cheeks, as much as Mark could determine it, telescoped—were long sessions of questions.

She broke the stance and turned off the light. Mark found his comb and began drawing it through his hair. The light in her other room lit momentarily, but he could not find her. Then it went off. And both frames were dark. Mark grabbed up his coat, shoes, glasses, case and book, and rushed to the door. The corridor was unlit, but he found the staircase and rushed down it, nearly dropping the book and glasses in his descent. A young doorman sat sleepily on a bench in the lobby, and Mark ran past him, slipping on his suit jacket as he moved.

About halfway up the block he saw her, moving toward Broadway. He slipped on his shoes and, keeping to his side, fastpaced himself to follow her. She had an almost athletic stride, nothing at all casual, fast and sure, and with the slight incline of the street, moving up from the river, he sensed strain and imperfection in the pumping of his heart.

His breathing seemed to begin to match a grumbling in the truck sounds along the street, and it surprised him—because he thought he was in better condition than that. His image in magazines certainly was.

Ahead, on the diagonal corner, she stepped down slightly into the road, searching the stretch of it uptown. Mark felt his breath constrict even more and struggle. She was looking for a cab. He would lose her. He imagined the cab, hump-backed yet sleek, fading to a dot down Broadway, his waiting for her with the glasses through a day again and then, tomorrow morning, her moving off in a cab, the pattern endlessly repeating, like the traffic lights down the infinite blocks. He could move in now, ask to share her cab, but it would be too sudden. He could note the cab's company and number, but then . . . he could not see himself playing detective.

One cab moved toward them now. She had her arm high, hand spread, to signal. It was practiced, he noticed; she did it almost professionally. The cab slowed and he held his breath and, almost as if it had grown out of the frozen distance of his held breathing, the vacancy bulb of another cab appeared up Broadway. Her cab stopped, the cabbie stretching a long arm over the back seat to flip the door handle. She stepped in. The door shut. Mark stepped from his own curb, and as the roof light of her cab shut off and the cab pulled away and past him, he shot an arm out, and at the same time a whistle, just barely catching the second cab. It stopped beyond him and he entered it on the run.

It was ridiculous. "Follow that cab," he said, pointing, almost unable to believe the melodrama of his words.

"Yes, sir, Mr. Tracy." The cabbie laughed. "You a crime-stopper?" he asked.

"O.K." Mark apologized.

"Who's in the cab—Flattop?"

Mark was at his mercy. But at least they were moving, at least she was still in sight.

"Listen, I don't want no machine-gun bullets in my cab —O.K.? No dumdum bullets in the upholstery." The man roared.

"There's an extra five if you can do it." Mark thought that would quiet him.

"Yes, sir, Mr. Hoover, sir."

"It's a girl."

"Oh—romance?" He ran a red light, went into a movie-background music routine. They were cutting east now, moving toward the park.

" 'It's no good.' " The cabbie started in on dialogue, taking both parts. " 'What do you mean?' 'It just won't work. I'm leaving.' 'Don't.' 'Yes.' 'No.' She snatches her alpaca coat from the back of the chair where she has left it. Daaah-dha-dha-dhaa-dum-dah. . . . She is out the door. . . ."

"Look, can't you just . . ."

They started across the park.

"He stands amazed! Has it come to this? Is it really over? He bolts out the door and down the stairs. 'Wait!' But she is running, tears in her eyes, for a cab, and his words only catch on the wind and are blown back to him."

"Cut, will you?"

"What's the matter?"

"Save your bits for the Carson show."

"The Carson show?"

"Yeah." They were approaching the museum now. And Fifth Avenue. The two cabs were separated only by a green Mustang convertible.

"Well, I've been on that show, buddy. So suck!"

"O.K."

They moved across Fifth Avenue with the light and continued east. "I been on the Carson show, I been on it *twice*. I been at the Bitter End! The Gate! I'm cutting an album in December, 'Follow-that-cab-Mr.-Tracy-Sergeant-Friday-sir-Mr.-Hoover-Rock-Hudson-baby.' Fuck you, buddy!"

"It's stopping."

"You know what Johnny Carson said to me?"

"You just passed her."

The man braked and turned suddenly around. "Just let me tell you what Johnny Carson said personally to me!"

"Here." Mark gave him a ten, opened the door and stepped out. He saw her standing less than a halfblock away, looking into a store window on Madison. He started slowly, vague words from the cabbie about "his material" fluttering like torn week-old newsprint around him. He heard the cab's wheels squall, heard it pull away behind him.

It was light now, getting light, nearing seven. He could smell the daylight reflected up at him from the pavement. What was she doing here at this hour, he wondered, after she had risen so early and with such seeming purpose; why now was she standing almost absently, reflecting in a store window on upper Madison, all sense of rush or time or destination gone? It seemed almost incredible that someone could so determinedly come to this point of reverie, the street wide and sparse, the light early, quiet, all stores and offices still shut. He stood, half seeing her, half looking into the window of a silent bank, seeing its enormous vault, amazed.

Now she broke and faced toward him, down the avenue, starting a slow free wander downtown. He pressed himself close to the window of the bank, and, head turned and featureless to her, waiting for her to pass, he thought of something from the margins. He remembered it especially, because it had closed the book. Camus had said, "Any fulfillment is a bondage," and she had said—Mark marveled at how he had memorized her in less than two days—she had said, "Only when it becomes conscious. . . . If I could only, for a change, become so enslaved. . . . Polishing boots would be like Bach in sunlight." He heard the light tap of her shoes and watched her reflection sweep past the vault. He wondered if she was aware at all of him. He wanted to turn and say "Susan!"—see what her response to his voice would be. But it was too early in the day. He knew. So when there was about a block between them, a respectful distance, he followed.

They walked unhurriedly down Madison Avenue. She would stop and check a glass, and he would stop. He noticed that her stops were almost always art galleries. And her taste—the length of her considerations in relation to what Mark judged the quality of the art—seemed precisely right. If she had dismissed something, paused only a second or two in front of something that he then liked, he would have felt stung, depressed. But she dismissed the dismissible, considered the considerable, pondered the ponderable; it quite excited him, their stroll and mesh.

In the mid-Sixties, she entered a coffee shop and he followed her in. She sat at a table and he took the counter where he could watch her in the mirror above the grills. She refused a menu, as he knew she would, and ordered. He tried to read her lips, but wasn't sure. He saw "coffee," saw that said last, but couldn't determine the items that preceded it. He tried to guess, echo the order for himself: "Unbuttered toast, orange juice and coffee," he said to the girl, but, moments later, when his toast arrived, he saw the waitress bringing *her* two boiled eggs. He'd miscued. It bothered him slightly, but he was close. She had orange juice too. And no cream in her coffee. It was close enough, sufficient for now.

She took a copy of *Vogue* from her thin briefcase sort of bag and skimmed it, glancing from pages to the people around her, sampling, measuring. Mark measured her and her measuring of others against memory images of *Vogue*, against his memorization of her from the book, against the others there and remnants from an imperfect past. It spliced, exchanged, refrained, became a melody: known, recalled, expected, hoped for. The pulp from his orange juice bred, multiplied in his mouth.

She paid and left. He paid and left. They walked once more down Madison. There was a haze of sun now, colder and more cautioning that yesterday. By now it was nearly 9 a.m. He saw her move into a high office building just ahead and he ran.

When he got to the lobby of the building, she was not visible. She had gone, caught the elevator and risen. Two large and facing silver lobby wall clocks both read six to nine. She worked here; that made sense. In some room on some floor above, she had an office—or served an office, more likely *had* one. He scanned the building directory, more than two hundred firms and companies sectioned there through twenty-two floors, most of indeterminate function, simply named for people: "Allen, Gibson & Wahl," "Pace-Papodopoulous," "Westlund, Westlund, Rothwell & Scaggs." Who were these people? What did they do besides naming offices, rooms, blocks, cells? Was there a Weiss? Starting over with "A.A.A. Agreement Inter.," he combed the list. It took him almost an hour. There was one Weiss, but it was Brian. Brian and Susan Weiss? No. Brian Weiss's daughter Susan? No, again. No, Brian and Susan Weiss were not related. She worked here somewhere else.

He tried an elevator dispatcher. "Do you have a Miss Weiss working in this building? A Miss Susan Weiss?" He smiled, trying to play it as business.

"Can't say." The man leaned against the marble facing beside his elevator, watching a girl adjust her stockings in a far corner of the lobby.

"What do you mean?"

"Don't know." The man's eyes finally met his.

"I see. . . . Do . . . Is there . . . is there some way or place I could find out?"

"Sure. Ask Grant."

"Who?"

"Grant. The other elevator." He pointed to the clocklike hand that was in motion above the other shaft entrance: 12—13—14—Stop—15, etc.

"Thanks."

"Sure." The man was checking someone else in the lobby now, another woman.

Mark watched the dial, saw it climb to 22, then descend. It moved down to 12, then climbed again, up to 22. Then it descended, with uneven stops, once more to 12. Then it rose again; descended to 12; rose. Mark watched the pattern, waited for the operator he had spoken to to descend in his unit and appear again. He did.

"Does Grant ever come down?" Mark asked him.

"Huh?" He was looking for women again.

"Grant."

"Yeah?"

"Does he ever come down?"

"From where?"

"From the twelfth floor?"

"Grant?"

"Yes."

"Uh-unh." He shook his head.

"Why is that?"

"He runs twelve to twenty-two. I run one to twelve."

Mark stepped into the stationed elevator and waited. "Twelve," he said.

A half-dozen others entered, and when they were in and had called out their floors, the operator swung from his post leaning against the marble and joined them.

Susan Weiss got in on the way up, at the seventh floor. She was carrying a manila file folder and her mind was distant. Mark's veins and arteries snarled. His eyes went white. They reached the twelfth floor and everyone but Susan Weiss got out. She was obviously heading down again.

"Mister?"

"Hmm?"

"This is twelve."

"I forgot something."

The operator shrugged. Susan Weiss seemed not to have noticed the moment at all. And so they rode down, Mark pulseless the entire way. She stepped off at the third floor. Mark stepped out at the first and did not breathe until he was outside in the air again. His eyes watered. His lips were dry. It felt as if the hairs in his nose had doubled.

What now? She either worked on the seventh and paid visits to the third or worked on the third and paid visits to the seventh. Camus had written something about a morning sticking in his throat and she had answered that it was the night that always stuck in hers. In any case, what they had both been talking about, perhaps it was simply time or moment, now stuck in Mark's. And the sticking made him sweat.

He decided he should be patient, stay put, wait, gather himself until she broke for lunch. He was patient for almost an hour and then became, again, impatient. He rode the elevator up to twelve, found Grant and asked about Miss Susan Weiss. "That'll be Artists' Talent Associates, seventh floor," Grant told him. Mark quickly caught the elevator down, dodged across Madison and stationed himself with a clear line on the building entrance, ready for her when she came out.

And as he stood there waiting, he tried, not without some interference, to incorporate this latest fact. Susan Weiss was an agent. S. Weiss, who had drawn and shaped herself in the margins, first of a Camus *Notebook* and then of his mind, was an "artists' agent." He repeated the two words: *"artists' agent."* They formed the first uncomposed shadow, the first dissonance.

It was after one when she did come out. She was with a young actor whom Mark was sure he had seen on some television series but could not name. He followed them to a Japanese restaurant where he managed to secure an adjoining room. Sitting there, without shoes, he could hear on the other side of the reed-curtained wall voice sounds without words, senseless, but resonant and percolated as early-morning coffee. He strained for sound divisions, for words, for even a separation of voice, but for some reason his stockinged feet under the low table seemed to muffle syllables and to separate from his body, enlarge and take dominion inside the room.

Then his drink came and he ordered a second and drank the first quickly and smoothly, and his feet joined him again. He forgot about them. He began to catch sense, words—sometimes his, sometimes hers—as being separate and isolate. It was strange, because as much as he had to reach, when a word came, there was no question about it, no fuzziness or blur; every one he *did* catch was absolutely distinct. He heard the young actor with her say "chant," and about two minutes later he heard her say, "Mall." ("Maul"?) Each word, like everything *in* the place, including the notes of broadcast Oriental music, was rodlike, reedlike, lightweight, highly lacquered.

He heard her say "arrogant." He heard him say "truck." He heard her say "consequence." He heard him say "longer." Then his tempura arrived and he only heard general sound for about five minutes until the man's voice came through again with "constant." Almost directly after, she used the word "child."

Then came the phrases, like splinters and quills, lodging somewhere in his skin. He would later have an image of himself as a Steinberg cartoon, crouched over tempura and hot tea in a Japanese restaurant stall, with words and phrases stuck like darts and spears and broken lances, all of different sizes, all over him—finally bound and gagged with the whole hemp and cloth of sentences. "Shall we say" was the first stretch of more than one word that he caught; then "but I want" from the man.

"Modes of," someone said, but he couldn't be sure who. "Appearances! People always . . ." the actor said very soon after, finishing it with something which made her laugh, a throaty and animally delighting laugh which became an almost immediate sexual prompt for Mark. Then they both started saying the word "Anew" back and forth, as if in some kind of game, each time laughing. "Anew!"/(laugh)/

"Anew!"/(laugh)/"Anew!"/(laugh)/ etc. Then she said, "For all I know, I'll forget," and then there was silence.

Had they left? Were they in the process of leaving? Mark leaned forward over his black-lacquered table, his glazed and calligraphed teacup between both hands, the steam rising to curl the fringes of his eyebrows, listening, listening so hard it hurt. But there was nothing, not even the percolation any more. He rose, banging both knees on the table, almost tripping on the cushions, slid open his door and looked out. Their shoes were gone. He looked beyond. There was no one in their room.

He went inside. He caught the scent of her there, despite the teriyaki and the green-tea smells. She smelled like clove. He touched the least pressed cushion for her warmth. He could sense her, even in absence, smell her, taste her, feel her still. Mark held her words—the quills, arrows, strands —separate from the man's: *maul, arrogant, consequence, child, shall we say, modes of, anew,* finally, *for all I know, I'll forget.* They were all intimate and small, but what did any of it mean? He laughed, adjusting: the question itself made no difference, anyway, *what it meant*; that was ridiculous; it was of no importance.

His waitress, surprised, found him there. He said he had gone to the men's room and had gotten lost. She said that his shoes were next door. He said "Oh, yes," put them on, paid his bill and then left. Knowing that his wrists would smell of soybean for at least two days but not really caring, he headed back for her building to wait.

Just after four, she exited again, this time alone. She was buoyant, smiling, pleased about something, about herself or the day. Things—whatever they were for her—had gone well. He could see that. She swung her thin black briefcase bag unusually high and started moving across town, looping past other people, almost in dance. Mark, a half-block behind, coy and amused, tried to follow her exact pattern, choreograph himself with her. It would have been a nice thing to watch from above.

She went into a small bar with a lot of people standing, drinking, beginning the week's unraveling of themselves; happy hour at 4:30 on a Friday. Mark worried, looking in from outside, that she had come here to meet someone, but she seemed to be alone, no special purpose; she did not seem to be waiting for anyone. She drank and watched others and was watched and seemed to enjoy the ritual, the aura of light appreciation and prowl. She drank, stood by herself, both professional and animal; distant, instinctive. There was a sense about her and about the entire place, a sense charged somehow almost electrically with irony. It was in all the mirrors: irony. You could taste it in the Irish and in the smoke. You could feel irony crackling from texture of wool on all the coats, dresses and suits. Everywhere: Pre-Weekend Irony. It ignited her, like an icespear coated with fulminating light, a frozen Fourth of July sparkler. Mark paused in the door once more to look at her somewhere near the center of the room. What did she mean to him now? How was he obsessed with her? Could he say? Was it as man obsessed with woman, or some part of him as model obsessed with agent?

He ordered Scotch, because he could see from the way the bar lights struck and passed through her glass as she lifted it to drink that she was drinking Scotch too.

"Scotch-rocks."

"Scotch-rocks."

She could be picked up. He saw that. She may even have

come here for that. He had not planned to meet her, actually to *meet* her, be *with her*, for a week or so. Still, he could tell that the chances tonight were particularly strong. Like the night she had written about, the night she answered the ad and brought the man who peeled oranges home with her, she seemed set, ready to explore tonight, test something, determine, find out. Mark, from his spot near the jukebox, leaning, watching, understood that. Inside, inside herself, her head, her *person*, as she glanced around studying people, as she reordered her drink, she was running through questions, touching possible combinations, posing moments, weighing. Mark could see a process going on now; he could almost *ride* it, like the silent excitement of gliding: lifting now, dropping, adjusting, modulating air currents, seeing the earth come near, then drift away, being only in sky. It became a precise fantasy for him for a moment; his dark glasses became goggles and he piloted the essential her: cold, warm, hot, totally stilled a moment, then rushed, an updraft, a turbulence, intense. Then they both seemed to settle down, to land together on an open beach in a night the precise temperature of their bodies—silent, stationary, weightless, fixed.

Then he moved. The moment was devoid of any meditation at all. It was total impulse. "Anyone here from Columbus, Ohio?" he asked resonantly to the people at large. There was a pause. The murmur quieted some. People looked at him. "No one here from Columbus?" he pursued, catching her eyes hard on him, knowing that, whatever the impulse had grown from, it had worked. Mark held up his free hand in a gesture which said to all, "Thanks anyway," set his drink down on the jukebox and moved through the crowd, heading out.

He gauged his passing by—close enough, close, just

about right. She would catch the search and the nostalgia on his face. He continued to feel her eyes, like two blind fingertips, slipping gently from just below his eyes, gliding softly left, circling, shifting past his left temple, touching his hair, fixing, as he moved finally out the door, on the back of his head. And his shoulders. Mark assumed a wandering and melancholy gait, moving crosstown. Within less than a block, he was aware of her, there, drawn, connected, traveling behind him.

"Wait!" she called out. He stopped and turned back, a studied turn, watched her hurrying toward him. Her movement was nicely awkward. She seemed in motion behind a window. He could smell hamburger and the harbor. He could hear a distant conversational sound of buoys. There was the sound of water lightly being cut. "You asked for somebody from Columbus," she said.

"Yes." He nodded.

"That was very good."

She had a small smile and was breathing hard from the run. They turned together and walked on. She took his hand. Mark listened to their footsteps move on the stone, an easy slip, and to the pigeons signaling like gulls on the dark ledgework above. There were blown brine-colored webs of paper in store doorways looking like foam.

"When you asked—in the bar—and I saw you, I could tell that was where you were from."

"I guess you never quite lose the look."

"No. No; that's right. Not if you've made the trip."

"No."

"No. Not if you've made the trip."

They gave each other a smile. They had come nearly two blocks. They stopped. "Where are we going?" she asked. Her voice floated, had small quiet wings.

"No real plans."

"Back to Columbus?"

Mark paused. He felt the hair at the back of his neck and hands catch, rise and turn in a current of warm air. "Are you hungry?" he asked. "Would you like a drink?"

"Well, you did interrupt my Scotch."

"Scotch. Right. Good." Mark nodded to a bar just beyond. They entered. It was overlit and ambling, filled with a low dusk of cigar smoke. Voices exploded throughout it, and everything smelled of corned beef. Mark touched and squeezed her elbow slightly and she took the cue, standing at the spot to wait while he moved up to the too long, too wide bar to order. "Two Scotch-rocks to go!" Mark called across to a large, purple-pored man with an apron.

The man laughed and, drawing two glasses from a shelf, repeated the order: "Two Scotch-rocks to go!" He laughed again, brought Mark the drinks and said it a third time, the laugh now a crumpled grin on his face, "Two Scotch-rocks to go!" Mark paid and took the two drinks, and he and Susan walked out again into the street.

Susan carried her drink and smiled. "How long has it been since Columbus?" she asked him. "Roughly." She drank. He smiled.

"Pretty close to five hundred years." He said it thoughtfully. "And you?"

"About the same."

"I see."

"Close to. Give or take."

"That's very interesting."

"Yes, it is. It's a remarkable coincidence." They looked at each other. Then they both drank. "I like these better taken out. Don't you?" she asked him. They were moving east now on Fifty-seventh Street.

"I like all things better taken out."

"Don't be so goddamn cute all the time!" she stopped and snapped at him, almost spitting the words.

He took her face and kissed it, lightly. He wanted only to make simple comment, press her lips. They looked at each other. They laughed, each laugh inflected like a question, traced with caution; then they walked on. "Did you enjoy the crossing?" she asked him. "The trip?"

"From Columbus?"

"Yes."

"Well, most times . . ."

"Most times you regret it. Right?"

"Well said," he said to her. "Well articulated."

She stopped. "What's happening?" There was something strangely vibratory and serious in her voice, like a moth caught behind vines.

"You mean right now?"

"Yes."

He paused, and caught the unmistakable drift and odor of damp ink. "My name's Mark," he said. "Mark Eliot."

"I'm Susan Weiss."

They kissed again. She held on. Neither one spilled his drink. Two cabs with large glowing roof ads drifted away up Third Avenue.

Then, somewhere nearby, they heard party sounds, two or three floors above. There was music, the loud garbling of voices, the sound of glass. They could see people pushing and sliding past each other like cells behind a window.

"I hope we're not too late," Mark said to her.

"If the damn hairdryer hadn't broken," she went along, "we would have made it without fuss. The damn hairdryer, and my damn stockings, and the damn cab driver."

"I hope there's still some booze left!" Mark said as they

entered the building. He fingered ten apartment buzzers simultaneously. Someone buzzed them in.

They tracked the sound, found it on the third floor. A man standing near the door looked at them somewhat cautiously as they approached. "Went to check our car," Mark said to the man. "Last time we got a ticket. Listen —have you met my wife?" he asked.

"Yes." The man adjusted quickly. "Harry Gordon. I think it was at the Silversteins'."

"I remembered the Harry, but not the Gordon," she laughed lightly and said to him. "Susan Eliot."

"I remember," he said smiling, checking her body out.

"Mark?" Susan said, tugging at Mark's coat, pointing across the room, "Isn't that . . ."

It worked. She planted Mark's name in the air. "Listen, you guys," Harry Gordon said to them. "Have you met the Lubbicks? Arnold and Julie Lubbick?"

"No . . ."

"I don't . . ."

"Arn! Julie!" They were drifting left. "Some friends of mine I want you to meet. Susan and Mark Eliot. Mark . . . you still doing the same . . ."

"Acting. Yes."

"That's what I thought."

"I *knew* I'd seen you somewhere before!" Julie Lubbick said. "Weren't you in that play—?"

"Yes!" Mark said. And they all laughed.

"No," she pushed on, "the one about the man—oh, it was about two seasons ago—there was a man in it who had left his wife. . . ."

"You sure that was a play?" her husband, Arnold, asked, and again they laughed.

"Left his wife. And he got involved with this bunch of hippies or something. And then one of them, or someone who looked very much like one of them, terrorized someone."

"I don't think so," Mark said to her.

"But I just *know* I've seen you! Recently."

"He's been in a lot of skin flicks," Susan said, and Mark kept his face tight.

"Oh, has he?"

"Oh . . ."

"Well." Then there was a round of jokes:· not recognizing Mark with his clothes on, screwing one's way to success, bad and nervous conversational adjustments to what Susan had said. "Doesn't it make you jealous?" someone finally asked her.

"I'm not really worried about competition," she tossed off. "But I do resent the money we spend on cures."

"Oh . . ."

They became "the couple whose husband was in skin flicks." The Lubbicks introduced them to the Patchmans. Warren and Cass Patchman introduced them to the De-Greggios. The DeGreggios passed them along to the Kotts. In less than an hour, they had set up their own mythology of pornography. Small crowds gathered to listen.

"Is there actual penetration?" someone asked.

Mark now approached being professional. "In the early days," he began, and told the story of the "early, pre-penetration days"—before *The Accident*. "After *The Accident*, an appropriate contract was drawn up, and there hasn't been any problem since."

"What's it like? With the camera on you and everything? And the lights?"

"No problem."

"Really?"

"Is that so?"

"Actually," Susan began, and he saw her daring him to meet the moment in her eyes. "Actually, the only problem was at home. We went through a period—before we brought in the klieg lights and set them up—of real flatness and depression."

"Lights?"

"Yes. And mirrors. That did it."

"Brought things back," Mark inserted.

"Would you like us to do something here?" Susan asked, looking around. "We'd be happy to." She pinched Mark's arm where she held his jacket. He held his breath.

No one in the group around them actually said anything. There were half-aside glances and finally someone stepped back as if to clear a space and others did the same. In a matter of just a few moments, there was a small circle with Susan and Mark in it, all with a sense of pre-curtain waiting.

They looked at each other, trying very hard to hold on to what was going on, maintaining against a breakup or a scream. Eyes locked and they moved together, each one concentrating on the other, on the other's lenses, trying to understand where they mutually were, play the moment as it was and should be played: exchange, catch up, learn, enter, adjust so that whatever happened next, it happened to them both, a joined instinct.

But there was so much, in a matter of seconds, that they had to understand and clarify about one another first. Each of them stood before the other's near-darkened window, peering in, searching, catching some shapes, some forms, then finding a sense of color there and texture. At the same time there were reflections. Mark, standing in front of Susan's shadowed glass, saw there a shape. And the shape was circular—no, more a sphere. And at the same time he made out that sphere, now irregular, there was the reflection of himself *doing* just that, searching, exploring, finding a shape, a circle, a shape, now a vase, a double-handled apricot-and-black-colored vase. And in the reflection of himself in her eyes was a reflection, and in *those* eyes, *his* reflected eyes, that *glass* was the reflection of her searching him, reaching through his windows to find and understand there: . . . a line, a pipe, a teakwood flute.

Their hands rose together now, also reflected. His hands between hers. Her hands around his. And they were, very slowly, unbuttoning. Mark could see now, simultaneously, Etruscan figures of dancers on the vase beyond her glass and the reflection, in that same glass, of him, of him and his glass reflecting her, her, Susan searching and finding now the exact grain and note openings on the teak, the flute. Without perceptible word or signal, they both turned to the people studying and immensely silent around them. "We, of course, need partners," Mark said.

"Would you help," Susan asked, moving directly toward Warren Patchman.

There was a mute but terrible hysteria in the crowd. "Not me, baby," Warren Patchman said, almost choking on the anxiety of his laugh. The circle widened. The crowd moved back. Mark and Susan scanned the partners, and their eyes were averted almost chorally. There was an awesome sense, somehow, of shame in the room—of nakedness and something criminal and shameful. Mark and Susan turned back to one another, redid the few buttons that they'd loosened and left.

Susan held on to him all the way down the stairs and, when they reached the street, stood and clutched him hard. They were both quiet for a long time. "I'm hungry now," she finally said.

They ate nearby, at a German restaurant where a man in a patched tuxedo played an accordion and sang, many of the customers singing with him.

"Order for me," she said, still holding tight and close to one arm, shivering slightly, almost as if she were afraid.

"Are you cold?" he asked when the waiter had gone.

"No," she said, and then, as if she had decided on the rightness of it, repeated, "no."

"Your eyes." He looked at her.

"What?"

"You're upset."

"No."

"But . . ."

"They're just watering. That's all. It's nothing bad. They're just watering. Water's coming out. It's all right. It's just water. Drill far enough and you strike."

"What?"

"It's an oil metaphor. A natural-resource metaphor. Drill far enough and you strike. Anyway, your eyes are watering too."

"No, they're . . ." He felt high on his cheeks. They were wet. There was water running down his face from his eyes. He looked at her, confused.

"See?"

"But I'm not . . . crying."

"I know." She smiled.

He blinked and wiped it away with his hands to shut it off. It kept up. He went to dry her face with a napkin.

"No." It was not angry; it was just clear.

"O.K.," he said, putting the linen back in his lap.

"It's not bad." She wanted him to know that. "It's not bad at all. Water on the . . ." She groped for the right word, but had to use a rough substitute. "Water on the . . . soul, *sol*arplexus, something like that. You probe in enough, down enough—you strike. When we were staring—that moment —or week or year or whatever—it was the most amazing . . . time of my life."

Mark took in a great breath and held it. And then nodded, staring finally down at the table. He could feel her looking at him. He looked up and they linked eyes again.

"Did you know Betsy Briggs?" he asked.

"In Columbus?"

"Yes."

"I *am* Betsy Briggs."

"I knew something about you made me think of her."

"But you just can't live in New York City, not with a name like Betsy Briggs."

"That's a good point."

"It destroys you. People make jokes. People make up country and Western songs about 'Betsy Briggs.' So I changed it. No one notices 'Susan Weiss.' No one singles it out. It's neat."

"The girl that I've tried to shake from my mind for fourteen years is Betsy Briggs."

". . . Oh. Yes."

On the street, after dinner, standing outside the restaurant and hearing the crowd sing with the patched accordion man, they thought of sailing back to Columbus, and caught a cab down to the piers to find a ship. The ships there were all too big or too filled with cargo and the smell from the Hudson was too rancid, and so they took another cab uptown to Susan's apartment. Mark saw the rest of what he had seen in part from across the street. It all seemed whole; things filled in.

There was Charlie Mingus on the sound system and the light drill of rain which had begun outside. The paintings which she had on the wall were all muted desert colors, animals and natives, all done on sand. They sparkled like warm sidewalks in the small single lamp. On the floor were rugs that Susan had made herself and against one wall was a rug frame with a new rug on it. "I have a rug fetish," she told him, laughing, undressing. "Eventually I'll have them on the ceiling and all the walls." They were drinking Scotch again. Everything in the room seemed a sort of liquid earth or mineral color. "I just love yarns," she said, shaking loose her hair, letting him run his fingertips very lightly over her breasts.

"Would you like me to tell you one?" He kissed her eyelids and temples and cheeks.

"One?" The breath was coming deeper now. She found herself swallowing. She took one of his hands and pressed her lips rhythmically against the fingers.

He moved both hands to her back, pressing softly, one place and then another, playing her. "A yarn."

"Only if you weave it," she said, and they kissed hard, bodies adjusting, bones aligning beside bones. At a point, he took her shoulders and set them apart. Her eyes stayed on him and her mouth continued to move—just slightly, involuntarily. He stepped back and moved his hands to the buttons of his shirt.

"Please," she said, touching the buttons herself.

"Get the record." It was a request and she understood. She nodded and moved off. "Who're you going to vote for?" he asked her, flexing his cufflinks so that he could slide them out of their slots.

"In the election?" She was leaning over the cabinet, her breasts waxed and warm as the rosewood.

"Is there other voting?"

"You'd be surprised."

"Not any more." He folded his pants and noticed that the cuffs showed soil.

"Is the other side all right, Mark? Of the Mingus?"

"Do you have something that lasts about five hours?"

"Only five hours?"

"It's a start."

"I'll see what I can do."

"That's precisely what I like about you."

"You mean 'us.' "

"I do. Yes."

"Are you going to leave your socks on?"

Mark looked down. "I thought you had a yarn fetish. I was doing it for you. I thought you liked yarns."

"Yarns, yes—but mostly tales." They looked at each other from across the room. "I almost have the feeling," she said to him quietly, "that we're making it—just like this."

He took a deep breath. "Wait until you see the close work," he said.

She put a high stack of records on and moved to him. The hairs on their skin just barely touched and set up an electric field between them. Again, there was an overwhelming intimacy in the postures of their eyes.

"Who are *you* voting for? she asked and ran her tongue along his shoulderblade.

"Buckley." He said it into her hair, which he held like the bough of a tree and kissed.

"No." She pressed her teeth lightly against his neck, repeating the name, syllabicating it, "Buc-kley" and with one hand touched his leg.

"Yes." His arms, both of them, swiftly and firmly wrapped her and lifted her up. She let her head fall back, went light and limp for him and he brought her higher up and kissed the flat of her stomach.

"I don't believe you," she said, her head and voice down somewhere near the rug.

"But it's true." He moved with her, carrying her toward the door which separated one room from the next.

"You're not the type," she said, running her fallen hands along the back of his legs.

"I think he's a good man."

"You don't mean it."

He set her down on the bed and stared at her. "Wanton," he said.

"Churl," she answered.

He snarled lightly and slowly let himself down toward her. She beat at him mockingly with her fists. "Away! Away!" she cried in delight. They had a mock struggle, which left them both laughing and breathless. Points of touch, even with their playing, were explosive now and they were both careful with them. They were ready, but they should take time. They lay beside each other, cooling somewhat, breathing to relax.

"Do you know what happened yesterday?" Susan asked him.

"Yes."

"What?"

"I shot a cigarette commercial."

She growled. "I meant to *me*."

"No. What happened yesterday to you?"

"A pervert called."

Mark's body temperature dropped; although he had not caught exactly in his mind what was to come, the blood of him knew. "A what?" he asked.

"A strange little man. Said he was a bookman. Said his name was Appleby. Said I sold him secondhand books." She laughed, stared at the ceiling and laughed again.

Though his body stretched prone, his heart crouched. "Had you?" he asked, almost distantly.

"Had I what?"

"Sold him books."

"Who?"

"Appleby."

"He mentioned Camus. Camus! Good God! Camus and" —she said it all as one word—"Jeanpaulsartre." She laughed.

Mark shut his eyes. He could feel the nerves, one by one, go slack along his arms and chest. ". . . Well?" he finally asked.

She skipped up playfully on an elbow. "Mark," she scolded him, brushing his chest with her nose. "Mark, Christ. Christ, Mark—*Camus*. I mean, D. H. Lawrence is *one* thing. But *Camus*." She poked his scrotum lightly with a finger.

"You never sold a bookstore a Camus."

"Darling, I've never even *bought* a Camus. Good Lord, things are dark enough as they stand. My life is no light-show. And I'll be damned if I'm going to shadow it any more. I mean, I've seen pictures of Camus. He has *caves* under his eyes. He and Samuel Beckett and Humphrey Bogart. No, thanks!" She poked him again, continued it, prodding. "Now," she said, almost whispering it. "Now. Please—now."

. . .

"Where are you going?"

"I can't stay!" Yarn hairs between the toes.

"What do you mean?"

The jamming on of clothes. Heat all over the face. "I can't stay!"

"Mark, I need—!"

"Susan, I have to get out of here. I have to get the hell out of here."

Her on him, grabbing. Him pushing, hitting, almost sick. "Get away!"

"Away? But why?"

"It doesn't matter! I can't stay! Christ, let go!" Pushing; her falling down on the floor, the sound of bruise.

"But I don't understand!" Tears. Mud on her face. Shit. Streaked. Bruises and dirt and mucus and shit streaked. Hollering. Hurt. Backing against chairs. Knocking them over. Rain smashing through the windows. Raging inside. Water—mud—slipping—sick—heaving—starting on her—smashing—striking out—heaving and smashing—cutting—wanting blood—wanting out and blood and peace—wanting quiet but blood—needing to hurt—scared—wretched.

"MARK!"

"Mark—Darling, now, please . . ." The soft underside of her lip was against his ear.

It had all flashed inside him for less than a second; then he took it and jammed it behind his eyes somewhere: the refusal, the anger. It could only fire on the far side of his retinas and along his blood. Beyond those points it would be ugly, be unstatably cruel. She had come, she had gone as far as he—had *let* herself out that much, which meant incredibly and inhumanly. And he would not—would not, would not, would not—amputate her or that.

"Yes," he said, concentrating as he had never concentrated before, for a gentleness, for something right. It was like trying to get to the exact center of sound in the most delicate of seashells without breaking the least flake of its enamel. He took her, brought her, lifted her. She moved in waves. Time. He was so careful with time, with placement, return and time. The small of her back, along her legs, all the quiet places on her ribs, her neck: Mark took fine time, delicious time for her with each moment, each part. And the parts which opened and received, those which requested, called, all the spaces between lips and lobes filled with notes, scales and finally more. And gravity died away in her, even in them, in a way. There was rising; there was flowering: swell and lift . . . swell and lift, swell and lift . . . until the moment, for her, of absolute weightlessness, memberlessness, dissolve, her eyes washing her face again, as in the restaurant earlier, not in any way anything to be called tears.

And in the afterdrift, they lay joined and she talked, talked as if he had never heard a woman talk before, about herself, about her life, a steady, soft, pure, continual rippling at his shore. But he could not really comprehend any of it. It was there. It was soft and true and fine, but it all slipped into the margins, into the margins of his mind, her voice, telling, remembering intimate scribbling in the margins so incredibly happily and beautifully. He had never taken such care in his life. He had never felt so taken inside himself. It was all gone.

Later, when they separated, she lay beside him in deep sleep and he lay on his back crying, sore. Then he edged from the bed, gathered his things and left, enormously careful about sound. Outside, he stood for a moment in the middle of 123rd Street and felt the cool outside dampness on his hands and cheekbones. He wondered whether it was actually raining or whether the air was simply condensing on the lifelessness of this city and on him and on their mutual corpse.

$\mathcal{V}$

Jan rose from her sleep with a young man named Ted to find Mark unconscious on her couch. She stood naked in the slightly arched doorway between the bed and living-rooms and watched him, the wide twist of his face, his almost desperate breathing. All the corduroy was wrinkled, and his shoes were still on. And he looked old. She was excited to have him back again; she was pleased that he had come back to be with her. But there was no question that, unshaven and bunched there in corduroy, Mark did look old.

She moved closer. She looked at his hand where the chainsaw had cut it and they had bandaged it two days before. The bandage looked like a patch of week-old snow and the skin around it looked white, sick and puffy. She knelt and kissed the hand and cried suddenly for a reason which she could not determine, certainly not name. She became angry at someone, someone she did not know, but someone who had taken Mark, taken her Mark, and in two days done things to him, widened his mouth, reset his eyes. She breathed deeply, rose, went and put on coffee. She could hear the small travel clock, distant, beside Ted in the bedroom, even above the cold water running over the back of her hand. It seemed lodged right there in the small map of her wrist.

Mark heard the water and without opening his eyes knew what it was. On Saturday mornings he would always sleep. And she would rise first. She would make coffee. Then sometimes they would make love. And then he would fall back to sleep and she would go out to the delicatessen and get food, bagels and creamcheese and Nova Scotia, fresh for their breakfast. It seemed comfortable being back with these things. He wondered what she had thought seeing him collapsed on the couch when she'd come in for the coffee a few moments earlier. He wondered if she was pleased. He knew he looked terrible. He *felt* terrible. Or maybe he didn't feel terrible any more, maybe that was all over. He supposed he'd have to wake up to really find out.

With his eyes still shut, he listened to the sounds; the water running, the pot being filled, the water off, the basket being inserted, the lid off the coffee canister, the basket being filled, the lid back, the basket filter on, the pot lid on, the pot on the stove, the stove on, footsteps. The footsteps came close, came beside him and stopped. She was looking down. He heard her hair rustle, felt her body bend; then she kissed him. Part of him wanted to take hold, but part of him held off; part of him seemed dead, deadened. He felt her lips again, this time against the bandage on his hand, then felt her rise and heard her steps move off, away, into the bedroom. He heard the scratchy hangers in her closet slide on their metal rack.

Mark opened his eyes and—weak and tired, drained— still felt comfortable. He knew this room. It was almost as if he'd spent his whole life here. He was Jan's husband— or father—or something. Something *like* that. It was the apartment that he and Heidi had had, the wonderful second one on West End Avenue with the blind Czech super. Blind? Yes; that's right; he *was*. And that's what this was, *where* this was. And they had never gotten a divorce. No. No, and it was Heidi who had made the coffee. And he had never plagued her with those phone calls, pressed her. Why had he done that? Made anonymous obscene phone calls to his own wife?

Had it been some kind of test? Well, they weren't really obscene. You couldn't actually call them that, no. What they'd been—they'd been the calls of an "unidentified lover," ways of saying certain things that he hadn't managed to even filter through their pillows in intimacy. They had really been *good* calls. Beautiful. But somehow they'd only scared her. They'd turned her against New York. And she'd finally given him an ultimatum—her or the city. "Love me, love my city," he had said flippantly—no, not really flippantly. He wasn't flippant.

Why hadn't she recognized his voice? Or had she? He'd never considered that. But briefly, all that, that past, had never happened. Just briefly; and this was not Jan's. It was West End Avenue—West End Avenue—*home*. And Mr. Rzchaclav was outside in the hall, sanding the banisters. And Heidi was just beyond him in the bedroom, standing beside a mirror. And Rachel, yes, Rachel was there too, there sitting on the floor in the kitchenette piling jello molds inside one another.

Or was it before that? Was he twenty and just living with Heidi? Had he ever really left *that* Heidi? *That* Heidi would have talked. She would have talked to the caller. It would have been *easy* for her. She would have asked him questions. She had been that clear. Too clear? Not clear enough? Why, when he had walked out on her that morning, that twenty-one years ago morning, had she, by noon, moved, totally moved, left—traceless and without address? And why had she changed herself, become, by the time he had caught up with her, someone else? Had Susan Weiss moved by now? Had she become the *real* S. Weiss? And how had she managed to come so close, made him believe the margins were actually *hers*? And yes—yes, what about that? If not Susan Weiss, who *did* occupy them? Could she have moved?

Jan moved in again from the bedroom, and he shut his eyes quickly and feigned sleep. She moved past, ruffled his hair slightly with her hand, walked and turned off or down the coffee and left, the door clicking heavily behind her. Mark could smell the coffee now, done. It smelled good. It smelled like Saturday, and for some reason, right now, he thanked routines, familiarities. He opened his eyes and breathed deep. He heard the street for the first time now, filled up with Saturday sounds.

But when he lifted his head to sit, his neck felt fat, thick and heavy. And his skull seemed scooped out, strangely hollow. He saw his chainsaw sitting like a starved, mean animal in the corner and smiled. He felt hot. He slipped his jacket off, checked the Camus, still in his pocket, and rose. He took a step. He started to black out, grabbed at a chair and steadied himself. He could feel his hands trembling on the wooden back of the chair, and there were something like thumbs bearing into his brow, moving over to his temples, then sliding back to his brow again. Slowly he felt the pressure leave. He coughed, walked to the window and stared outside, where there was sun. Then he moved to the sink, took a cup, and at the stove, with fair steadiness, poured himself coffee. He smelled Susan Weiss on his wrists.

Back again at the window, he waited. He watched for Jan's return from the delicatessen, though he knew it would be some time. Below, a covey of young blacks scrambled on the hood of a Buick, and he watched the sun crumbling there, beneath them, in reflection. All the voices seemed to come from the metal of the car. It was as if the chrome spoke—"Get that motherfucker! . . . yo' ass I am!"—obscenities in its light.

Then, gradually, he awoke to somebody else, somebody waiting there at his back. He could feel the skin on his neck tighten in signal. He took a long drink of his coffee and turned. "Hi," he said, then crossed back to the stove to refill.

"Hi." Ted stood in his green boxer shorts, legs wide, about five steps into the room. He watched Mark pour the coffee into his cup. There was a caution about his stance, his regard, even his voice.

"Mark Eliot," Mark said, setting the pot back in place, keeping his voice flat and level, keeping himself reduced, apart.

"Ted Sands." Ted kept the exchange, gauging it, never taking his eyes off Mark's back.

"Jan made coffee," Mark said, tapping the pot. "There are cups up there, over the sink."

"Thanks," Ted returned. His hands were slightly open, arms forward, like a wrestler.

"You want some?" Mark took a step toward the cabinet.

"I'll get it!" The reply was fast, positioning.

Mark turned to him and smiled. "Sure," he said, then wandered back to the window with his cup.

Ted nodded slightly and moved up, moved carefully across to where the coffeepot buzzed faintly on the coil. Mark focused out through the window, trying, once again, to listen to the voices reflected in the chrome. Instead, he heard the sounds of cups rustled, one cup found, the coffeepot lifted and poured. Ted kept on watching him. His skin kept up its signals. He could feel Ted's study tightening at the calves of his legs.

"I was worried that you might be Jan's old man or something." Ted finally said. Then there was the grating suck of his coffee.

"Yeah, I was worried about the same thing," Mark replied, his voice angling among the patterns of light, the geometry in glass.

There was the coffeesuck again. "What's that supposed to mean?" Ted asked him over the cup's steam.

"That I was worried about the same thing?"

"Yeah."

"It's a paradox." Mark kept his back to him.

"Maybe I'm just trying to find out if you're a fucking burglar, so I'll know whether I should throw you out on your ass or not." Coffeesuck. Pause.

Mark tried to see if Ted had any reflection in the pane.

"Because if I don't find out soon, then I'm just likely to . . ."

Mark turned. "Look—cool it, fella—will you? Just suck your coffee and cool it. Jan ought to be back before too long." He looked at the boy—*boy*: he caught himself using the word, thinking it—looked at and resented him, disliked him with his thick blond hair and mustache and premature beer paunch trying to establish any authority in this place.

"*Are* you related to her?" Ted finally asked.

"Yes. Yes, I am. I *live* with her." Mark said.

There was a pause. Ted smiled. He smiled and nodded. He ritualized it, smiling and nodding, and moved out arrogantly into the room. "That right?" he asked. "That right?" using his tongue to fold back a portion of his upper lip.

"That's right."

"Oh . . . well . . . well . . ." He laughed to himself. "Well, we certainly missed you last night." He laughed louder. Mark wanted to punch him. Ted raised his cup. "Good coffee." His straw mustache curled down into his smile.

Runty smartass little fucker, Mark thought. He watched Ted bobbing, nodding and smiling a moment more, then turned back to the outside. *Screw him.* He could feel Ted's jaunt, his bounce moving along the floorboards in the space behind.

"You . . . been out of town?" The words seemed to loll in Ted's mouth.

"What's that?"

"Have you been out of town?" He overenunciated.

"I've been away."

"Away."

"Right."

"How was it?"

"Shitty."

"Shitty. That's too bad."

"Yes, it is. I'd agree."

"That's too bad when things are shitty."

"I think you should know that you're beyond beginning to piss me off."

"I see."

"Mmm."

"Sorry about that." *Suck*. Silence. Pause.

"Just thought I'd mention it—as a point of information."

"Gotcha."

The door handle slipped and rattled and Jan walked in, breathless, carrying a paper bag. "Breakfast," she said, gusting it with a smile. "I guess you've met."

"Kind of," Mark said.

Ted took the bag from her and kissed her on the lips. "How do you feel?" he asked. It was all very assertive and coy.

"Fine," she said, "fine," checking the moment uncertainly against Mark.

"He said he's been away," Ted went on to her, pushing for dominance.

"Yes, he has," she said. Her voice was soft, close. "And I hope now he's back."

Ted dressed, and the three of them sat having breakfast together, Saturday breakfast as Mark knew it would be. The tension eased some. They even joked. But the joking didn't really do what they pretended it did, didn't clear things out of the way. Ted pushed to tell the detailed story of his picking Jan up at The Ginger Man and of his coming home with her. Mark took enormous, precise time spreading creamcheese on his bagel, setting the pink-fleshed slice of fish on it precisely, but remained polite. It became clear that Jan wanted to spend time alone with Mark. It became equally clear that Ted would work to postpone that for just as long as he could. He was not a person who had the grace to fade.

There began to be questions and friendly observations about Mark's age, his strength, his condition. "You play ball?" Ted asked.

"Ball?"

"Yeah."

"You mean professionally?" They all laughed.

"No, I mean for exercise. For recreation."

"Oh, I'm a great believer in recreation."

"What about ball?"

"Those too." They laughed again.

"Think you could last out an hour's tag game this morning?"

"Sure."

"In the park?"

"Sure—if I'm the star."

"That's up to you." Ted smiled. His mustache cupped down into his mouth again.

Jan watched Mark's face. She saw him through and beyond his eyes, studied there apprehensively. Mark took a neat, scissored bite out of his breakfast sandwich. He imagined the tightness of his body, his remembered speed. He smiled to himself. "Sure," he said.

"Mark? . . ."

"What?"

Jan cut herself off. ". . . Nothing . . . nothing—I'd just . . . just like to come. If it's O.K. And watch."

"Great!" Ted struck the fisted handle of his fork against the table. "Great! Terrific! Great!"

As the three of them moved along Fifty-ninth Street toward the park, no one spoke. It was a good day. Mark could still feel the weight of Susan Weiss on his chest, but the sunlight that came in textured folds and was cool slowly reduced that. From his drawer of weekend clothes at Jan's, he had taken a pair of frayed chinos and he wore those, together with a blue crew-neck sweater which he had been caught in once in a downpour and now always hung like a loose blue blanket, low below his hips. In it, Mark almost felt that he was Anthony Perkins—elongated and lank.

Their walking was strange—in that it left no sound. Jan and Ted had on sneakers, and Mark wore a pair of canvas shoes. Somewhere on the near distance of Fifth Avenue, a parade played, moving its music away and downtown. Sounds of brass—polished and cool as the light; crisp as the leaves—made the day seem unexpectedly wide and possible. A blind man in a black turtleneck passed, and as he did—Mark wondering if it was again the man he had been seeing for days—the moist nose of his dog caught Mark on the back of a hand. Mark thought he heard the dog fading behind him, whining, wanting a return touch, his thin voice sounding like Susan Weiss's singing, her closed whisper in the dark, notes climbing her milky cigarette smoke, verses recounting explored boxes in her childhood's Ohio attic. Mark turned and caught the blind man and his dog both standing, watching him. He saw the three of them reflected across the street in a wide and highlighted store window, then followed Jan and Ted, cutting abruptly, diagonally into the park.

He hurried slightly to catch up. They moved past horses and old men and others sitting, playing, singing on the grass. Then, at the far side of one of the meadows, were seven or eight young men in sweat and polo shirts, bell-bottoms and cutoffs, all sneakered, all standing in a crude circle slapping a football among them in the air. They were rallying, urging each other, "Keep it going!" "Keep it moving!" "Keep it in the air!" "Hey!" "That's it!" "Keep it going!" Finally, someone struck too hard and the ball looped up and beyond the circle, dropping on the ground just outside. A collusive groan went up. The circle broke. Someone spotted Ted.

"Go out!" they yelled at him, and he broke from Jan and Mark, suddenly became more tight and compact and darted out and across the grass. The ball sprang up into the air, a nice spiral, a strong pass. Ted gauged it, slowed down slightly, cut to his right, then took it with bravado. Mark stood still beside Jan for a moment to watch.

"Do you really want to do this?" she asked.

"Why not?" he said to her.

"I'd rather talk," she said. "I think maybe we ought to talk."

"We'll talk," he assured her, watching Ted return the pass, arch his shoulders back and heave it, high and long, into the air.

"But what does this *prove?*" she asked him, pressing it.

"Prove?"

"Being the jock."

"Don't you like jocks?"

"I like them in their place," she said, and smiled smartly.

"*Hey, Mark!*" Ted shouted to him, across the space. "*We're gonna start!*"

Mark waved to indicate he'd heard and would be right there. "Who knows." He grinned at Jan. "Who knows—I might make the All-Park Team."

"Sis—boom—bah," she said, and Mark moved off away from her and across the grass.

He had played football once. In junior high and high

school in Norwood, Massachusetts, he'd been a running back. He'd played pickup touch games in college too, and in the span of twenty-odd summers since college he'd averaged a game or two on the Vineyard's beach. He felt he could handle it. He still had speed. And he'd stayed in really trim condition.

Introductions moved fast. The others, all around Ted's age, shook hands. They divided up. Mark fell with Tom and Phil and Yanko and Gary. Gary took charge. Since Ted's team had had first choice of player, Gary opted to receive—he and Yanko staying back; Mark and the other two ahead to block.

Someone imitated a referee's whistle. The ball thudded up. Mark set his sights on Ted. Keeping him within vision, Mark headed up field, aiming as if for someone else, then angled low and straight, directly in Ted's path. Ted joined the air, floated almost in slow motion, then nosed down hard into the grass. Mark stopped and watched him for a moment while the play swirled on around him. He just barely heard Gary's voice, coming up fast behind, yelling, "Block! Block!" But by the time the words registered and he caught the image of the man he was to take out moving up past him, it was too late for anything but a sloppy lunge. He landed skidding on the ground and the tag was made.

"Nice block." Ted said, jogging back past him.

"Yeah."

The next play was to be a short pass from Gary to Yanko over center. Mark avoided lining up against Ted. He did not want to push what he felt—or allow Ted to do the same. The ball snapped. Ted made the tag, and Gary blamed Mark. "He's your man!"

"He's what?"

"Your man! Where were you?!"

"Nobody said anything about man to man."

"Well, they are now. Keep him away."

They tried the same thing again; Mark faced Ted in the line. With the center, Mark felt Ted's forearms against his mouth, hard and then past. Mark touched his gums for blood and found it. But the pass had gotten off and Yanko had caught it, making another ten yards before he was tagged. This put them only twenty or so yards from the invisible line sighted from a bench to a tree, their goal. Playing five downs, they had two more in which to score.

"I'd like to try running it," Mark said back in the huddle.

"You?" Gary asked, annoyed.

"Yeah."

"Can you run? Are you fast?"

"I can be," Mark said.

"Let him try."

"It's early."

It was grudging, but Gary said, "O.K."

"Which side?"

"Left."

They lined up. Mark back for the pass from center; Yanko back slightly left to block. Waiting for the snap, Mark calculated an awkward right-leaning of his body, as if to test the wind resistance on that side. He caught Ted eying him, digging his toes into the turf, waiting for the snap. It came and Mark feinted once hard right. It worked; Ted charged hard right, pulling the rest of the defense off with him as Mark pushed and swept left. He made the end and had only one backup man to outrun. Twenty years peeled away. He drove his legs, slamming his feet hard into the ground, running, and as the gap closed, he could feel his chest tighten and pound. The backup man fell far short and Mark dashed down easily and across the line.

Yanko was there almost immediately beside him. "Fantastic!" Tom and Phil hailed him too, but Gary just stood off, toeing the ground. Mark looked over at Jan. She did a quick, compressed cheerleader act. He felt embarrassed. Yanko yelled out "Suckers walk!" and Ted's team turned and trotted off toward the other end of the field, where Ted huddled them a moment before they spread out and dispersed.

Being the first to score lifted Mark. It made him believe, for an instant, that he had found the girl in the margins and was living with her. He flashed on the image of Susan Weiss, double-exposed, at once gray-skinned and bony, seen beyond curtains in the circles of his binoculars, at once that, but also liquid, her eyes warmly colored and always wet. Yanko kicked, and Mark began a jog down the field, Susan Weiss's words, her stories and reveries in the dark, jangling around his ankles, his wrists and neck, sonorities of his disconnection, like an enormous mistake.

Ted parted him at the waist. He felt all the breath leave, total exhaust. He lay doubled on the ground, his ribcage pleading for wind, his bones feeling brittler and drier each second. He could hear the sounds of play somewhere beyond. Then someone came over. It was Phil. "You O.K.?" he asked. Mark could only answer with his eyes.

A short time later, when Mark once again had his breath, Ted tapped him on the shoulder. "Sorry," he said—mustache in mouth.

"Nice block," Mark volleyed. The words ached.

Ted looked around at the others, and there was some kind of silent exchange.

It increased. It became clear that it wasn't just a question of Ted and himself any more; Ted had allies. Each of the next three downs found him taken out, double-teamed each time. He caught a foot hooking his, then an elbow in the mouth, but he didn't say anything. One of the results of the collusion was that Ted's team, concentrating on other things, wasn't moving the ball, and Mark thought he could settle for that.

On the fourth down, Mark tried something he had seen a coach do once, years before, in high school. He hesitated in charging so that the two blockers trying to wipe him out both misjudged and moved into each other, Mark grabbing their shoulders and making the impact sure, then moving around them to make the tag, catching the side of Ted's face in the reach.

"Nice play," Phil said to him.

"Nice play, Old Man," Ted echoed.

"God, Sands, you didn't say you were going to bring a veteran," one of the blockers pushed.

"Which war?" Gary said, and then laughed.

"Didn't see you make that tag, Gar." It was Yanko.

Mark knew he was in trouble. He looked over at Jan, and she shook her head. Ted picked up the signal. "See? His daughter thinks he should quit."

"There's always Medicare."

"Jesus, you guys have pretty big mouths for a team that hasn't scored." Yanko called at them. That broke it; they drew in and huddled.

They would push to prove Yanko wrong. There was something tightly serious about the knot of them, backs bent, heads together, constructing their plan. Mark, crouched on hands and knees on the scrimmage line, waiting, caught the deep odor of earth. It smelled to him like blood. He could taste it on his teeth. It was the taste of ink and handprints from the margins of his book. Mark sensed that he should probably stand up and leave, but couldn't.

They broke. Ted lined up to the right, and from the way he pushed his toes against the turf, it was clear that he must be going for a long pass. Again a part of Mark tried to step off, step away; but it didn't work. On the snap, instead of charging, he dropped back and followed Ted. He dug in. It became a race. He was thirty again . . . twenty-five . . . twenty. Then, for both of them, the event had nothing to do with the ball. It was a proof of bodies.

At the same moment Mark pulled ahead, he focused back out of the contest and on the ball. He saw it leave the thrower's hand, checked himself, let Ted, who had lost place sense, overtake him, then turned, slowing almost to a stop to take the pass. Ted caught what was happening and checked himself. Mark had only taken one step with the caught ball when he felt both of Ted's closed fists hard on his shoulders, slamming him to the ground.

He was up immediately. "This is *tag*, you asshole!" he shouted. "Not fucking karate!"

"You got tagged."

"Bull*shit!*"

"Can't you take it?"

"It ruins him for the young chicks!" Someone else edged himself in.

"Why didn't you just *knock* it down, for Chrissake!" Gary shouted at him. "We could have *had* the ball back *there!*"

"Trying to be the flash, and you really fucked it up." Ted kept coming in from the edges.

"You're really an asshole—you know that?" Mark kept his eyes straight on Ted.

"Come on; let's play ball!"

"How'd you like a punch in the mouth?" Ted moved in, setting his feet apart.

"How would I *like* a punch in the mouth?" Mark asked him.

"Yeah."

"That your idea of a really sharp and clever question?"

"Hit him, Sands!"

"Floor him!"

Yanko and Phil broke them up, moved Mark with them back to a huddle.

"He's just trying to make you blow it," Yanko said.

"Forget him."

On the next play, Mark caught an elbow. On the second play, he was tripped—someone else each time. On the third play, Gary sent him out for a short buttonhook. He ran, cut, turned, stopped to take the pass, but the minute he had it, he felt the pressure on the back of his knees, felt himself losing contact with the ground, going up and over backward. He stood up slowly. The whole thing, from Gary's call on down, seemed like a setup. He caught some exchanged glances. Yanko caught up with him, walking back to the huddle. "Cut out," he advised Mark in a quick aside.

Mark considered it. "Can you pass?" Gary asked him as they gathered.

"I think so," Mark said without weighing it.

"Throw me a long one," Gary said. "Long!"

"I'll stay back and block," Yanko said, and Gary slid a side look at him.

They broke. Mark stayed back for the snap. It came, and all five defenders rushed. Yanko took out one of them, Ted, sending him back on his rear, but the other four were all over Mark, slapping supposedly at the ball, knocking him to the ground, one falling with a knee against his ribs. "Sorry," whoever it was said in the blur. Then they all started congratulating each other: "Nice rush!" "Nice rush!" congratulating and laughing.

Yanko helped Mark up. "If I could help you, I would, but it's gotten too big. I'm a joke to them anyway. Make up some excuse, man. Split."

"Mark!" Jan called, concerned, from the sidelines.

"Mark!" "Mark!" He heard a couple of muffled mimickings and waved her to keep quiet. He trotted over to the huddle.

Gary made a mock production out of asking "Where the hell was the blocking?" and received appropriate mock-grumbled excuses. "Can you kick?" Gary asked Mark in the huddle.

"No."

"No?"

"No!"

"Shit, man—I thought you were an all-star! Tom, you boot it. Everybody else down field for the tag."

The punt was strong, high, distanced, and Mark started down with the others. He caught one of Ted's players waiting for him, waiting to cut across him on a block and he shot ahead, readying himself, keeping a steady sidelong eye.

The blocker feinted away and then came for him, lunging his block. Mark lifted his knees hard, as though he were jogging through surf. There was a crunch and cry. Somewhere ahead a tag was made. Then everyone converged.

The blocker sat on the ground, rocking, cursing, holding

his left hand to the bloody right-hand corner of his mouth. Mark waited until most of the others were around. "Sorry," he said, squatting down, regulating it as coolly as he could. "If you hadn't left your feet for the block, though, I don't think it would have happened."

"Fuck you!" Blood spit from the player's mouth at him. Mark felt a strange pride and strength. Ted and another picked their man up and walked him back to the huddle. Mark stayed squatting close to the ground, smelling soil and blood and ink and handprints again. "You shouldn't play so rough, Old Man," somebody mocked him from outside.

The huddle time drew out. It brewed a quality of group revenge. Ted said they were waiting for the bleeding to stop, but there was a great deal of intense exchange, a lot of diagraming on the earth. Finally, tightmouthed, they split apart to resume play.

"Watch it." Yanko nudged Mark.

"I know." It was a hurried, throaty return.

Standing at the line, waiting, the voices began coming back, calling from all the bordered hallways, chorusing at the edges. Mark heard Heidi—or was it someone else? "You'll go away. You'll go away, I know." Could he have stayed with her? Could they have kept it up? The center leaned forward over the ball as she returned: "You have no sense of the realities, Mark; you cannot love this city and love us. I'm taking Rachel. . . ." *Taking? Taking!* What gave anyone the right to *take?* The ball floated back through the center's legs in slow motion to Ted. Mark started ahead, bumping, then sliding off the arms of an opposing man.

Take—in the margins she had said . . . She? . . . Who?

. . . Heidi? . . . Which Heidi? The one nearly twenty-one years ago? Or—? No . . . *she* . . . *she* had said—to Camus, to him and to Camus (Had Heidi ever read Camus?): "Imagine *me*—expecting nothing—taking—assuming it in my hand." Mark moved in in a direct line on Ted, who cocked and recocked his arm for a pass. You don't *take* things, take them away with you; you *held* them; that was it at most. And who *said* that? Who was she? And where were the margins? How did you get *into* the margins? Susan? Heidi, is it you? But you're not "S. Weiss." "Susan Weiss." Who is *she*? Mark's feet floated in, charging, nearing, one soundless canvas foot after the other. Something in his vision saw Ted's arms float down from the cocked gesture of pass, saw him offer the ball there in front of him, like a punter, but Mark's weightless legs kept on bearing down. If he could get into the margins more himself, if he could find them, then she would just appear. It was a question of borders, he thought. If you could find the right borders and then just take one more step, *after* them and into the margins . . . the margins were magic. That's why he had chased down the book. He knew that. The margins were magic. What had happened with Susan Weiss? Had she lied about never owning a Camus? Sure: Heidi lied. Heidi lied to him about lots of things. Lied, went away, changed. That was *possible*.

Ted was taking a step toward him now, offering the ball low. And Mark moved in on it. Ted's right foot was poised back, his spine inclined diagonally, his eyes hard ahead. *Susan Weiss could have lied*, Mark thought again. Lied as part of the magic. No, not "magic" . . . what? Ted wasn't passing, he began to realize through the drift. He was kicking. Kicking. *Art! Not magic—art.* And he, Mark, was right there on him, charging, floating forward, unable to stop. *Art.* Ted's foot was describing a hard low arc, swinging down and beginning its trip up. Mark tried to shift the position of his body in the charge. *Yes!* If he could find the margins—if he could find them again and find their art—then he could find Susan Weiss—and know if she had lied—*art*fully lied—and if she was really Heidi—the first Heidi—grown up and in disguise—no—not in disguise—in . . . in *form*—in costume. Ted's foot slammed frontally into Mark's crotch. And Mark dropped.

It was like death. There was a circle around him of standing and distended figures, all of whom looked like mourning balloons. He felt a constant contraction, a shriveling into his grave, a final journey of desiccation. He saw Jan moving among them, moving among the mourning balloons in a fury, her mouth menacing, her hands beating at Ted. The light was always being drained out of the sky; the sky out of the air. Everything was descent and contraction and vacuum.

Then the pain started. The death and burial ceased and the pain started and the reconstruction began. And he wanted it away. He wanted nothing to do with it. Whoever it was who was responsible for reversing things, Mark wanted to shout at him and tell him: "*No!* Let it go! Let the death be death. Let me sink to the flat vacant end!" If this was the way it had to happen, if reforging meant an acetylene torch held hard on the groin, then let me go. He felt the terrible heat force all his juices to the surface, felt his face and entire body bathe and dry, bathe and dry.

And with it all, with the pain, came sound. Voices. The stupidities of forced remorse there above him. And Jan's anger, her screams. Mark did not want to rise again, did not want to reverse what had started—the sinking, shriveling, fading—and step up to that. But there was no question now.

There was breath again. There was air. He could feel air moving, beginning once again to ventilate him. And as it grew, as it grew it became quite strange. It became the ventilation of laughter, a hysteric revival. The balloon figures became comic bobbing above him. The last hour, his involvement in the game, became a cartoon, and he watched the animation of himself, sat bent double, the double harp of his ribcage sore from what now seemed forty-one years of laughter.

Jan knelt to touch and help him. And when she did, the entire scene inverted. He was floating above them all, and they were looking up, and Jan was standing on tiptoes reaching up to him trying to bring him back: "How are you?" she was saying. And her weightless words echoed.

"How are you?"

"I'm O.K."

"They did it all on purpose."

"I know."

"Goddamnfuckingsonsofbitches."

"It's O.K."

"I hate them."

"There's no sense."

"I do."

"There's no sense in it."

"I don't care."

"It's all . . ."

"What?"

Mark giggled. "Who are you?"

"Mark, I'm Jan!"

"I know." He began to set his feet under him.

"Are you all right?"

"It's O.K."

"Can you stand?"

"Sure." He rose slightly, giggled again, then slowly straightened himself out. "It's O.K."

"Mark?"

"You O.K., buddy?" somebody outside asked.

"Mark?"

Mark started stiffly off—toward the city, outside.

"Mark?" She trailed along.

"Hey, buddy, you gonna be O.K.?"

"Mark, what's funny?"

Behind him, one particular voice raised in impatient anger. "Well, you could at least answer, for Chrissake!"

"Mark?"

He shook his head and kept laughing to himself.

"Mark, what *is* it?"

"Fuck you, man! You deserved it!" The words flapped like grimy kite-tails in the bunched branches of trees behind.

"Mark! Please! At least say something."

He did. Later, in a bar on upper Lexington, over whiskey sours, Mark talked to Jan about himself for the first time in their two years. He told her that he had once, when he was a student in this city like herself, given half his blood to a girl named Heidi, whom he had found nearly frozen to death inside a jungle gym in an asphalt playground on Houston Street, and later married and still later made obscene—no, not really obscene—telephone calls to, Heidi, who, restored, had moved on to restore a house in Dover, Massachusetts, taking . . . *taking* with her their child, another girl, perhaps now a woman, Rachel. He told Jan how he felt about her—relaxed, soft, but very terminal. He watched her across the table, unwrapping sugar cubes and stacking them in silence.

"I'm in the margins now," he told her—as if it would be, in any way, an explanation.

Soon afterward, when they left the bar, he could actually smell the dark coming on.

vi

Outside the city, the wind, scrubbing the bordering rivers
to a fine corrugation, sliced in and tried to puncture the
Pan Am Building's glass. All the concrete smelled damp,
like foam. All the cab aerials glistened in the wind like
straws. From gutters on almost every block, fractured
umbrella ribs caught automobile headlights and seemed to
discharge sparks. Things looked blue. There was a taste of
alum in the air. In Grand Central's men's room, Mark, his
mouth opened to the exploding chrome showerhead, gargled
country and Western songs. He had soaped and lathered
himself like a sheep. His bones felt raw. Beyond him and
beyond a discard of wingtip shoes, whose toes stared like

eyes from the top of a wire trashbasket, the black attendant trimmed his nails into a urinal.

Also beyond, beyond and apart, above in a booth in Cobbs Corner, Jan sat waiting. She ballpointed overlapping rectangles in blue on napkins, then shredded them into a glass of water, watching the ink filaments slide up like hairs around the air bubbles in the water, then cloud. Her face looked bruised and gray. The coat she wore looked too big. Her hair appeared to belong to a woman twenty years older than herself. And the wind, trying to dislodge the station from outside, made her feel cold.

When Mark, wearing a bluish tweed suit and a fine navy turtleneck, joined her, he looked shiny, and their hands together on the formica tabletop looked variously metallic and strange—his buffed, hers lead-colored and struck. They ordered club sandwiches, turkey and ham, and Mark talked on and on about a place called the Pemigewasset Wilderness, somewhere in New Hampshire in the White Mountains. He said the rocks there were worn smooth as tubs and you could ride their channels a half mile.

"And at the end," he said, "at the end there's a huge chute and fall. And you go out into the air and then fall down into this clear pool. It's like a heart attack, the shock there, when you hit. When you go under when you hit."

He looked to Jan for some response. She only checked a piece of lettuce in the corner of her mouth, pinched the insides of her eyes above her nose and drained her coffee cup.

And so they took a cab back up to the apartment, Mark whistling louder than the wind whistling outside. He asked Jan to see a movie, but she didn't want to, and so he went alone to a small theatre around the corner and watched *Beneath the Planet of the Apes* twice through. It was an awful movie, terrible; Mark laughed, a thin tinselly laugh, through most of it, but there was something about the images of bombed-out New York subway stations that quieted him. He carried them with him into a bar called McDaniel's, where he sat and saw coils of subway track wrap and unwrap his two bottles of beer. Around 11:30, he went back to the apartment and made love to Jan, but it was bad and they both knew it. And after she had shuddered herself secretly to sleep, he got up and went through Camus again. It was fine! He fell asleep with his eyes feeling charged, almost electric, inside his head.

Sunday morning Jan refused to get out of bed. She said she planned to stay there until she died. Mark tried stuffing pieces of sweetroll into her ears to tease her out of it, but she just pulled herself under the covers and cried. So he went out and bought a *Times*. He scanned it in a delicatessen booth, checking each newsphoto for the appearance of "S. Weiss," his now retouched image of what she must be. He found one in the Society section, but she was getting married and her name was Cutler. She was marrying a man named John Pearson, and Mark began seriously to question his instincts. He found another photo in the Book Review section, this time a woman named Rena Davidowiz, no mention of Miss or Mrs., who had written an existential novel of children growing up on Mott Street. Could S. Weiss have married, remarried? Might she have a pen name? She looked incredibly much like his abandoned Susan: Susan Weiss, who had told him in their mounting of passion that she had never read Camus. Could she have lied?

From a crucial section of the book, one in which Camus had stated, "There is consciousness only in city streets!" and S. Weiss had margined, "Yes, in the trash and offal, in the

discarded rings and waste-love," Mark drew his list of addresses, phone numbers and names. No more guesswork!
No more intuition! There was too much what? Too much
pride in that. He would call, and if necessary call *on*, each
possible S. Weiss in the five boroughs of New York. He
would make sure. He would *find* her. And he would con-
vince her. They would go off and live somewhere, somewhere marginal: the Pemigewasset Wilderness, West End
Avenue, the men's room in Grand Central Station. But he
would bleed again; they *both* would. They would transfuse
each other.

By 11:30 that evening—except for a Sylvia Weiss in
Queens who could not be reached by telephone and whom
he would definitely check the next day—the list was
exhausted. Thirty-six of thirty-seven names called, inter-
viewed, cross-questioned, handwritings checked, and Mark
was thrown back two days, onto Susan. Had Susan lied?
Did that fit—a kind of margin on her own margins? Everything else except the fact, except the yes-or-no ownership,
of the Camus had seemed so right. He remembered the
feel of her bracelet against his neck. He remembered the
way she said the syllables "Buc-kley."

As he set his key in the apartment lock, Mark heard
Jan's barefooted scrambling beyond. He opened the door,
stood in its frame, listened. He heard bedrustlings, squeaks
fading away to silence. He shut and locked the door again
behind him and wandered into the small kitchen. Before he
saw it, he could smell the beer which drained still, trickling,
from the horizontal can set on the drainboard. He smiled.

"Jan?"

No answer.

"Didn't you want the rest of this beer?"

No answer.

"I thought you were going to stay in bed till you died!"

No answer.

"And either you have deceived me—or there is a mad beer-draining rapist loose in the place."

Something like the reclutching of bedclothes two rooms away.

Mark moved back into the front room, carrying the empty beercan, clanging the side of it rhythmically with a spoon.

"And someone's been drinking *my* beer—and they drank it *allll* up!"

Not a sound.

"Jan? Are you dying?"

Resolute silence.

Mark dropped the spoon into the beercan and, moving to the door of the bedroom, rattled it like a dinner bell. "Come—and—get—it!"

Improvised death.

"Are you passing? . . . Have you passed? . . . Is that a decomposing shape there under those covers?"

"Go away!"

"Ah *ha!*"

"I *am* dying! I *will* die!"

"You don't think that beer will keep you alive."

"I don't know what you're talking about."

Mark flipped the beercan and spoon against the wall. "Get out of bed, lady; I want to talk."

"Not in your life!" The words pillowed up with the strength of a doll.

"Last warning! I want to talk."

"Fuck!"

"O.K.!"

Mark exited again into the front room, searched, and

behind the couch found his chainsaw. He checked it for fuel. There was still enough. He carried it with him back through the bedroom door, then stood in silence and watched the lump that was Jan shift slightly, breathe.

"I'm really going to die. I don't care," she said, muffling through. "I mean it this time. I'm never getting out of this bed."

Mark pulled the cord, and the chainsaw spun into life. Jan screamed. Mark, watching the bedclothes to see if the miniature voice beneath them would surface or recant, felt his hand ache. The shape only drew itself together more tightly than before. He sawed one leg off the bed and, as the bed tilted to one side and dropped, watched the shape's arms reach out and clutch the mattress—to avoid being spilled.

"It won't work!" she said.

He sawed another leg, and the bed inclined at forty-five degrees. He paused and watched. The form splayed out, locking both arms and legs around the upper incline of the bed. The bedclothes rolled off.

"Well, look who's here!"

"No way!"

"Ma'am—how come the lower left-hand side of your body is blue and the upper left-hand side is white?"

"Eat shit!" The words sounded softly tinny as they passed down through the mattress, spiraling down the springs.

"I believe I'm ready to," Mark said, mostly to himself, set his key to Jan's apartment gently, like a thermometer, between her buttocks and, shouldering his binoculars and chainsaw, left.

.   .   .

He wandered the city, staring into it like an immigrant, touching the brick sides of buildings as if they were braille. Everywhere there were beautiful women riding taxis alone —everywhere, and broken bird feathers under all the leafless avenue trees and at the corners of too many streets. No phonebooths stood unoccupied. Why? Why were there semicircles of people waiting, waiting upon waiting to keep them full? Why did the wind smell mulled, like unclean wine? Picking through trash, Mark found a suicide note typed on a 3 x 5 card. It was paperclipped to a recipe for chocolate mousse. He wound in toward the park, where, sometime around 2:00 a.m., laughing, he started up his chainsaw and its vibration shook the laughter out of him. He felled a tree bordering his football meadow and carved the remaining seven-foot trunk into a cross before he drifted away and took a hotel room for the night.

In the morning, with his eyes still closed and under the street noises from outside, Mark could smell the grain of the manila window shade. Was he waking earlier still? Later now? Was there any pattern? He had a vision of himself stretched out on cereal, of his small sixth-floor overnight room six inches deep in—no, not cereal, not Rice Krispies, *sawdust*. He dropped one hand over the side of his bed; his chainsaw and binoculars were where he had set them. Would the *Times*, he wondered, carry an article, a picture?

Mark rose and dressed. He walked the few blocks to Grand Central, where he lockered his chainsaw, shaved and took a sunlamp in the men's room. When he called, his answering service told him he had a 10 a.m. wine commercial filming at Grant's Tomb. Unbelievable, he thought: Greek tragedy.

There was still the last untracked name, still Sylvia Weiss in Queens to be checked out, with a little over an hour and a half left in which to do it. When he called, she answered. "What do you want?" she asked, and sounded somehow like a talking sponge, porous and far.

"Well, I have very specific reasons for trying to locate an S. Weiss who once owned a copy of Camus's '*42–'51 Notebooks*."

"Of *who*?" Her words had tunnels in them.

"Camus."

"What's that?"

"Are you going to be home until ten o'clock?"

"Yes, but what—?"

Mark hung up and taxied to the address. It was a neighborhood where the sidewalks, even the buildings themselves, were the color of old bones. There was a chain of four dark men strung sitting across the chalky top step outside the door to the building. Mark rehung his shoulders and started up.

"Where you goin', man?" one of the chain asked.

Mark, basing his feet fairly solidly, paused halfway. "There a Sylvia Weiss living in this building?" he asked.

The men looked at one another; then one turned to him and said, "Not here."

"It's her address."

"We said not here." One of the men started unbuttoning his shirt.

If you are in the margins, Mark thought, then that is where you are. He looked at the man—strong, in his mid-forties—then at his blue-checkered cotton shirt. "Well, then, I guess I'll just check," he said.

"No, you won't."

Mark ascended one more step and the men rose silently together. The scene froze.

"Is that him?" a voice called from the second-floor window above, the same voice, one with airpockets in it.

"I think so, Gramma," one of the men lifted his head straight up and called.

"Does he want taxes?" Some shards of urine-white hair dangled and swung vaguely beyond the cracked, dusty frame.

"We don't know." Then ahead: "*Do* you want taxes?"

"It's all right," Mark said quietly and started down.

"Tell him I'll be dead in two months and it won't make any difference," the voice called out from above, each word shattering like a dry spore in the air.

"Gramma's just living on a shoestring," one of the men said behind him as he set a foot onto the skull-colored sidewalk and jammed his finger up to hail a cab that would take him up to his appointment at Grant's Tomb. Scratch Sylvia, he recorded; scratch the last.

The cameras and the sound booms were set up at the tomb. The crew was there, shuttling about almost weightlessly, like paper scraps. There was a sense, although it was not quite cold enough, that the air might fill with a light snow at any minute. Mark checked the tower of Riverside Church for a colored light, a weather beacon.

The director handed him his wardrobe—offwhite double-breasted suit, black pleated shirt, black shoes—and pointed to where the trailer was pulled up. Mark went inside to change, interrupting an assistant director's make of a continuity girl. They left and Mark thought he smelled powder smells, smells of a shooting gallery, at sea somewhere in their wake. He dressed quickly and wondered if Susan would be at work. It felt good, dangerous but good, to accept her margins. He was sure she had lied about her rug fetish too.

Outside, the director introduced Mark to the girl he would be working with. Her name was Shelly or Shelby or something like that, and she had the tightest skin Mark had ever seen drawn on a moving frame. He thought about how percussive lovemaking would have to be with her, and smiled.

"That fucker's a real asshole," she said to him, of the director who'd moved away to arrange the wine bucket and glasses on the small round table before the Tomb.

"I don't know," Mark managed flatly.

"Watch out!" The words escaped, somehow, through her cheek. "He sucks cock."

"Well . . ."

They filmed the spot, an hour attempting to hold their wine glass lips kissing in toast, while cameramen on the ground with zoom lenses tried to shoot up and through the glasses, tried to capture romantic and swimming images of Grant's Tomb behind; a zoom from love, to wine, to the rose-colored tomb.

"What is this shit?" the girl kept saying. "Get some wipeass to hold up my fucking arm!"

Mark stared continually at her skin, the unbelievably taut forearm. He kept searching for a seam, afraid that if he found it, he would do so only to see it split, see the entire girl instantly shrink into a lingerie of herself and collapse, like a water balloon. He had the recurring thought that she had been pumped up, that under the tanned tight skin pressed a strange, somewhat colloidal solution of sharp jagged pebbles and wine. He kept imagining the spots on his white suit each wine-colored, blossoming into a rose, then, on the instant, dying, clutching, dropping its petals, gathering musk. Oh, yes! And one of the pebbles in her, one of the sharp-edged pebbles, when she burst, would have, in exploding, struck him dead at the temple. Then the cameramen would bury them both, Mark and the spent roses wrapped together in the girlskin, there in Grant's Tomb. With the director giving the last rites.

When it was all over, Mark and the girl got to finish the wine. It should probably have been chilled, but it cut the nearly noon hunger and sense of fatigue.

"This fucker I live with's really down on my cunt," she started in.

Mark looked out and away at the Hudson River. It seemed either to be all shore or to have no shore at all. He couldn't quite decide which. He thought he felt Susan Weiss's eyelashes pressed against his chin. He smelled the party they had been at together in the wind. He heard a small German accordion play. All the air—as he drank and looked out and listened to the skin-girl's words . . .

". . . like to take a blowtorch to his balls. . . ."

. . . all the air seemed suddenly to be textured with Saran Wrap.

The thought of sculpting another tree in Central Park drifted in on him during lunch, and he remembered that he hadn't even checked the *Times*: 2 a.m. last night, probably not discovered until dawn—*no*; he'd have to wait another day. He might become famous, a Phantom. Did they have silencers for chainsaws? What other forms could he make?

He called Susan at her agency, but the girl answering said she wasn't there.

"Is she out at lunch?"

"I don't know."

"Do you work there?"

"You mean *here*?"

"Yeah."

"Yeah."

"Do you—would you have any idea where Miss Weiss might be?"

"No. I don't actually hang out in her office."

Mark thought that he perhaps heard roaches moving about inside the earpiece of the phone. One corner of his lips felt chapped. "Could . . . could you please . . ." He was trying hard to sound harmless, nice: "Could you please ask someone who would know; ask whether she's been in today or not? This . . . well, It's fairly important."

". . . Just a minute."

"Thanks."

Mark let the mouthpiece of the phone drop, and breathed deep. In the other voice's brief absence, he looked around. He brought the phone back up. He felt crowded by the penciled phalluses on the walls.

'She hasn't been in. She hasn't called."

"Thanks."

"Sure. Goodbye."

Maybe she *had* cleared out. Like Heidi. Maybe that's why she hadn't come to work. She was spending the day moving, vacating, just as Heidi had vacated, vanished on him years before. Maybe she was Heidi's orphaned younger sister. The phonebooth began to shake, tremble with the nearby passing of an enormous, steel-pipe-carrying truck. Mark stood and felt the cartilage vibrate in his neck. He thought he felt the booth unmoor, rattle free of the concrete and begin to tip. What a strange bier it would make, he thought, glass shivered through wire mesh, horizontal and funereal on the sidewalk. And suddenly the binoculars' case dangling there at his side seemed antique, macabre, like a leather reliquary.

The seatcovers of the slow black cab Mark took to his unfurnished apartment across from Susan's were made of something like satin and whistled when, after paying his fare, he slid across them to get out. He thought it strange that the cabbie should never utter a word the entire way and, watching the cab pull west, he saw it vanish around the corner. All the people moving up and down the street were coughing lightly. Mark coughed once himself, then moved into the lobby and took the elevator up to his apartment.

The main room smelled like cold hamburger and moist paper. It was unaltered, just as he remembered having left it. The light too, the way it fell from the windows, seemed preset, just exactly the same; unusual when he had departed at dawn and it was now midafternoon. He followed an impulse to explore the entire base surface of the space, testing each floorboard, moving first in diagonals, then in circles, pressing with deep bends of his knees, shifting his weight. The floor seemed fine, solid enough. And the room had heat. The cold-meat smell from before had sunk away someplace, gone underground.

Mark went to the single window and tried, standing slightly above it, to look across. But the other side of the street looked two-dimensional, like a drop; it lacked depth. He shut his eyes. He felt the tips of Susan's lacquered fingernails on his ribs, felt the weight of her entire frame somewhere within his back. He heard what sounded like Wagner from some other within-range apartment and wondered if it also might not be hers.

He unclenched, opened his eyes. He stared straight at the glass and it appeared rippled, like overlays of stretched clothesbags or a design, thousands of fine white parallel threads. It made him want to squint diagonally to the left. Something prismatic, perhaps some imperfection, bent his sight. He could feel the nerves strung to his eyes bind and pinch. He could barely see across the upper air's emulsion of grit. And Susan's window seemed merely a dim gray basting of milk.

Mark unslung the binocular case from his shoulder, opened it and, with a piece of Kleenex from his coat pocket, rubbed each lens. He remembered her ears. He checked his watch; it was close to 2:15, nearly the half-day anniversary of his chainsawed park cross. Binoculars down, he looked again at her windows, knelt, then lifted the large glasses to his eyes.

Still, focus came slow; too much near resolution, then too much far. But finally he had it, had it down: the dust particles vibrating on her pane like cilia on some organism under a slide. Mark smiled.

He searched the entry-room window where he had, three mornings before, seen her last. But nothing seemed there. Not even her lamp was on. He shifted the glasses to the right, to the bedroom, and scanned that. Furniture: he tried to recall the exact position of the bed; where? . . . Then he found it, just its edge, the near footpost first. He traced the border of the mattress up toward the head. A thin white arm dangled over the edge. He trapped it, circled it, saw where it landed in bent fashion, palm-down on the floor. It didn't move. It seemed gray, disembodied—

as if Susan, in the rush to get wherever she had gone in the morning, had forgotten it, forgotten one arm, forgotten to pick it up from where it lay sleeping on the bed and put it on. But it was all the glasses could find. The rest—shoulders, hips, knees—was too far away, chopped off by the upper window line.

Mark brought the glasses down. Was she asleep? Had he, sixty hours ago, exhausted her that much? Was it possible? Or had she bought another Camus, bought another copy of Camus and in a new frenzy remargined it, stayed up and frantically written for forty-eight hours and then collapsed? Or had she, had she, had his Susan Weiss, like Jan, gone to bed never to get out—to die? No. No, she was too strong. That was set down, had been set down for him: "strength." Mark smelled the hamburger re-enter his room, felt the wallpaper grow pulpy and moist. He felt his wristbones begin to shake.

O.K. O.K.! He would study her skin. O.K. He would watch that. He would search closely and see what was happening there. He set his elbows on his knees to hold the glasses straight, adjusted the sighting slightly again. He watched for tics, contractions. He tried to see if he could see her pores relax. If he could get a sense of *texture*: smooth, porous, slackened, dry, damp—*that* would tell him. . . . O.K. O.K., he had it. Yes. O.K., he was studying something . . . studying something dusty, cracked and sleek. Or was that her window? Or his? Had the arm or hand changed position at all from the time he had first caught focus of it? Check. No; it seemed precisely the same.

Mark tried to chart it. If he gave it a map, diagramed it, he could better tell. His billfold had a pad of paper in it and a pen. He took them out and, working back and forth between them and his binoculars, drew. He sketched the lip of sheet fold, where it lay only one inch from her upper arm. He caught the precise arm angle as it projected stiffly over the edge. He drew—almost perfectly, he thought, or at least as perfectly as he could determine it —the exact focal triangle: arm, floor, vertical side of the bed. He placed the exact folds in the hand: base on the floor, two fingers tucked under—just right. And . . . was her bracelet there, the thin silver one he remembered? No. Would it have been on the other wrist? Didn't remember. Was there a watch? No. Had she been wearing a watch? Wasn't sure. Mark tried to calibrate the exact tension of her skin—but it was like the textures he had tried to search before; spoiled by the intervening panes, the windows, his and hers. They cut in and obscured any kind of ideal judgment.

Still, he worked, drew in fine painful detail all he saw, taking well over an hour before he was done, checking at regular intervals for any measurable change. But there was none. His sight started to squeeze and blur again. Objects, even the air, blanched, grew whiter. He closed his lids, opened them. His own skin looked to him like fresh coconut meat. His blood began to stutter somewhere in his veins. The room's unbroken planes moved about him with the ease of light.

He thought of gas. He brought the glasses up again and tried to check for it. Had she had a gas stove or gas heater in her place? Had there been? . . . Nothing, blank; couldn't evoke it, remember, know. What would air in a room *look* like filled with gas? Through binoculars? Would it be liquid and wavy? Sheetlike as heat is sometimes, seen from a distance? Did gas rise or fall? Could he detect layers of air in the room above her and her angled arm? And would it be colored; would gas be slightly blue? Again, it was so hard to tell, *see* with that goddamn imposition of the glass. The *window* might be what seemed blue, the damned window: and it was there, closed, locked! Jesus, if there *was* gas there in the room, if there was gas, it would be locked totally *in*. Was she alive?!

He checked for blood. Every surface that he could find and explore, he checked for stains or smudges or clottings that might in anyway be taken for blood. There was one spot on the floor carpet about a yard or so from her hand which might have seeped from her. It was amoebic in shape and about four inches across at the widest mark. But, no —no, if she had *done* something like that, cut her wrists, the blood would not be a yard away from her but *there*, draining, at the juncture, on the floor. But of course, it could, just as well, have been the other wrist. Or her throat. What time was it? How long had he been studying her? Mark scanned what he could see of the mattress and its sheet covering, but there were no visible or spreading stains. How long? . . . How long would it take someone to bleed to death? Mark felt his skin getting cold. Mucus formed at the corners of his mouth. He checked the graph of her arm again—against the details of the sketch. The sketch itself looked bloodless. Nothing, for nearly two hours now, had changed.

Once again, Mark had trouble with his eyes. They began to blur and sting. His lashes seemed to be angry, to be curling in, clawing the corneas. And the window in front of him grew, somehow, thicker. He shut his eyes, tried to readjust and fix everything—window, pain, room, Susan's stiff whitish arm—inside. He would not, no, would not concede to her death. Even danger. She was not a person who fell into that sort of thing. She was—well, why search? She had said it herself: "exceptional"! A seeker of "strength." "Exceptional." And so . . . He kept his eyes shut, wiped his mouth. He crouched and dropped both hands down to feel some solidity on the floor. He felt his fingernails scratch at gravity. Inside his head, the walls and floors and ceilings and windows, even segments of the street and river, were shuffling and reshuffling themselves like 3 × 5 index cards.

He shook his head. He stood. He raised the binoculars up and looked again. The arm behind the windows and across the street had, he was sure, grown much more like quartz. Mark walked. He circled, toured the room, feeling the walls, checking that they were substantially plastered, studded and nailed in place. He began to cry, though he could not locate, with any precision, his reason why. He remembered Heidi, Heidi saying to him once, just before the fury and the cries and her vanishing: "More than anything else, I love to watch your shoulders when they are asleep." "Why?" he had asked her, very much in love, quite adoringly amused. "Because your neck makes love to them," she had said. *What did that mean?* "And when you wake up, when you rise, they have given birth to something new and wonderful in your head." Mark started rubbing heavily at his face with his open palms, tearing pinches of hair from his arms. The light was fracturing in his room. Outside, now almost 4:30, it was growing dark.

Mark started bunching skin up with his hands, punching irregularly at himself. He remembered doorways along Riverside Drive; the smell of lilacs; the taste of an unlabeled brand of wine; the vision, on upper Amsterdam Avenue, of a departing cab; waiting in the rain by St. Luke's Hospital for a bus which he hoped would never come and then, when it did, go. But who . . . who abandons whom? Who abandons whom in this life? In this city in this life? Who is it always—hasn't it been always?—who stays? And who leaves? It began, almost terrifyingly, to come in: airports, scrambled eggs, a motel in Chicago, an off-season men's dormitory room in Pennsylvania, a month-long journey through a subway, the reading and rereading of *Cain's Book* by the also now vanished Alexander Trocchi—who abandoned Trocchi? Mark was not aware of the moaning sounds which he made.

Then he thought again about the gas. What if it *was* there? A stove or lamp or heater that she had left on? And it was, breath by breath, taking her air away? By *accident*. Not by loss of strength or will or any exceptional quality —but by accident. Jesus! He squeezed his hands. Jesus, Mark! Jesus, come *on!*

Someone should break the glass. He checked the arm against the sketch again, and it was the same. Someone should hurl something through the window and, if there was deadly gas inside, let it out. Someone should act, should puncture the poison cell.

Mark bent the penclasp back on his pen and, using the end of it as a screwdriver, unscrewed the doorknob on his door. It came off more easily than he would have thought. He held the brass globe like a baseball in his hand. He swung his arm, loosening it at the shoulder, checking his body strength. The football game had been a disaster; would his old left-fielder's arm see him through? He crossed over to where he could see better, using the rough plane geometry lingering in the transit of his mind to attempt a distance guess. No more, really, than to second base, he thought. He should, despite the near doubling of his life, still be able to throw it.

He knelt again by the sill; once again, with the binoculars, checked the arm against his sketch. No change. The lock at the top of the lower frame had in his brief absence been painted over, and Mark had to beat at it with the doorknob to chip and shake it loose. When he could slip it ninety degrees, he did so. Then, putting the brassplated knob carefully down by his side, he set his two index fingers in balance along the underside of the upper frame. He paused a minute before lifting. There was a buzz around him from the walls. He could feel the room heating up. Somehow the floor under his carpet seemed to be sweating, giving off the contained odors of its grain. Mark felt the muscles in his chest swell, set his shoulders in perfect harmony with his neck, shut his eyes and gave lift. The pane gave. In its proper frame, it released, rose up.

The wind keened around the edges of the frame, smelling like old soap. Coats and awnings flapped on the street below. Mark imagined the water in the Hudson, not far beyond, struggling, around the corners of debris, to lather and make up. In opening, it felt now to him, he had set something in motion.

The knob seemed to glow in his hand, glow and grow heavier. Outside, when he threw it across the early dark, it would thread the two buildings like a small meteor. Mark imagined himself a kind of cosmic sniper, hurling small chips of planets at his personal targets across city streets. Then the knob began to beat there, beat against the slight pressure in the curl of his fingertips, like a heart. He would have to use a well-aimed sidearm shot.

He took slow aim. He moved his arm—his whole body, in fact—in practice, in warm-up several times. He wished, as with the lead bottles in all the traveling carnivals, impossible as the whole task may have seemed, that he could have had three tries. He checked down to see if anyone, because of his open window, had noticed him, had stopped to watch. Everything seemed clear.

In preparation for the energy of the throw, he began to take deep breaths. Like professional football players he had read about, he would psych himself up—no, that wasn't exactly right; *that* dimension was there—he would *body* himself up. Now with the rhythm of his breath, he swung his arm back and forth, rocking his body, shifting his weight slightly from one foot to the next. He was building, building, storing power, teasing the energy, exciting it, mounting his own power with it, getting the sight, getting the object in his sights, getting his purpose, what he wanted, at a point, seeing that point, driving, rocking toward it, taking his time, building his strength, concentrating his hope, moving, storing, building, ready, ready, ready for the release, ready for the release, ready for the release— *now!*

The knob left his fingertips.
It sailed.
It rose up slowly   like a brass balloon.
It scaled into the sleepy dark.
It moved quietly enough to bloom.
It retained a warm, blood-colored glow
It mounted slowly . . . up and across, moved.
Passing thin tiny owls
Making folds in smoke
Tracing an arc.
Mark could see its connecting arc.
He could see the knob.
He could see the dark.
He could see Susan's window.
He could see himself.
He was aware of the curve.

He held his breath.
He held his breath.
He held his breath,
It wound down.
It rained.
It sailed like a child's small moon toward the glass.
And everyone in Manhattan became mute.
Everyone in the city stopped, statuary still;
All the birds turned white and posed.
All the rivers jelled.
It was going to go.
It would shatter.
It would hit.

Then Mark recaught his earlier image of the knob as meteor. Meteor! My God! No! *Meteor*; her room was filled with gas! God, please, *no!*

He had a sudden vision of her entire building exploding, in an instant's time becoming nothing but dust and debris. He could see the whole thing as a chain reaction, buildings popping east to west, uptown to down, thick white puffs of smoke, like corn kernels going off faster and faster in a mesh basket. *I'm sorry, Susan!* his mind screamed. *I'm sorry; I didn't think!*

Then it hit. The glass burst. There was no blast. There was no reduction of New York City to a rubbled cloud jungle. Just snapped glass. Just the far splintering of glass, sounding bright, crystalline. Mark heard, recorded it, realized—then dropped to the floor for fear that someone on the street below, seeing him, would look up, catch him at the window.

And when voices began to grow and gather on the street outside, he reached up, groped around, found and pulled the window down, re-rotating the lock. He wished he might have had some more white paint, *quick-drying* white paint, to paint the lock over and alibi himself. For a minute or two, he just lay there on the floor, at the foot of the window, breathing hard. Then he crawled across the carpet to his door, opened it with his fingers, slipped out quietly and descended the stairs. He found a service entrance leading out to a back alley, and from there squeezed his way past enormous barrels to the street.

There were about ten people gathered on the sidewalk near where the glass had rained. Mark caught a sudden relief that no one had seemed to be injured by the splintering fall. He decided to walk down to the corner, cross and double back, then mingle to see what might be disclosed. He heard sirens. They grew closer as he moved down the block and across. He saw red rotating lights turn a corner two blocks up and begin a growing, glaring light straight on down. He arrived on the site just as the ambulance and policecars did, a patrol of white and blue uniforms moving into the building.

"What happened?" he asked a man standing back somewhat from the group.

"I don't know. Someone busted a window up there. I don't know."

"Why the ambulances?"

"Don't know. Guess we'll have to wait and find out."

Mark stood there waiting, the lids tight down on both eyes. Around him, from the street and from inside the building, more watchers arrived. Soon the stretcher bearers carried a fully wrapped small linen form through the lobby, out through both sets of glass doors, quickly through the crowd and into the back of their van. Mark felt himself go dry, from the center of himself, spreading out. Anything aqueous in his body seemed to be squeezed, through his eyes, down over his entire face. How had she done it, he wondered. Had it been gas?

"Who was it?" one of the tenants already on the street asked another exiting from the building.

"Old Mrs. Dagleish, in 3-D."

"It figures."

"What was she? In her nineties?"

"At least."

"Just happen? Do they know?"

"They went to check when her window broke. I heard someone say they thought about a week."

Three-*D!* Mark thought. Three-*D!* Was that possible? Had he, in his glasses, somewhere in the eye mirrors of his mind, reversed left and right? He stood back somewhat, turned his back flatly to the street and looked up. Jesus Christ!

"I heard the other one went too. What's-her-name."

"Weiss."

"Yeah."

"Went today."

"Did she take her———with her?" Mark missed the word; it blurred; something like "*smorves.*"

"I hope so!"

"Well, I guess that leaves the entire third front free."

Mark moved himself slowly away and up the street. So Susan, just like Heidi before, *had* moved. He heard the ambulance start up, begin, once again, to spin its light. He turned and watched it pause at the down corner before it turned and disappeared. "I'm sorry, Mrs. Dagleish," Mark said to himself; but out loud, "I'm sorry I broke your window. It was a mistake." Still, as much as it honestly bothered him to have violated the death privacy of Mrs. Dagleish, he could not restrain the shared knowledge that Susan Weiss was alive. And now that his blood flowed again, he knew, knew he would find her.

vii

She'd left no forwarding address. He checked that first. "Strange woman," the superintendent of the building said. "Strange."

Monday night, Mark carried his chainsaw into Central Park in a large green schoolbag, felled another fairly broad tree and carved the trunk into his own three-dimensioned version of Norman Rockwell's praying hands. Tuesday morning, the *Times*, one step behind him, carried a story and photo of his cross: "PHANTOM SCULPTOR VISITS CENTRAL PARK." It was fairly tucked away on an inside lower corner of the first section.

Mark had no filming to do on Tuesday. He called Susan's

agency. They knew nothing of her, where she was; they had not seen her since Friday. She was not at the bar where he had picked her up; the bartender offered no help. Mark found Puccini on the jukebox and had a beer. He spent the afternoon walking the length of Riverside Drive along the park. He had an intuition that he would find her, reading a volume of Sylvia Plath's poetry, sitting there on a bench.

Tuesday night, in a far Morningside Heights corner of the park, he felled two small low-crotched trees, trimmed and carved them up and left them lying in the middle of a path: two clutching hands. On Wednesday morning, the Phantom Sculptor was on the front page of the second section. But they were still one day behind.

Wednesday, again, she had not shown up at work. Or they were covering for her. He taxied over to the building, rode the elevator up to the seventh floor and, finding the offices of Artists' Talent Associates, walked in.

"Miss Weiss's office, please?" he asked the girl at the desk.

"Down that corridor to the left. But she's not—"

Mark bolted off at a trot, locked away from the voice going on behind. He found her door. There was no light shining in it behind the glass. It was locked. The girl at the desk was just catching up.

"I *told* you. . . ."

"*Open* it!"

"What?"

"Open it."

"Why?"

"I want to see."

The girl looked angry at first, then surly, then arrogant. She had the proof.

"Sure," she said in a voice that was, if anything, serrated.

She took a key out and undid the door. The office was dark, untouched.

"Satisfied?"

"Thanks." Mark disappeared back down the corridor at a trot.

He called Jan. She answered the phone. She was not martyred to the bed.

He felt panic. S. Weiss *was* Susan. Now he knew. Yet there was no system, no system which he could think of by which to look—gone from apartment; gone from work; gone . . . *Gone*. A whore tried to pick him up at Fifty-first Street. When he didn't buy, a slight Levi-jacketed black followed in her wake, asked him for a cigarette and clearly made him a pass. Five minutes later, waiting for the light to change so that he could cross Eighth Avenue, someone asked him if he'd like to pick up on some grass. Was something showing in his eyes? He bought a pair of dark glasses at the first available store, descended into a subway and searched on.

Thirteen hours later, at 1:30 a.m. on Thursday, he rose up to the street again. He had ridden every subway in the city, every line, followed green lights and red through miles of connecting white-tiled tunnels. His head still shook and jangled like loose change. His eyes were like graphite smudges: vague, dwindled down. Like a blind man with a mouth organ, he had rambled from car to car, always, it seemed, uphill. His feet had felt like stumps; his head and shoulders like butcherpaper flared in the wind. There was no weight in his hair. He searched for her, looked into long lines of faces, all the time peered down upon by flat advertising images of himself, infinite rows overhead—his paper body drinking wine, smoking cigarettes, wearing unbelted slacks.

He would spot her again and again. She would be two doors away in the next car. There would be a strawberry-faced lady in a torn navy-blue coat on one side of her and a wiry black art student with a huge portfolio just beyond. She would be looking lost, her face very singular and in pain. So he would take one of the doors and move through it: the tunnel space, like impossible memory, moaning past him; grit, like a shrapnel of high-velocity gnats, on his face. He would stand in the gap, on the violent metallic coupling porch, and stare, try to make sure it was her, squint and search in. Then he would open the second door and it would always never be her. Wrong eyes. Wrong hands. Wrong knees. Wrong hair. Wrong neck. Wrong fold. Wrong incline. Wrong bones. Or she would disappear —into a rip in the lady's ratty blue coat, or a woodcut in the student's large portfolio case. Then, suddenly, again he would see her—train already, and too late, in motion; doors tight shut—standing on the Fifty-ninth Street platform, buying gum.

So Mark stood, at 1:30, on the street level, taking at least ten minutes to readjust, set a new clock to his blood, let his bones re-engage. The windshield of his face was flecked with dirt. His hair was blown. If he had murdered someone on the spot, his image would have been right. He crossed to Grand Central, unlocked his saw, walked to the west side of the park, around Sixty-seventh Street, and carved a dove.

A policecar moved in on the sound. He was almost caught. But the dove was good. He had talent. The *Times* had it in the late city edition that morning; the Phantom

Sculptor made the front page. But there was such meek gratification in it. In his fourth successive shrunken hotel room, Mark looked at the picture of his dove and felt blank. No sting. No victory. He had a need to do what he was doing, and that was all he knew.

He put his saw back into its green schoolbag and carried it over to Grand Central. He showered, shaved, changed, despite the rain outside, back into corduroy, hoping it would bring him luck. He had his shoes shined for no reason he could explain. He wanted to have highlights on himself somewhere. He liked the earth smell of polish. The buff and motion untensed his feet. He didn't know why. He watched the tan and black raincoats come and go all around him. They carried lawn and leaf smells in from Connecticut with them: lawns yellowing, leaves collecting into mulch. Or perhaps it was all just the smell of newsprint, damp on all the *Times*. Mark swore one of the attendants, white-coated and standing just back from a row of sinks, was a woman, a girl.

At his morning appointment, the filming of an aftershave ad, he seemed a mere paring of himself. He began to think that he actually *was* an ad, a slip of colored print only millimeters thick. When he turned his back on people, it was conceivable to him that he might vanish, that they might see, instead, only a B.M.W. car or a feature about "Campus Maoists at Purdue." In two weeks, he would be used to start a fire—or to wrap crystal being moved from East Orange to Beloit. The huge white towel which he wore for the ad clearly had more texture, more dimension, than he had himself. And the four girls crouched adoringly at his feet: they would all surely be used to cushion the matching crystal salt and pepper shakers in an adjoining crate.

He wrapped up the ad and called Susan's agency.

"I'm sorry; she's on the Coast."

"West?"

"Yes. Los Angeles."

"When will she be back?"

"We're not really sure. It's indefinite."

"How does she seem?"

"What?"

"How does she seem? I have reason to be concerned."

"Her *voice* seems fine. She called in and had me make flight reservations for her. But I haven't *seen* her since last Friday."

"What is she flying?"

"Pardon?"

"What is she flying? What line?"

"Oh—United."

"Kennedy?"

"Kennedy. Listen, is this the guy who was here last . . ."

Mark caught a cab to Kennedy—to camp out by the baggage claim.

In the terminal, he got a schedule of all arrivals from Los Angeles and began meeting them all. It was a strange ritual, hour after hour, the repeated meeting of no one. Yet those filing out of the connecting telescope all seemed deeply engaged in it too: arrival at nowhere; arrival from nowhere; meeting and met in their arrival by no one—incessant, habitual—and always looking at a watch. Motion. That seemed paramount. Remain always in motion. Move. Check your watch, assume a direction, point, head and move. Still, once in a while, someone would wander from the chute and appear to be uncertain or in awe. Usually it was someone who was alone, or a mother carrying one child and towing another. Mark could catch the sense of chance and improvisation in their eyes. But usually most flowed straight ahead and without mystery.

By the fogged predawn of Friday, Mark had seen no one, really, who looked anything like Susan. He had caught brief naps, left for random snacks, but had not, to his knowledge, missed a flight. He caught an airport guard viewing him with suspicion. After sunrise, checking out the next flight, he saw the same guard talking to another guard and throwing off slight head-feints in his direction. What potentially did they see him as? An assassin? A double revolutionary agent? A narcotics contact? What sort of people spent whole days in Kennedy Airport meeting every plane from Los Angeles?

Again, there was no Susan. Mark left the guards to their inventions and moved off to the United desk.

"Do you have passenger lists?" he asked.

"Well, yes; each flight . . ."

"I mean is there any specific way of knowing *who's* coming in? And when?"

"Sir, I'm not sure I . . ."

"My wife . . ." Mark liked the conviction he gave it. "My wife is coming in from Los Angeles. There's been a terrible confusion about which flight. Is there any way you can check against existing lists—so that I might know?"

"Well . . ."

"I've been waiting here almost a full day."

"Oh, *you're* . . ."

"What?"

"Nothing."

"Is there any way?"

"Well, we could check with L.A. United. Their departures. If your wife's name has already appeared, then she's in flight or has already arrived and you've missed her.

If it has not appeared yet, we can page or call you when it comes up."

"That would be great."

"Fine. What's your wife's name?"

'Susan Weiss." Mark spelled it.

The man wrote it down. "It's not exactly an uncommon name."

"No. I know."

"But we'll be glad to check."

"I appreciate it."

"When we find something out, we'll be sure and page you, Mr. Weiss."

"Mark. Mark Weiss. Thanks."

Mark left and met another plane. No Susan. The guard no longer watched him. The man at the United desk must have called up. It was nearly nine o'clock. Mark went to the Savarin shop and had a coffee and some scrambled eggs.

"*Mr. Weiss. Mr. Mark Weiss. Would you please report to the United Information Desk? Mr. Mark Weiss . . . Mr. Weiss. Mr. Mark Weiss. Would you please report to the United Information Desk? Mr. Mark Weiss.*"

Mark left half a plate of eggs and four sliced halves of toast and paid his bill. He jogged across the glossy tiled floor.

"Hi."

The man looked at him quizzically.

"Weiss. Mark Weiss."

"*Oh*—yes." The man checked a pad of paper to his left. "We have a record of a Susan Weiss—but this is recorded as a *Miss*. . . ."

"Probably a mistake."

"At any rate, departing Kennedy last Wednesday . . ."

"That would be her."

"For Los Angeles. With an open ticket for her return. Los Angeles reports that, as of now, there has been no confirmation for return on the open ticket. If you'd like, you could leave us your home and business phone and we could call you as soon as we show record of the return ticket being confirmed."

"Could you just page?"

"Suppose it's several days?"

"Oh. Yes. Well . . ." Mark gave the man the number of his answering service. "But *page* first."

"What?"

"*Page* first. Before you call. Even if it's in a week. I might be here."

"In a week?"

"I mean . . . off and on. I might just, just to check, drive out."

"Yes."

"So page first."

"I'll put a note."

"Thanks." Mark smiled and started away.

"Mr. Weiss?"

"Yes?"

"Don't you work?"

"Work?"

"Work—yes. I'm sorry; I was just wondering how you could be around the airport, off and on, a whole week."

"Sure I work. Arms work, legs work, spine's in fairly good shape." Mark moved himself, puppetlike, for the man; then laughed. "I'm an actor," Mark explained. "I work in movies, in films, in pictures, on celluloid."

"Oh."

"Sometimes."

. . .

Mark took a room in one of the airport motels. He called and got the man at the United desk he had talked to. "I've got a new number," Mark told him. "A working number. I can be reached here."

"Fine."

Mark numbered it slowly out. The man repeated it. "Good," Mark said, "but if I'm not here . . ."

"Page."

"Right. Thanks." Mark stretched back on the motel bed and fell asleep. He dreamed of people tubing up and down; growing, shrinking like telescopes, but always in motion. The people began to lie down, to lay themselves end to end like pipe, and he dreamed himself walking through them, the hollow of them into or out of some enormous plane. Then he was in flight. And Susan was the stewardess. She served him stuffed mushrooms and wine. Her lips were wet. He sat across from the curtained flight kitchen and could see in, could see huge blown-up poster-size pages from the Camus and see that every time she went back into the booth and slid a new tray out of or into the steam drawers, she would pause, her face a soft liquid wash, to write herself into the enormous margins. Such incredible suffering—so composed. And then the plane hurtled down, nosed to crash. He could feel the seatbelt tugging, slicing him almost in half. Yet the most important thing to Mark, as he watched himself, was to keep his wineglass steady, keep the wine level, hold his hand just so—while he listened to the equally doomed Susan's violent scribbling in the booth beyond.

When he woke up, it was noon, Saturday. He called the United desk. "This is Mark Weiss."

"Still no word."

"Thanks."

He showered and wished for a change of clothes. He wandered back to the terminal, had a steak, felt the need to *do*, not just wait. He bought a paperback copy of *The French Lieutenant's Woman*, but he kept seeing the words as lace and could not make sense out of them. He decided to meet somebody. He had never met anybody from Butte, Montana, so he decided to do that. There was a flight which had stopped in Butte due in in about an hour and a half. In the meantime, he watched other arrivals, trying to select just the sort of person he would meet. It was in the eyes. Then he began to see it in dark glasses, a line between them and the slight hesitancy of a body.

Mark checked the clock, then the proper Butte gate. He moved off to meet the flight. It was right on schedule. Not many others waited. People from Butte weren't met often at Kennedy Airport on Saturday. That was either a bad or a good sign. Then they began coming through the gate and Mark toned himself for the role.

Dark glasses—about twenty-seven—a woman. The body paused, slightly uncertain, shifted.

"Hi!" Mark stood directly in front of her.

". . . Hi."

"Right on time! How was it?"

". . . Fine."

"No problems?"

"No problems."

"Want me to carry your coat?"

"No, I've got it."

"Great! Meals O.K.?"

"Yes. Just fine."

"Gee"—a hand on her upper arm—"it's good to see you!"

". . . Yes. Yes, you, too."

"Well, shall we get your bags?"

"Fine."

"*Mr. Weiss. Mr. Mark Weiss. Would you please report to the United Information Desk? Mr. Weiss . . . Mr. Weiss. Mr. Mark Weiss. Would you please report to the United Information Desk at the far end of the concourse?*"

"Excuse me."

"Yes. Certainly."

Mark ran.

She was up in flight. Mark felt his veins inflate. She would arrive at 5:25. Thirty-one was the number of the gate. There were two hours, slightly more, during which to prepare. How would he handle it? What would he say? The girl from Butte, Montana, was standing alone, a trunk-sized piece of luggage at her feet, in the center of the United lobby.

He would follow her, tail her back to Manhattan, watch her for a couple of days, perhaps a week, two, three, whatever it took to make irreversibly sure that she was, in fact, S. Weiss. He would need a disguise. In a terminal drugstore, he bought a pair of child's scissors and some paste, went to the men's room and made a mustache for himself out of his own hair. It wasn't bad. Then he bought a hat. He had never worn a hat in his entire life.

The mucilaged hair under his nose itched like a rash. He had a cup of coffee, and the steam from the coffee melted the dry paste and some of the hair fell in his cup. He had twenty minutes for a repair. He made it—though it wasn't as balanced as the first job, not as carefully in proportion. The whole mustache, anyway, seemed to be too far out, too much spread from the center of his face.

Mark checked the monitor, and the flight was still on time. He bought a copy of the *Times* to hold up in front of him and could hardly believe his own melodrama. At Gate 32, where he had decided to wait and watch, he looked out and saw her flight taxiing into place. He saw the square tube go out to meet it; plane and terminal touching, making love; bird and earth, spirit and flesh. God! Even his own imagery was becoming absurd!

The first passenger emerged. It was not Susan. Then they came bunched, filing fast, all in motion. Then he saw her. She wore small black glasses, a plain, light khaki raincoat and carried a small attaché case. In an easy habitual drift, she separated from the others and moved down the hall, her soft shoes making hardly, among the others, any sound. Mark followed, kept about thirty feet behind. She neared the bottom of the escalator as he moved himself on. He held his copy of the *Times* up hard in front of him.

She stood on the far side of the luggage claim wheel, waiting for the bags to start down the chute, studying the other passengers with a deliberate, wondering care. The scan of her head was irregular. It was impossible to predict where she would turn, what she would settle on next. But wherever it went, her vision settled in, searched, wondered. Mark thought she was probably transposing people, placing the passengers in bedrooms and at breakfast tables, taking their vests and raincoats away, finding them at moments of loss, unexpected change, testing them against such surprise.

Then she found him, watching, the *Times* only covering his chest. She ticked. Her frame tightened up. Mark understood fully that he should cover himself, but his arms took on a sudden weight and he couldn't move. She bore in; she backed away. She turned quickly and moved off. Mark's feet first, then his ankles and calves—all were casting themselves into bronze. She was at the terminal door before he could move.

Then he dashed. The paper hurtling out of his hands, the hair flecking off below his nose like paint, he ran across the United lobby and toward her door. She was trying to get a cab; he pushed the door when he should have pulled, thought he heard a crack. A cab pulled up and she climbed in. He pulled the door, his arm up for a second cab. It stopped and he entered. "Follow that cab!" It was impossible! It was not happening. He could not believe the words —twice in just over a week—but what else could he say? And the cabbie didn't break it either; he remained true. "Yes, sir!" he said, foot slamming down onto the gas. "Yes, sir!"

The chase was pathetic, absurd. Two cars separating them, moving through traffic five to seven miles an hour along the expressway. Yet Mark was afraid to get out and rush her cab, for fear that the whole pattern might suddenly accelerate, clear and speed up. At one point, Susan jumped from her cab and scuttled up an embankment, trying to get to an overpass where she hoped to hail a different cab. He followed her up, amazed at her agility and speed. And when he got to the top, she was gone and he could not understand it—until he saw several people in cars checking out the embankment on the other side of the overpass. She'd crossed over and was scrambling down again. He turned and started after her, tripped and rolled down the embankment about forty feet behind. She ran and recaught her cab. He ran and recaught his. And they were back in the slow-motioned chase scene again, both panting, both having to explain themselves to their irritated drivers.

Then the slow pattern broke, the traffic speeded up and

the chase scene became quasi-classic. Feints into a left lane
—sudden veers into a right—double circlings of clover-
leaves. Everything speeded up, became properly rushed and
anxious, until both cabs, still only now about four cars
apart, moved into the margins of the city. There the traffic
paused and timed down again. Breaths became more regular.
Muscles connected in a more fluid way, began to shake out
their knots.

"Your wife?" the cabbie asked in slowed traffic on the
F.D.R. Drive.

"Lot of people chase their wives?" Mark kept his stare
ahead.

"Their wives—or anything." The cabbie laughed.

"Yeah—or nothing."

"Right! Or nothing. That's for sure."

Mark thought he saw Susan moving in and among the
traffic on the drive ahead. But it wasn't.

"Then she's not your wife."

"No."

"Just a chick."

"In a way."

"You live together?"

"No."

"Lot of people just live together these days. They prefer
that."

"Yes, I know."

"You doing that?"

"I guess; trying to."

"Ain't got no wife?"

"No; just trying to live together . . . by myself."

"I don't—"

"They've pulled out! Left! Don't let them—!"

"Got it!"

Around Forty-second Street, Susan's cab moved from the edges in. And Mark's followed. She was heading toward the station. She was taking him . . . was that what it was? They were going to *his* place! To Grand Central. To the lockers and the men's room. She was taking him *home!* Or was she just going to use that enormous expanse of tracks and tunnels and lines and lights to evade him, to get away? He checked the meter, took fifteen dollars out, preparing for any exit. But they *were* going there. They pulled near the station. She leapt out. He threw his bills into the fare tray and moved out too.

"Susan!" he called out, "Susan!" but she was gone into the terminal before the sounds even broke out. He followed her in. She was running down the ramp. Mark thought he heard crying, a throaty, high-pitched, withdrawing sound, and envisioned tears dividing past her head, splitting the air. He imagined one of them hitting him in the forehead. He had a sudden and awful fantasy: of her stopping, swirling, taking parts of her body off—breasts, forearms, ears —and hurling them angrily, *spitefully*, at him. He could feel her, the flesh of her, thudding against his chest. *Stay whole, Susan*, his mind pleaded; *stay complete and whole; Jesus, please!*

Still he closed the distance, even with her good start. She was heading, he was following, down . . . down toward— Amazing! He'd been right! Or close, anyway— the women's room. His home was Grand Central's men's room. She was making hers the women's room. Incredible! She *was*. She was, beyond any question, S. Weiss!

She moved down the stairs past the identifying sign. He paused only a half breath, then followed on. Then she stopped, static, at midflight, froze herself, and he drew his own body to a quiet, an awaiting, halt.

"O.K.!" she said, spitting it, her back still to him, slapping one hand against the tile wall. "O.K.—I don't want a scene. What?"

Mark searched out as much breath as he could. "I want . . ."

"Bullshit!" she said, screeching it at the bottom of the stairs.

"That's not true."

"Yes, it is."

Their space stayed photographed. Neither of them moved. She broke it first. "Why did you leave?"

"I thought . . ."

"Yes, you certainly did!"

"Let me finish . . ."

"You mean, again?"

"I mean, what I was starting to say."

She turned and looked at him. The look bent and folded him inside. He saw that, somewhere in flight, she had discarded her case.

"Your comment . . ." Under Mark's groping for the right words, she started an ascent of the stairs. "Well, the Camus . . ." He watched her, and it slowed him down even more. "I . . . I didn't see *through* it. I thought you . . ." She was even now. His eyes followed her. Now she was one step above. She stopped. "Well, I just accepted it . . ." She pushed him, catching him turned clearly off balance, and as she rushed up, he began to tumble like a padded gourd down the steps.

He reached out, up, caught a rail, stopped himself, swung his feet out around his body, got them under him. Then, not losing motion, he started up again, a renewed stumbling pursuit after. He caught her rounding a corner and rounded it too, descended a slight ramp into the vaulted main station.

All kinds of people stitched past him; he tried to find clear space, a line, a direction, *between* them, spot her *down* it, He tried to sight over the heads of others. He jumped.

Across the station, moving toward the paperback-book corridors, he could see her. He moved right after, leaping like some small fitful ground-animal to keep her form, keep a steady check on her direction. She moved out of a far train gate, and he accelerated, unbalancing a small woman carrying packages in the rush. Like a perverse tenpin, she did not fall until he was out the train gate himself. By the time she went, there was a small circle of passengers standing around her—would she or wouldn't she?—watching her bob and tip.

One of the trains had begun motion, and Mark looked down its ramp to catch sight of Susan boarding it. He could not tell whether she had looked back and seen him finding her or not. The last car pulled slowly away. He had no idea where it might be heading, but he started up again, moving closer, closer and closer for a while, almost reaching the last car before their speeds equalized and a ten-foot gap stayed steadily between Mark and the train. There was a driving, a near-breaking pressure, inside his chest, but Mark tested himself against it one margin more, closed the space, caught hold of the moving car, pulled himself onto the platform and felt his whole head go red. He stood there blowing breath out again and again into the cindery tunnel as the train moved on underground and uptown.

They passed men working in the dark on the tracks, and the men seemed mute and unreal. At one point the workers were welding, and flurries of sparks flew out all around them, sudden light spilling into almost instantly dead flowers. Mark had once made a beer ad with a welder's mask on, lifted up on his forehead. He tried to find himself in a face of one of the men, bent and quiet below. Maybe that's where he really was. He stared. One of them gave him the finger.

Mark stayed on the rear train platform. He felt the underground spin off him like dark hair or wire, like spider's thread. He had lost his new dark glasses in the chase somewhere, perhaps on the women's room stairs, and when they surfaced in Harlem even the slate-colored November light seemed harsh, seemed to chew at the corners of his eyes. A market smell rose up from the streets below. There was a dominating sense of fruit rind, of lettuce and cabbage leaves. Mark could see scatterings of it on the streets. He searched into all the shameless and unshaded windows at eye level. They became frames in a strip of overdeveloped film. Everyone seemed to be in underwear, lying in bed watching television, covered with climbing children. He began to see himself in the rooms, facing away in the background, always staring into a mirror.

As they slowed at 125th Street, Mark had a strange sensation. It was a feeling that his eyes had been bored back another half inch in his head. There seemed a new dimension to what he saw; there seemed more room to visualize inside his skull. The rooms he had just been staring at, watching, set up repeated spaces inside his head, fused even with the hotel rooms he had been occupying before he had gone to camp out at the airport. Not only that, but there was something of his future caught in the penetration of the repeating image. He was thinking that he should probably move into and through the train, wherever it might be heading, to search for Susan when he saw her move past him and toward the descending stairs to the street. He jumped off.

When she reached the bottom of the stairs, Susan looked

back on impulse and found him starting down. She ran. He heard a strange sound unwind from her mouth when she started off again, moving somewhat tiredly now and unevenly down 125th Street. Mark picked up the chase.

At first, nearly a block separated them; then Mark began to close it down. The people here seemed more leisured too; they stopped to watch the two of them run on, seemed to find narratives in it. When there was less than half a block between them, Mark started shouting after her, *"Susan! Jesus, come on! Susan!"* but, if anything, the calls just seemed to accelerate her. Then she tripped and fell in front of a fishmarket.

Mark slowed so as not to totally rush and overpower her. The man who owned the fishmarket had an outside sidewalk cart, and as he scrubbed the fish by the fallen Susan, their scales flew up into the now-darkening air like small coins, skin-thin stars. Mark thought of the men welding in the tunnel. He was walking now. Susan was on her hands and knees, crying, watching him. The fishman was bent over her trying to help.

"Susan! . . ."

The fishman straightened up, lifted a cleaver from his market cart. "Back off, man," he barked at Mark.

"Stay out of this," Mark said.

"Who *is* he?" he heard Susan say to the man with the knife. "Who *is* he? Get him *away!*"

"Back off! Stay away!" The fishman set himself between the two of them. He put one hand behind his back to help Susan stand.

"Susan!"

"He just started chasing!"

Mark stopped. "That's a *lie!*"

Susan was up now, talking nonstop to the man, denying

any previous sight or knowledge of Mark. People were gathering, enough to call a crowd. There was a good scattering of advice.

"Take off, man."

"Cool it."

"Better move you' ass."

"Disappear."

"He just started chasing me!" Susan had a good audience now. "I just got off the train and he started chasing me. I don't know who he is. He tried to get me. He tried to grab me. He chased me all the way from the train. I've never seen him. He's crazy. He's crazy. Get him away. Help!"

Mark pointed. "Her name's Susan Weiss! What she's telling you is a lot of bullshit. Her name's Susan Weiss. I know her. I just want to talk to her. I've been trying to *find* her. This has nothing to do with the rest of you people. This is between *me* and *her*."

"My name's Estelle Lampieri," Susan shouted. "He's out of his mind! He's insane!"

The fishman stood there like a warrior. He reached into a pail to his right and pulled out a severed fish head. He extended it at arm's length: a trophy, a sign of what would become of Mark if he took another step.

"Kiss off, baby."

"Turn your butt."

"Just a minute, you gonna be dead."

"Don't be crazy. Run."

Susan had them all! He had no leverage—none. It was all hers. She spun on: "My name's Estelle Lampieri. I live at 1025 Amsterdam Avenue, Apartment 5-D. My husband, Carl, works at Tad's as a grillman. Our kids go to P.S. 339. What does this man *want*?" Mark couldn't help being thrilled by her. Even *he* believed her. She was beautiful!

He'd try once more. "Susan . . ."

The crowd tightened. The fishman set his feet slightly more apart. Somewhere—he had no idea whether they might be connected or not with him—Mark heard sirens.

He took a step forward.

Susan screamed, "Help!"

The fishman threw the fish head at his feet. "You come any closer, I'm gonna have ta carve you up with this," he said.

Mark paused momentarily, then took another step. Susan screamed again, this time "Don't!" The fishman cocked his cleaver by his right shoulderblade. The crowd came more alive with advice.

He moved ahead. Susan began to scream at him: "Stay back! Don't be an idiot! Stay back!" "I'm warnin' you," the man kept repeating, "you try ta touch her, I'll carve you." He stepped again. "*Mark!*" She was calling him Mark now. That was good. "Mark, don't! Don't! He *means* it!"

Mark looked straight at her. "Will you talk?"

"No."

"Why?"

"What's the use?"

"*Lots* of use."

"You don't understand."

"Yes, I *do!*"

"Do you want me to swing this on him, Ma'am?"

"No!"

"I'm moving to you, now, and I'm not going to stop!"

"Don't!" She was crying hard, shaking her head.

"Man, I'll send your head right out into the street!"

"*Don't!*"

Mark took another step, and the cleaver sliced a half-arc

threatening jab at him. He remembered a subway drawing with its announced gang, "Butchers."

"Please!"

Mark took another step and the cleaver swung back—violent, violently ready now. Susan grabbed the fishman's arm.

"No!"

"Lady, I thought . . ."

Her words choked up and out, through phlegm and tears. "Let him . . . See if he will. See if he'll come *to* me. *See*. Wait—*see!*" And then she cried, her face crumpling, badly distorting, her head shaking back and forth.

Mark moved and took her head between his hands. The fishman kept the cleaver raised above the slight incline of his neck. Mark leaned forward and kissed Susan on both eyes. They left together, Mark supporting Susan, moving quietly back down the street.

Susan had moved to West End Avenue, to a building only a halfblock from where Mark and Heidi had once lived. Mark spent the next three days there with her. If they had kept a journal of that time, excerpts from it would have read:

Saturday night. On the floor, drinking:

"Why did you lie about the Camus?"

"Sorry. Can't hear you. I've got a foreign body in my ear."

"I said, why did you lie about the Camus?"

"Maybe Camus lied about me."

"Never thought of that."

"Could I please have another small, very full glass of that champagne?"

(Pouring) "I really *would* like to know."
"Well, it can certainly be arranged."

Saturday night. Later, in bed, as Mark would have recorded it:

When I had remembered the cut of her bracelet against the back of my neck, I had forgotten the small jade stones—pressing like eyes.

Same. As Mark supposes Susan Weiss would have recorded it:

There is something in good men's shoulderblades that is like the anatomy and freedom of wings.

I believe it possible that the light splinters which agitate sometimes at night above a bed are, at least the most prismatic of them, what has risen earlier from fine love-making.

The truth of any man is in the topography of his back.

Sometime between Saturday and Sunday, quiet awakening.

Mark: First of all, the body remembers. Twenty years gone just in sensing the exact weight of eyelids. And West End Avenue smells just the same. Reason against suicide: that the evicted memories can't comprehend. They panic. They swarm the corpse. They grope all the locks. Finally they turn and consume each other. Only the most unendurable survives.

There is a terrible loosed nostalgia above a quit battlefield in war.

Along a seacoast, in deep winter, you can find foamed, frozen memories of the too early dead. They are always trapped in black ice among the rocks.

Similar but later. As Mark supposes Susan might record such waking:

I'm awake. He's asleep. I have little sense of time. What a good, what a perfect sense of *the random*. What I notice most about myself at such moments—is that I breathe.

Sunday breakfast:
"This is fine."
"You're fine."
"Yes, I am. . . . And you?"
"Just fine."
"Yes."
"This is a silly conversation!"
"It's all right."
"We wouldn't like it if we overheard it."
"It isn't meant to be overheard."
(Pause)
"Pass the goddamn butter."
"That's better."
(Susan's fingers scooping butter, spreading some on Mark's. Buttery fingers fast-lacing through each other.)
"God."

Sunday morning, later. Mark:
Today I could be a ringer of churchbells. Even in a city of siege.
In all three rooms, on the walls, there are only woodcuts. No paintings. It is so much as it should be: the print, *im*-print, when something is gouged out, of what remains. Nothing layered. Cut wood on pressed wood. Natural. Re-union.

Sunday. Outside walking:
"Did you ever try suicide?"
"I'm not sure."
"Mmm."

Mark supposing Susan: The city is owned by pigeons. It is not even a case of dispute. They understand. What anyone smells, after a time of quiet regular rain, is their wings. If you are clever, you can ride from the day on that. Or on oranges peeled by a lover; or on the sail of a man's shirt.

"Who is Estelle Lampieri?"

"A forty-seven-year-old sadomasochist woman who lives above a fishmarket in Queens and entertains young Puerto Ricans by the score."

"What score?"

"Forty-seven to nineteen."

Sunday. In bed:

"Do you have any pictures left of your modeling?"

"What do you mean?"

"When you were in *Harper's Bazaar* and places like that."

"No. I gave them all away."

"To the lover who peeled oranges?"

"To all visiting Puerto Ricans."

"From Columbus?"

"I don't know anyone from Columbus."

"What about Betsy Briggs?"

"Betsy Briggs is a fifteen-year-old runaway with no boobs who O.D.'d on diet pills in a Holiday Inn in New Hope, Pennsylvania."

Mark: Camus talks of celibacy. There must be strength in it. I worry that we may be making love too often. Or too much. Can there be celibate lovers? Would it contain more *art?* Nuns and priests marry God. Do they touch? It would be hard to give that up. Is touch finite? Threatening word when you actually try to follow it: "consummation."

Mark supposing Susan: What do you do when even the insane wallpaper seems kind? Distrust. When there is no precise memory of having climbed a flight of stairs? Same. Such calm. Calm hysteria. If I jumped screaming from the bed and peppered the livingroom with fresh eggs, we would both feel better than we do now.

Monday before dawn:
"... nine, ten: ready or not, here I come."
"You'll never find me."
"Great bunches of hair are sprouting on my face."
"Oh, help; the Wolfman. Help. No. . . . I'm not hiding in the closet."

Monday midmorning:
Mark supposing Susan: Why is this better? Watching him "repair a cantaloupe," opening it with a screwdriver and pliers. "Just a minute, Ma'am," he says, lifting the pulp out with the pliers. And I laugh, preferring it somehow to soft touches on eyelids in the dark.

Monday, later. Mark:
I am unnecessary when she is listening to music. No. Not right. I am partly why she listens to *this* music. If I could rest my head against the inside of her head. I love the way she, simply, weeps: clean and without actual hurt.

Monday dinner. Mark:
I can believe she modeled. Further: that she has already or might act. I would believe her as Antigone—Antigone cutting braised mushrooms, handling the fork just so, lifting it, carrying her wrist, touching her mouth. And that is the color of Antigone's wine. And her parsley. What a marvelous small shrub.

After:
"Tired?"
"I have to go to the office tomorrow."
"Life gets real."
"Gets?"
"Just teasing."
"Are you sure?"
"I think so."
"What will you do?"

"I might . . ."

"What?"

"Go to Boston. I'm not sure."

"To see your wife?"

"No."

"Your little girl?"

"She's sixteen now."

"Probably a very good idea."

"Should we finish off this wine?"

"Do you like to finish things?"

". . . No."

"Well, then . . ."

During the night. Mark:

I could act. I could do that again. I know it's there. There's so much in residuals now that I could leave the other alone. Act. God, how old am I? I can't think. Act. God, do an O'Neill play! But first, fly to Boston tomorrow. Meet the woman I helped live. *Rachel.* Still like the choice of her name. Act.

Sometime before dawn, thought or dreamed. Mark:

Why am I constructing and preserving this—*us*—like a journal?

viii

Mark and Susan rose early and walked crosstown together. They kissed, before they left each other, on the corner of Madison and Fifty-fourth Street.

"See you tonight?" Susan smiled and asked him.

"May be close to twelve," Mark said.

"Will you want dinner?"

"Probably have that, if I can, with Rachel in Boston. But thanks."

"Something light? Cheese—wine?"

"Wonderful."

"See you later, then."

"Yes."

"Have a good day."

"Yes. Yes, you too. Have a good day."

They started apart, Susan moving down Madison, Mark moving west. He stopped and called nearly a halfblock across to her. *"Susan!"*

She heard him. "What?"

"Don't move away again!"

"I won't."

"Goodbye."

"Goodbye."

At Grand Central, he showered, shaved, took a sunlamp, had his shoes shined, and dressed in light tweed, a brown suit. Closing his last locker, he noticed the chainsaw there in the green schoolbag and smiled. He was not through with that yet. The Phantom Sculptor had not disappeared entirely; he was lying low a bit. But he would surely be back.

The cabbie who drove him out to his shuttle flight at Kennedy didn't speak. He simply pointed to the meter, took his dark glasses off, turned to the back seat and stared. When Mark opened the cab door to get out, it almost blew back against him in the cutting wind. There was practically nobody on the walks.

A man in airline uniform stopped him before he went in. "There's been a bomb threat," the man said.

"Which line?" Mark asked him.

"I'm afraid, all." The man was trying to look very confident, yet grave.

"What sort?"

"Someone's called all the lines. Each time the message

was pretty much the same: 'You might like to know that a bomb's going off there today.' No place. No line. Just the general threat."

"Then there aren't flights?"

"No, we're flying. We're on schedule. We're just warning everybody about the risk. So far, most people have been holding off. Most of the terminals are fairly empty."

Mark looked into the Northeast lobby through the double set of glass doors. No one milled or moved; it was all surfaces and geometry. "Well," he said to the man, "thanks," then nodded and moved past him to the doors.

"You going to try it?" the man, behind, called.

"Might as well," Mark said without looking back, and pushed on in.

He paid his shuttle fare. "Did someone mention our scare?" the ticket agent spoke to his pad.

"Yes. Outside," Mark told him.

"You'll be a test case, then," then man said.

"What do you mean?"

"Well—as of right now—on the eleven o'clock, you're the only one."

"No pilot?"

He looked up. "Well, of course, *that*, but . . ."

"Well, as long as I'm not alone," Mark said, picked up his ticket from the counter and wandered away.

The vaults of large space without people all composed themselves with ghostly neatness. Huge transparent blocks of light and air made stacks of height and stretched themselves into tunnels and corridors. There was an overpowering smell of wax, wax and newsprint, unnaturally high stacks of the morning *Times* at the variety counters. Empty up and down escalators moved steadily past one another, no commerce between them except a constant and regular stretching of the elastic air. Steps rose up and vanished. Steps descended and fell. Mark stared down a row of unwatched TV schedule monitors—all as regular as the daily paper, as the winding and unwinding stairs.

There were random boarding announcements, but they were flat, less than recorded, disbelieved. Planes carrying only their own crews taxied off from the terminal, paused and lifted with a dull rush into the sky. Very few seemed to arrive. Except for the scale, the entire complex was like a mock-up, an ad, a promotional model for Johnson's Wax. Mark imagined it all being ripped suddenly by a bomb, like a fist suddenly punched through a huge photographic page.

He boarded, and the boarding agent asked him if he knew and he said yes. He walked alone down the connecting tube. He had a fleeting urge to stay in the middle of it, to live his life out there. But he boarded the plane. The stewardess smiled at him; "Have they—?"

"I know," he said. "I do this with full knowledge."

"We just want to be sure," she told him.

"That's only reasonable," he said.

"Take any seat."

The captain gave his spiel. He ended it by taking notice of the scare. "My whole life's been flying," he said. "It's what I always, when I was a kid, wanted to do. It's what I've always done. If this crate shreds the sky between New York and Boston—which I certainly hope it doesn't—I'll at least know I've done what I wanted." Then the stewardess gave her oxygen-mask emergency-door speech directly to Mark. He felt compelled, the entire time, to maintain eye contact with her. It made his throat ache.

The takeoff was smooth. It seemed to Mark soundless, and like a kite.

"I certainly hope it isn't us," the stewardess bringing his lunch said.

"No. I hope not." She had given him two steaks.

"The captain said you could have a couple drinks, if you wanted them, on the house."

" 'Plane.' "

"Yes."

"Do you have splits of wine?"

"Red or white?"

"Oh, *red*. Let's take the drama of it all—and the symbolism—all the way."

"One or two?"

"I'll start with one."

"Fine." She started away.

"Oh! . . ."

"What?"

"Tell the captain thanks. Thank him for me."

"I will."

Mark had his steaks and wine and talked to the stewardess about her growing up in Tulsa. She rattled on about her not really giving her parents a chance, about rushing and misjudging them. She said she'd always held their first names, Maud and Oscar, against them, and Mark agreed that that was silly. They had named her Sarah, and growing up had called her Sadie, but she'd nicely finessed that: "Sally Hewes," her nameplate read. "Well, if we don't get blown up in ten minutes," she told Mark, checking her watch and taking his tray, "then we should be all right."

"Good," he said, smiling. "Thank the captain again for the wine."

"Sure." She paused. "Sir, excuse me, but aren't you famous or something? I know I've seen your face before. I mean, often."

"Yes, I am," Mark told her.

"Who are you?"

"The Phantom Sculptor."

"Who?"

"The Phantom Sculptor."

"Oh."

The plane flashed fire and disintegrated in Mark's mind for a moment, then fused together again, clean, glistening and clear.

Mark called Concord Academy from the airport. "Is Rachel Eliot there, please?" He hadn't said the name, except in his mind, for at least thirteen years.

"Who?"

"Rachel Eliot." He spelled the last name. "One 'l,' not two."

"Oh—as in T. S."

"Yes."

"Ummm . . ." There was a long-drawn pause, the sound of index cards or pages being flipped. Was it possible she was no longer there? He'd been sending money for tuition every year. Had she shot a policeman or bombed Harvard's International Center? Was she hiding from the F.B.I.?

"She should be in the dining hall right now," the girl answering said.

"Could you page her?" Mark noticed how much busier the terminal was outside his booth than things had been just an hour earlier in New York.

"Well . . ." It was clear the girl did not *want* to page her.

"It's really quite important," Mark said. "It's not an ordinary call."

"That's what they all say."

"Well, this one's true."

"O.K.—it might take five or ten minutes, though."

"That's all right. I'll hold."

"O.K." The other end faded; almost silent, nearly dumb background sounds.

What did she mean, *That's what they all say*? What was the implication of that? Did she mean all that called Rachel? All that called girls at the school? Was Rachel hungered after? Loose? Mark laughed at his own thought-use of the word "loose," at his self-righteousness in it. If anyone was *loose*, he was *loose*. Loose as a goose. Where did that come from? He hadn't used that phrase since high school. Loose as a goose; what kind of stupidity was that? On the operator's periodic reminder, he kept dropping quarters into the phone. Finally, at the other end, there were the sounds of approach. Then a breathy voice answered—breathy and, he thought, somewhat unsure.

"Hello? . . ."

"Rachel?"

"Yes?"

"This is your father."

Mark should have known there would be a pause, but he did not expect that there would be one as long and glassed as occurred.

"Could I have that again, please?"

"This is your father."

"I see."

"I know I . . ."

"Look, whoever this is, unless you cut the crap and play it level with me, I'm going to hang this phone up right now. I don't like games. Especially that one. So you can decide how you're going to handle it, but I'm not going to string along with that."

Mark arranged himself. "Rachel?"

"Yes?"

"Will you give me a few minutes to try and identify myself?"

"Yes. That's what I'd like."

"I mean, as your father?"

There was another very carefully partitioned pause. Then, in a softly pebbly sort of voice, she said, "Yeah—go ahead."

Mark reviewed the facts, as tightly and concretely as he could organize them. Each time when he paused, hoping for some response, there was only some unseen hyphen of thought at the other end; unsure, immeasurable. Finally Mark asked her directly, "Is that enough?"

There was a shorter pause; some voice: "Is this some friend of Gerry's?" she asked.

"Rachel, this is your father. This is Mark Eliot," he said.

"Gerry's the only person I can think of that I've told most of that to."

Who was Gerry? Mark wondered. "Even things like the ebony animals?" Mark asked.

"I don't know. I don't know how much I told," she said to him, her voice a little less textured now. "I was pretty crazy at the time."

"Oh."

"Not exactly . . . sane."

"Well . . ."

"So, then, what do you want?"

"To see you."

"You're not supposed to."

"I know."

"That's breaking a trust."

"I know."

"If Mummy found out, she'd most likely slap a lawsuit on you."

"I suppose."

"And what if I say no?"

"I'm not sure." She was tougher than Mark would have guessed. No, "tougher" was not the right word—something.

"What do you mean?"

"I mean, I probably would come out there and try to see you anyway."

"Why?"

"It's hard to say."

"Do you need to *purge* yourself? Big plea for forgiveness, or something like that? 'Repentant Dad'?"

"Yes. I suppose that's a big part of it. Sure."

"What did you have in mind?"

"Supper?"

"O.K."

"Thanks."

"Did you say 'Thanks'?"

"Yes."

"Why?"

"For saying yes."

"Did you think I might say no?"

"I didn't know."

"Christ!"

"Is around four all right?"

"Four-thirty. God! I can't believe you'd have thought . . ."

"See you then."

". . . Fine."

"Thank you, Rachel."

He hung up and stayed in the booth until someone knocked on the glass and brought him around. "Sorry," he said to the man as he went out. He went to the Avis counter and rented a car. He drove it directly to the Commons' underground garage; the tunnel, Faneuil Hall and the Charles all, in passing, pushing in very hard on him.

He went to the Public Garden and walked around. He bought some peanuts and stood on the small bridge and fed the ducks. He and Heidi had done that. And before Heidi, he and Judith had once come there in the middle of the night, taken a midnight flight from New York with Times Square chestnuts; "Mr. and Mrs. Mallard!" Mark had called out somewhat drunkenly into the dark, summoning the true and storied ducks. And Judith had stood on the bridge with her face high and glistening in the rain: sounds of as much pleasure as if they had been in bed. What would Susan do here, he wondered?

He bought a small pad at a drugstore on Charles Street, an artist's sketch pad thick with paper. There were some stairs a halfblock beyond, leading down under a black cut-out sign of a man, lettered "The Shadow." It was a small coffeehouse, and Mark descended to it and sat there for almost two hours drinking fresh limeades, practicing sketches of Susan from a picture she had given him. He became quite good. Most of the time was spent refining her neck and eyes. Each time he got closer—closer.

"Someone you know?" the waitress asked; she wore Levis and a black turtleneck and smelled like the limeade she brought, that and coffee beans and marijuana.

"Yes." Mark said.

"Very unusual." The girl looked down over his shoulder at the last sketch.

"Yes. She is."

"Are you an artist?"

"Are you a waitress?"

"Not at night." The girl walked off. She stopped at the pastry counter, looked back and smiled.

Mark spread two rabbitear fingers in the peace sign for her and went back to his sketch. It was hard to get the proper sense of moistness below the lids.

Just before 3:00, he paid and left, taking a slow walk down Charles Street toward the garage. Behind him, above, he heard an M.T.A. train leave the Charles Street Station and head off over the bridge toward Harvard. He imagined sitting in it, looking out over the river, seeing the silent motion of the sculls and sailboats from the Boston University boathouse. He imagined Harvard/Radcliffe students reading copies of *Soul on Ice* and *The Possessed*. And there were people with shopping bags from Jordan Marsh's and Filene's. Was there an accordion-carrying blind man? No. No, not in Boston. No, that was New York. All the blind men here sat on benches along the river trying to record the precise whistle of kites. Or they fed pigeons English muffins in the Commons. Or they carried on research projects at M.I.T. Or they catalogued the braille collection at Widener Library. The Boston blind were clearly a different breed, a breed he would more like to be a part of—if he went. The Boston blind, yes, were all proud.

Mark was nearly run down by a car on Commonwealth. He dropped the sketch pad and stayed dangerously in the middle of traffic until he'd retrieved it. There was a difference too, he thought, standing back on the curb waiting for the light, in Boston obscenities. He wondered how much Rachel would be a product of all that. He wondered how much she would be his daughter.

The drive to Concord along Route 2 in his rented Nova was relaxed. He turned the car radio to WGBH and listened to an hour of Bruckner. In Cambridge, the leaves were just powdering, but farther out, through Belmont, Arlington, Lexington, they were already dust. He drove with the window opened, and it occurred to him that the leaves were not at all like powdered New York park leaves. Even dry they smelled moist. There seemed sufficient sap, enough juice.

There were stands as he approached and entered Concord, small white clapboard roadside places with extending tables of fruit, late vegetables, bottles of condiments and preserves. He stopped at one and bought himself two bottles of mustard pickles and a gallon of apple cider.

He was smiling; he felt good.

"Do you make these?" he asked the woman in charge. It was as if he were on his way to a week's fishing trip in Maine, off to New Hampshire, to North Conway to become a New England artisan, to devote the rest of his life to carving wood.

"Just a minute. Wait till I make this change," she said. She made it. "Now what did you want?"

"I was just wondering—did you make these?" He held one of the bottles of mustard pickles up, a murky cadmium yellow catching the light.

"Did," the woman at the register said.

Mark smiled again, setting it with his jaw. "I see."

"Too much trouble. Don't any more."

Mark thanked her, climbed back into his Nova and drove off.

He was still quite early, and so he drove out to the Concord Bridge site, parked the car and walked the brief path to it and stood. It was the second bridge he'd felt himself tied to during the day. He wondered about that. Perhaps he was developing a bridge thing. He laughed. He stopped. There was no one else there, no one in the small grove, by the statue and the waterside. Someone had put a bomb to all this a couple of years before, he remembered. There were still signs, ineradicable probably, of the repair. It seemed sick. There were bombs going off all through the country now—no immunity—and the whole idea seemed quite unreal, scripted, trivial and unfelt as the glib values it all objected to. But to bomb this, to bomb this place, *that* . . . Mark found his face awash the way Susan's often was. He had perhaps caught it from her. Tears. A female flicker landed just ahead of him on the bridge rail and he wished suddenly that he had the equipment to photograph it. He stood there. Real history was a quiet thing, he thought. Even real revolution. He stood composing conversations between himself and Rachel. But when he left twenty minutes later, they were all tangled somewhere among trapped branches under the bridge.

He found the road leading up to the Academy, turned through the entryway onto it and drove up to what appeared to be the central hall. There was a dance class being held on one of the sloped lawns, and as he stepped from the car he stopped and watched it for a while—afraid, partly, to shut the door, cautious that it might break the dance. If people could have that sort of respect for golfers taking shots, they could have it as well for lives which attempted to be graceful and in motion.

It was easier to leave the car door ajar; and he did that, almost tiptoeing toward the main entrance. The building was old—most likely central, at some former time, to an estate. He went in. There were more girls. Some moved; some lounged. There was a desk.

But before he could complete his cross to the desk there was a girl intercepting him, standing just to one side. She was quite short, still summer tanned. Her eyes were large and green and she wore metallically lustered hair in a large single long braid down her back. Her face was girlishly muscular, tight balanced bulbs of life toned symmetrically there.

"Hi."

"Rachel?"

"Yes."

Mark had no concept of what to do—hug, kiss her; shake her hand.

"Can you go?"

Her voice was slightly low and tight. "I've checked out."

They moved out the door, walked silently past the dancers still in motion on the lawn. "That's quite nice." Mark pointed.

"You get pretty used to it."

Mark opened the passenger door and let her, very soundlessly, slide in, settle onto the vinyl. He pressed the safety button down and pushed the door firmly until he heard it shut. The sound reminded him of a bone snapping. He thought that his lower neckbones and rib ends felt, for some reason, febrile and brittle. When he crossed to his side and looked over at the dancers, they were all sitting, scattered on the lawn; their dance had stopped.

He got in, turned on the ignition and turned off the car radio.

"You rent this?" Rachel said to him.

"Yeah . . . yeah." He bent slightly over the wheel, eyes hard on the row of trees bordering the Academy property. Generations of ebony animals flashed through his mind. "I can't think of anything to say right now," he told her, "that won't sound absurd."

"Then wait."

"There are about five dialogues stretching out like a gloved hand in front of me, none of them very real."

"Wait."

Mark drew a full breath, held it a beat; "O.K." He eased the emergency out slowly, even gently, and they moved off.

Ten or so minutes later, on Route 128, Rachel turned slightly more toward him. "You shouldn't think it's just you."

"Pardon?"

"You shouldn't think you're the only one. Struggling. Having trouble."

"Thanks."

"Where are we going?"

"I thought we might drive up by Gloucester and Rockport."

"Fine."

"Do you have the time?"

"I'm signed out till twelve."

"Good."

They drove on past Winchester and Wakefield. A chartered bus passed them. It had a large blown-up poster of Mark smiling, confronting a menthol filter, just above its exhaust.

"Oh, God!" Rachel said. "Oh, no!" And she began to twist in her seat almost hysterically. She laughed. Mark heated like an electrical coil, tried to toss off things like "I know" and "Pretty silly." But, like weak arrows in a fresh target, his comments only wavered an instant, drooped, then fell off.

After what seemed to Mark a very long time, Rachel finally slowed herself, gradually trailed off and stopped. The bus was far ahead of them, a shape, a shadow, nothing at all distinct. "It's incredible," she said, "that for almost fourteen years I'd been hung up by *that*." She laughed a final time, a hard-edged laugh mostly to herself. Then they drove on silently for a while. "I'm sorry," she said just before the Route 1 underpass. "I guess that wasn't exactly nice."

"I guess you don't have 'exactly nice' feelings about me," Mark said to her.

"I don't know what I have," she said.

"What does your mother say?"

"She asks me if I have enough pills."

"I mean about me."

"I know."

The traffic thinned around them, and the dark began to seem cleaner.

"Sometimes," Rachel went on very carefully, precisely, sadly, "sometimes, when I'm home—for a weekend—and we have something like a glass or two of Dubonnet together —usually a Friday—sometimes she says things about an apartment on West End Avenue. She giggles about a crazy superintendent. And . . . and occasionally . . . occasionally —at the end of her 'Nosto's'—just before I have to leave for a date or she for a party—occasionally she touches . . . touches on you. She says things like . . . 'He was a really fine actor.' 'I only wish you could have seen him act.' "

Mark's window was rolled down. There was something like a pre-salt smell in the air.

"Thanks."

"I go—I used to go; they've closed it now—to the Charles Street Playhouse a lot. Mummy subscribed. There was this one actor there. He was in a lot of their plays. He's a Greek. And I used to watch him. And I used to imagine he was you. *Like* you. *Some*thing. *I* don't know. It's all really confused. He was beautiful. Some plays—that he did —I saw three or four times. I remember one especially. By Brecht.

Mark tried to smile. "I could never do Brecht."

Rachel was kneading two left-hand fingers into the corner of her lower lip.

"But I'm going to start again."

She was staring through the windshield, assembling other thoughts and places from the dark. Her face tightened, rippled, seemed at random moments to go suddenly slack. "That's why I laughed so much at the bus," she said; she put both hands up and massaged her eyes. "Why now?" she asked. "Why did you choose now . . . to 're-establish ties'?"

"Let's wait until we find a place."

"You want to 'set it'?"

Mark held his breath.

"Find proper atmosphere?"

"I'm discovering that you can be quite tough."

"Sure. Why not? I learned it from Mummy. I mean, we both had to be the daddy, didn't we?"

Mark pulled over to the side of the road. He turned the ignition off. He raised his hands, trying to shape his words from a gesture.

"I'm sorry!" She was looking at him; sad, scared. He caught and held contact. "I'm sorry," she shook her head slightly, bit her lip, ". . . sorry."

Mark dropped his hands, turned front again, recharged the ignition and pulled out. When they were readjusted to traffic, he said, "It's not easy, I know."

"No; it's not . . . no."

"I've been independent too long. I tend to be . . . tend to be impatient."

"Like father, like daughter."

"Mmm."

". . . I *do* want to hurt you. You *know* that."

"I guess."

"I mean, something in me wants very, very much to hurt you."

"Yeah."

"But that doesn't mean that, at the same time, I don't want you to give me your necktie and tell me stories about giraffes in the dark. Because that's there too. I mean, I would have thought that you'd have figured that all out, before calling. Expected it. Been ready."

"I should. I probably should."

"It *isn't* easy."

"I know."

"I mean . . ." She grated her words somewhat through tears. "What the hell do you mean just calling me up on the telephone after fourteen years? Christ!"

They crossed the bridge into Gloucester. Another bridge. The Portuguese church on the hill was lit up and Mark saw it and thought of how long it had been since he had been here, even near. He turned them onto the coast road, toward Rockport. At a place called The Fin and Claw, they turned in, parked and went inside.

At the table, Mark asked Rackel if she'd like a drink.

"A what?"

"A cocktail. A drink."

"I'm under age."

"I'll get it."

"Do you think that's right?"

"If you'd like . . ."

"Fraudulently buying your own sixteen-year-old daughter a drink?"

"I'm sorry. You said you and your mother . . ."

"I'll take a G & T."

"A . . ."

"G & T. Gin-and-tonic. G & T."

"Fine."

"Hadn't you ever heard that?"

"What?"

"G & T?"

"Not for a while."

The drinks came. Mark started to raise his up to drink.

"Aren't you going to toast or anything? 'Reunion'? 'Dads and Their Girls'?"

"At this point, I think just 'Talking' would probably do."

"To 'Talking,' then."

"To 'Talking.' "

They drank. They both ordered the mixed seafood plate.

"Would you like another one of those?"

Rachel paused. "Sure."

"Two more, please." Mark touched the rim of the glass with a finger. The waitress stole a halfglance at Rachel, then moved off. She came back with two more drinks.

"You know what I think?" Rachel asked.

"No. What?"

"I think you're not my father at all. You're just an older man who's trying to seduce me. Who wants my body."

"Is that right?"

"What?"

"Do you really think that?"

She became suddenly sober, turned to her drink. "No."

Mark tried to drive quietly on through her dusk. "You're a very pretty girl."

"What does that mean?"

"You look less like your mother than I thought you would."

"When I'm perverse, she says I look just like you."

Mark laughed lightly to himself. ". . . Yes."

Rachel pushed herself back tightly against her chair. She set the distance between them with her eyes. "Aren't you going to ask me if I'm on speed or something?" She snared a small piece of haddock, added a clam and set them both in her mouth. Very carefully, she chewed—somewhere behind a nearly immobile jaw.

"Are you?"

"What do you think?"

"I think you smoke grass fairly regularly, but that you're too smart to try speed. I think you've dropped acid once."

She didn't move. But something in the slight tint of her skin and clarity of her eyes glinted with a respect for his precision. "Do I wear a bra?"

Mark's lips played quietly across each other. "I have a recurring dream," he said. He heard the breakers beyond the pier outside. They sounded like the gentle asthma of a large heart, the heartbeat of some sweet but dying god. Rachel touched a hand to her lip as if she heard and recognized it too. "It's my one, my single recurring dream. In it . . . in it, I always see you."

Rachel bent slightly to her plate, picked the batter off one of her scallops. "And? . . ."

"You're there. Usually different. Usually never quite the same. I mean, in looks. But . . . but it's always you. Looking at me. Too often, crying. But—and this will, I'm sure, seem strange to you—always ticking. Like a clock—my Rachel-clock—ticking. It's a terrifying dream. It always scares me."

"Were you scared to call me today?"

"I certainly was."

"Are you scared now?"

"Quite."

"Does that bother you?"

"I . . ."

"What?"

". . . Think partially that it may be a good thing."

"Should people try to scare each other?"

"Well . . ."

"Should they?"

"Your mother had the ability, once, to scare me. And I think our . . . our . . . *what*? 'Division,' 'breaking,' may have had something to do with her losing that. I don't . . ."

"Then they should? Try and scare each other? People?"

"I'm not sure I'd use the word 'try.' "

"Well, then . . ."

"I think someone's willingness to *be* scared is a good thing. I'm quite willing right now for you to scare me."

"And I do?"

"Yes."

"Was that the whole dream?"

"Just the middle. The ticking heart."

"What about the outside? The nerves?"

"The outside part was the most frightening. You would be there, as I described, slightly different, progressively older as we both, even apart, have grown. And then . . ."

Rachel kept turning a shrimp tail over and over in her tartar sauce. The rising of the tide, outside under the pier, made sounds which seemed to elongate. "Yes?"

"And then you would go off. Like an alarm. You would ring. And . . . and then . . ."

Rachel pressed her fork down into her plate, sliding the tines forward slightly.

"And then something would occur. You would be feeding a duck. Or bleeding. Or . . ."

"Bleeding?"

"Menstruating. Or wearing a bra. That's why I smiled. Or carrying a circus toy. Or bringing your first report card home. Or swimming without a top. Or making love. Or being drunk. Or fighting with another girl. Or falling from your bike. Or having your teeth drilled. Or squealing over your birthday cake. Tick, tick, tick—then the alarm —and then—some . . . *moment*, some moment in your life. And then, usually pretty fast, I'd be sweating and wake up."

He looked at her. Her fork was scraping violently across her plate. Her jaw seemed almost to be rupturing.

"I had no plan to tell you that."

"Excuse me."

She went off to the ladies' room.

While she was gone, Mark ordered himself a beer. He ate slowly, chewing randomly, like a broken machine. He folded and refolded his napkin—with no real design. Outside the pier looked unposted, like a flat raft bobbing absently, anchored in the tide. Mark himself felt a kind of perpetual sick buoyancy. The restaurant floor seemed to be set adrift. The tables seemed to be drifting on the floor. The tablecloth floated on the table; the silverware was adrift on the cloth. Beer drifted in his drifting glass. Light drifted down from drifting fixtures on a drifting roof somewhere above. Mark, swamped by his own peripheries, closed his eyes.

Rachel returned. "Gin's a bummer," she said. "I don't really like it."

"Would you like some of my beer?"

"No, thanks." She tried to look steady and sure at him "I would like one of those rolls, though."

"Sure."

"And butter."

"Here."

"Thanks."

She made a great calculated ceremony of buttering both halves of her roll. Mark got himself ready. She spoke finally to her stroking knife.

"So you've just been unscared and celibate for the last fourteen years?"

"Celibate—no."

"You remarried?"

"No."

"Sleeping around?"

"I suppose you could say."

"Trying to set an example for your dreams?"

Mark took the moment to say one of the few things he had planned, somewhere in the evening, to say, "I've found another woman. I found her in the margins of a book of Camus and tracked her down. She's allowed me to be scared again. Her name is Susan Weiss." Mark filled it all in as thoroughly as he could. And ended: "And somehow, together, we're in those margins. There *are* margins. They're strange. They're unsure. They're dark and troubled and dangerous as hell. But I'm in them. And I love them. I can *make* things. I can *act*." He smiled. "Carve trees." He could smell the wood pilings under the piers outside, their brine hearts. "Rachel, do you know what *risk* is?"

"Risk?"

"Risk." He leaned forward, toward her. "There is this —Christ, it's been *lives* since I've at all had it—this sense of . . . well, 'risk.' And I suppose that's what all this is about. I mean—finally. And so . . . God bless it! God bless the seafood plate! God bless . . ."

"Just like your first tree house?"

"What?"

"The sense of risk."

"Oh . . ." He leaned back again. "O.K., sure. Yeah." The waitress came.

"Something else?"

"Coffee. Black." He nodded at Rachel.

"Same."

"Two black coffees. Any dessert?"

Father and daughter both shook their heads. The waitress walked off. The tide outside seemed to be agitating the room. The fishnets seemed tremulous and shimmering enough for underwater spiders on the wall. On both sides of the table, there was the postponement of breath.

"How old is she? Your new woman. Your Susan Weiss."

"I don't know. Thirty-six. Thirty-seven. Near there. Why?"

"Is she 'pretty.' A 'pretty girl'? Like me?"

"Yeah. *I* don't know. For me—yes. Here . . ." He drew a pencil from his pocket, started to sketch Susan on the placemat under a lobster.

"And so you're both going to live 'happily ever after'?"

"We'll both live."

"Happily?"

"Marginally. It doesn't . . ."

"Ever after?"

The waitress brought the coffee. Heat rose up from it. It lent the air in the room a sense of being unmoored.

"Ever after?"

"That's not what's important."

"Really?"

"We'll live as long as we can."

"Which is?"

"It doesn't matter."

"No?"

"No."

"How long's it been?"

"What?"

"How long has it been? So far? What's your record?"

"Well . . ."

"How long?"

"Well, actually *together*, three days, but . . ."

"Oh, Christ! God!"

"Rachel, you don't—!" Mark thought he could hear the breakers lapping under the windows of the room. There was too the almost cocktail laughter of gulls.

"What do you give it? Five days? A week? Wow! At best she sounds like a *good idea!*"

Mark burned his tongue on his coffee. "*Shit!* Don't drink it. It's too hot." His eyes watered slightly. He set it down. He pressed his lips together, feeling the bone of the teeth behind.

"You O.K.?"

"Yeah."

"Use some ice from your waterglass."

"It's all melted."

"Not all."

"It's all right. I wasn't thinking. I was in too much of a hurry."

"I was pressing."

"You sure as hell were."

They gave each other very insecure smiles—then seemed, almost, to take them back. The light around them washed, became indefinite.

"You're a romantic." She lifted some ice shavings with her fork, carried them across the table and dropped them into his coffee.

"I am?"

"Yes." She dredged a few more out for her own. "But it's not necessarily a bad thing. Romantics just get disappointed. It's why you can't sustain anything."

Mark felt the first deep flash of anger he had felt for Rachel, for something which she'd said. "I can sustain something!" he assured her.

She stirred the ice into her coffee with her fork. "Can you?"

"Yes, I can."

"Really?"

"Yes!"

"Then why haven't you?"

"O.K. Let's let it drop."

"No. If you can sustain something, then . . ."

"Enough!"

"Then why—?"

"I can sustain *lots* of things! Lots!"

"Fine! Name one!"

"My dream of you ticking, for instance. Of you, like an alarm, periodically going off!"

Rachel pulled her fork back. She raked her cheek with the warm, curved back of it. It whitened four even, deepening lines over her bone.

"Don't do that."

"Shall we go?"

"I think so."

The drive along Route 128 back to Concord was relatively empty; the air outside warm and annoyingly cricketed. About ten minutes into it Rachel began to cry uncontrollably. She clutched her legs up under her and twisted, back to Mark, facing the dark and vinyled car door. He asked what was the matter and she screamed "Shut up! Shut up!" at him and shook and cried even harder. When the tears didn't stop but began to alternate savagely with bursts of laughter, Mark pulled over.

When he turned off the lights and motor, Rachel leapt into the back seat and crouched against it, feet up, facing front. She held her rough, bitten nails out like a ragged sloth bear and breathed wild animal sounds—the corners of her mouth wet and turned. Mark reached for her, but she slashed at him, once catching the back of one hand. He climbed over into the back seat in an attempt to press her there, stabilize her, settle her down. But she passed him, scuttling front as he achieved back. "*Rachel!*" he shouted at her. Still she only hissed at him, backing against the dashboard this time, claws out. Frustrated, angry, he made a lunge again over into the front, but he caught his left foot on the seat back and tripped off balance, veering head first against a solid part of the dash. The air-vent lever slashed a small half-inch gash into his brow and it began to bleed.

Rachel had scurried again against the door; she jumped toward him, hugging him, crying. They stayed there together embraced silently for about a half hour, the car and truck lights passing them randomly along the road. They did not try to talk. When Mark turned and started up the car, Rachel snuggled against him, one hand on his, her head on his right shoulder. He could feel her breathing against him and occasionally could feel her lift her head, turn and study him, although he never looked down. And so they rode that way, as if they were both twelve, and were both in the back seat, and were both aware that one of their parents had the wheel.

But once he had pulled into the parking area and had shut off the lights and had paused a moment, looking straight ahead, and had then reached for the key—Rachel bolted, opened her door, sprinted up the path and stairs and disappeared into a suddenly appearing block of light. Mark felt his throat constrict. He felt the corners of his mouth draw moist. He opened his door and got out and stood, the rented car feeling like a toy beside him. He walked around it to shut her door, and the air felt warmer there. He could still smell salt. Perhaps it was from the dancers' bodies, left there around the grass from generations of afternoons. He watched the punch card of tiny window lights in the building some distance before him. All the time he'd been with her, he had wanted, for some reason, to call his daughter "baby," but he hadn't, and so he said it now to himself in the dark, although, even with his lips moving, he could not quite distinguish it. It sounded, as he caught the word, more like another word, more like "maybe."

ix

Rachel's scent wrapped around the inside of Mark's Nova, moving back in along Route 2, like a membrane or a skin. He tried opening windows, but the fresh air only gave her more breath, and so he rolled them all up again. He could smell her on the collar of his coat too. And on his wrist. When he tried the air conditioner, it gave him chills. He began to think of Heidi. Somewhere in Rachel's scene was the taste and weight of even her dark hair. He stopped at a gas station in Lexington. There were directories in the outdoor phonebooth at the far end of the lot, and he went through them until he found her number in Dover.

He wrote it down. He stared. None of the digits were

familiar. Through the door and hinge cracks from outside he could smell dark puddles of spilled gas. And windshield-wiper fluid. And damp birds. And dry, pulverized leaves. And across the asphalt distance and pumps, seeming almost a perfect painting boxed there behind glass in fluorescent light, he could see the young attendant sitting at the station desk, wearing a baseball cap, reading something. Mark heard his coins, one at a time, drop what sounded a great metallic distance into the phone. He studied the numbers and, again taking them one by one, dialed.

The phone fluttered in some hollow inside and just above his eyes. It rang four times before Heidi answered. Her voice sounded almost too easy, as if it expected somebody that he had never known and could not possibly be. "Hello?" Mark held the receiver of the phone away from his head. He studied the mouthpiece and the receiver, two vented disks, absolutely regular perforations. "Hello? . . ." Her voice changed, tightened. She had never recognized his calls before. Maybe now.

"Where is Dover?" he asked her. He could almost see her draw back slightly, ripple her brow, pause. "Could I smell my way there? I've just been in Gloucester."

"Who is this?" she said.

He waited. "You have the most incredible elbows," he told her. The words escaped. But it was true. He remembered.

"I want you to know that I have this phone monitored," she said exactly, designing each word.

"Heidi . . ."

"Who *is* this?"

Why *was* that? Shit! He had a voice! Other people recognized it. Other people said: "Oh, Mark!" "Mark, hi!" "Hey, Mark!" Christ, and she had *lived* with him. He had found her! Given her blood! They'd had Rachel. They'd been characters in each other's dreams. Fuck! Why had she never, not once, known him when he had called her up? He could hear *her* without even *hearing* her; he could hold the quality of . . . *shit*—Susan would know him. *Three* days, and . . . "The thing about your elbows," he said, "the most amazing thing—is how they join. You can actually feel . . ."

She hung up. He got change from the attendant inside the station and called Susan long distance in New York: "Hi."

"Mark!"

His eyes dimmed. His voice clouded through. God damn! he thought; Jesus Christ, God damn! Amazing! Fantastic, amazing! Three days! Rachel is wrong; she's wrong! "How are you," he asked her.

"Lonely"

"Yeah."

"Are you here?"

"No. No, in Boston. I flew up."

"Should I wait? Up?"

Mark paused. He smelled the gasoline outside again. And the birds.

"Mark? Should—?"

"I'll be . . ." He wasn't sure what he was doing. "I'll be—I'll be . . ."

"Late?"

"Well . . ."

"Another day?"

"Yeah."

"Did you see her?"

"Huh?"

"Did you see your daughter?"

"Oh—yeah."

"How was she?"

"Good."

"It went well?"

"Well, I think. Yeah." Mark found himself struggling, very close to tears.

"Mark, I love you."

That was it. He couldn't answer, couldn't talk.

"Mark? . . ."

(Squeezing it) ". . . Mmm."

"Tomorrow night, then?"

". . . Yeah."

"Thank you, darling."

(Just barely) ". . . Yeah."

They hung up. Mark broke. He made sounds which sounded like small, very bare splashes inside the booth. How the hell had someone like Susan *come* to him? How had he discovered someone that flawless and fine? He looked down at his hands. Why weren't they folded on a shuttle plane headed back? What was he? What was moving him? He was opening the booth door, walking across the oil-stained asphalt toward the station, opening its door, seeing the college-student attendant look up from his desk and asking . . . what? *What* were the words he was saying? He listened: "Do you know . . ." He just barely heard: "Do you know how I would get from here to Dover?" What?

"Dover?"

"Yes." What was happening?

"Mass. or New Hampshire?"

"Mass."

The young man seemed to smile to himself. He took off his baseball cap, got out a map and drew lines. The lines connected Route 2 in Lexington to Dover. Somewhere in

Mark's mind, he felt himself obliged, bound to stay because of the lines. "Should take you twenty to twenty-five minutes," the young man remarked; and short moments later, Mark found himself headed unavoidably south along Route 128.

Dover was dark. It was an unlit town, houses distant from one another, and much of what Mark wove his Nova through seemed old, softened, obscured by trees. What he could see of random houses signaled a feeling of size and of the past. He found Heidi's street. He found her house. It was a small, neat, shingled saltbox set close to the road on a large lot filled with double-trunked oaks, willow and birch. He drove his car several hundred feet past her property, pushed all the buttons down, got out and stood in a dark which was almost tactile with the smell of bone meal and humus.

There was no clear sense or plan of what he intended to do. He could hear Susan. He could see the plums and nectarines in the fine wicker basket on her kitchen table, in the sun. He could feel the light in-the-dark dovetailing of their ribs. There was no *reason* he should be standing here. Where he wanted to be was back on West End Avenue with her. Absolutely no "why." He heard what he thought surely must have been an owl off at some distance to the right, then another—same sort of bird—responding left. He started off, moving behind trees, across Heidi's property, so as to not be apparent scanning her house from the street. It would be messy trying to deal with a vagrancy or attempted-burglary charge. In the nearly complete dark, the thatch of small sticks and fall leaves under his feet made him feel, in part, as if he were hiking across the tops of trees. He began to taste chimney smoke.

The only light that Mark could find on was toward the back of the house. At first, he watched it standing some distance away. He noticed how small all the windows in the house were and how viscous the light, as a result, seemed caught in one. Probably the curtains, he thought—though he was not sure, from where he stood, that there were any. He tried to make out walls, wall*paper*, pictures on walls, sconces, furniture, but the light stayed as thick and adhesive as pudding. So he started, slowly, to move close.

He began to see the smoke, an unsteady dark gray dissolving fast just above the house, ghosting momentarily before it went. And he began to see that there were curtains. They were white and seemed hand-woven and widely gapped. And beyond the wide lace of pattern he began to catch color—blue, soft, antique and, as he moved even closer, eventually, patterned. There was harpsichord music inside too. And he began to hear that. It fused almost inextricably with taste of smoke. Mark had a vision: embers of Bach or Scarlatti glowing quietly on a grate.

At last, he stood just outside the window and looked in. It was a study, or den. Heidi was sitting at a desk, a packet of elastic-wrapped envelopes to her right, typing. She was wearing a blue flowered robe. Her lips moved as she tapped. She looked up and off, picking words, lifting them as if with long fingernails, from somewhere inside her head. Mark watched her eyes—which seemed larger than he remembered them, somehow—drift, float, then pull tight on their strings as she began to type again. Was she writing a novel? Was she setting down the story of their lives?

He watched her skin. Her hands looked older, the knuckles oldest of all. Her neck seemed pretty much the same—maybe, possibly whiter . . . more blue . . . a bit more dry. He thought at first that she had gained weight, but no, that was not true; she hadn't; she was not heavier, not really, no. But something about her . . . He studied her face. Her brow seemed—perhaps it was the drapes and window glass—seemed flatter. There seemed to be a thin coat of wax over it. It had that shine. And her cheekbones seemed to have lost some of their point and spread. And her chin appeared—well, yes—less delicate in its shape. She had not gained weight; no. But she seemed more blunt. That was the precise word for it. Her body too, her shoulders, even her hair, everything seemed just a degree more *blunt*. Mark wondered if that happened to everyone. Had he, as well, blunted in the last fifteen years? He had begun more and more to think of himself, to worry about himself, as *paper*, as one of his own ads—but that wasn't really "blunt." Mark suddenly remembered Heidi stretched out in a New York emergency room twenty years earlier, receiving blood. He became aware that his left hand, tucked in his jacket pocket, fumbled an empty candy wrapper. It made thin, far sounds, not at all like the harpsichord.

He went around the house. He tried the front door. It was unlocked and he went in. The sounds of Heidi's typing and of the harpsichord record, the smell of her fire, took on more body. There was a carpeted stairway immediately opposite the door, and he climbed up it to the rooms above. There were three of them: bathroom, large bedroom, small bedroom. The large bedroom was Heidi's, he imagined; the small Rachel's when she came home for weekends. Mark heard the phone ring downstairs, heard Heidi's typing stop and heard her answer it. As always, she spoke in closed words, softly, and he could not make out what she said. He wondered if Rachel was calling her mother to say her father had visited her that night.

There was an upstairs phone in the large bedroom and

Mark picked it up very carefully and moved it to his ear. The voice on the other end was a man's:

"Why not?"

"I'm doing some typing tonight."

"Something 'crucial'?"

"You're loading the question."

"I'm sorry."

"That's all right."

Neither of them spoke.

"Are you still angry?"

" 'Angry' is your word."

"How come, suddenly, you're a semanticist?"

"Jesus, Richard, I *do* have some autonomy! I'm doing some personal typing tonight, and I just want . . ."

Mark pressed the disconnect button. He took a breath. He felt his neck and forehead warm, and very carefully set the extension back on its base. His eyes coated briefly with a thin film. He pressed his two hands together, palm against palm, setting them perpendicularly against his mouth, pinching with his two forefingers at his upper lip. Finally he brought them down onto his knees and stood. He walked to Heidi's tall antique dresser. Could she hear him moving up here? He opened a bottle of her scent that was sitting there and smelled it. He rescrewed the cap. He opened one of her drawers and set his hand inside. He never looked, but he could feel paisley there—and green cashmere. He walked to her closet door, opened it. He looked in. It smelled like the closet in the room they'd both lived in before they were married. The shelves seemed arranged the same way. He looked for his Levi jacket. He picked up one of her shoes, ran his hand over the toe. He heard a small dish break against the wall downstairs, then another. He smelled the smells of coffee grounds, and oak. He dropped the shoe and crossed over to Rachel's room. He heard Heidi coming up the stairs and hid under the bed.

Heidi threw her shoes against the wall. Mark listened as she swore. He heard rustlings, sounds of her robe moving against her as she crossed over into the bathroom. Then there was water, splashing hard into the sink. He heard the toilet flush, then the water continuing over it, filling in the sink. Then there were washing sounds, cupped water slapping against her face, blown with breath. Mark saw the bluntness of her bones again in his head. He imagined the sink basin coated with a film of wax. He heard her blow her nose, heard the water begin to run out. He heard it suck before silence. Then he looked out and saw her bare feet and ankles in the door.

Heidi had always had the feet of another woman. That hadn't changed. The woman that her feet belonged to lived in Maine. She was of indefinite age, and her husband worked in an ironworks factory, twelve midnight to twelve, and she was perpetually tearing long strands of old pillow-cases and workshirts and red flannel sleepers, all of which she hooked into rugs, flat concentric eggs, dozens of which lay all over her floors. But above the feet, there was Heidi. Mark could hear her crying. That had stayed very much the same; he remembered that. Did she know that he was there? What was she crying about, there at the threshold of her daughter's room? The feet turned and Mark heard Heidi above them moving away. He saw the light in her room go off. He listened to the dark house. He could hear the coals dying, playing Scarlatti in the fireplace below. He looked up at the bedboards and the faintly visible springs just above him. It seemed like only minutes before he fell asleep.

When he woke up and checked the treated and lit dials

and numbers of his watch, it was almost four. He had had no dreams. The house was still. The dark seemed almost weakeningly warm. And the warm smelled like wood. Mark slid out from under the bed, stood, went to Rachel's window and, undoing the catch, very quietly opened it. The cool moved in almost willfully and with unnatural weight. Mark imagined himself bruised by it. He closed the glass and walked across to the door, feeling his shoes there on the sill, just slightly unstable. He thought he could hear Heidi's deep nighttime breathing beyond, past her door, and he moved diagonally across the hall and into her room.

Her particular and recalled taste was there—hair, blankets, her skin. He crossed to her bed and looked down. She was sleeping as he knew she slept, on her side, arms wrapped around a pillow, close, yoking it. Her skin looked tighter in some places, looser in others and all much more yellow in the dark. Mark watched. He watched the bridge of her nose. He noticed one nostril flare. He looked at her temples and at the lines of her neck and jaw. Some of her bones appeared patched, as if sections of them, under the skin, had been shattered in the years between and had had to be replaced. He looked at the blanket, saw her shape. He watched the ripples as she began to stretch a little and turn. He wondered if she was going to wake. He caught himself, both shoes slipped off, hands undoing his tie, and wondered if it was the heat in the house or the fact that he'd slept on the floor under a bed in clothes or what. He picked his shoes up and left.

He tiptoed downstairs. Some coals were still alight behind the livingroom screen. Now, though, they were mute. Mark stared at them awhile. He walked around the livingroom in the dark, touching all the things that she had—figures, wooden chair arms, lamps. He wondered if she had a basement. He heard Rachel talking to him, saw her finger-nails slashing at him in the air, felt the air-vent gash on his head. He saw Susan's margins drawn in the air, heard the sound of pigeon wings, tasted Susan's wrist. He went back upstairs and crawled under Rachel's bed. And once more, very easily, he fell asleep.

Water running again in the sink and the toilet flushing woke him up. Heidi sang. He smiled. He listened to her singing and dressing and to a cardinal summoning warm air outside. What if he lived for months here, he thought, coming and going, moving always in other rooms, sleeping under Rachel's bed? Would she know? He heard Heidi hurrying down the stairs, pans and dishes ringing against surfaces below. He heard her making a phone call, but could not—except for "preliminary"—distinguish any words. He heard the front door shut, heard a car start up, rev, back, rev again, then fade very quickly away. Mark surfaced from under the bed. He undressed, took a bath, dressed again. He went downstairs and made some instant coffee. He drank some juice. He tried his hand at an omelet, read the Boston *Herald*, washed the dishes, left them drying on the drainboard, wrote a note: "Incredible elbows" on her telephone pad and, this time through the cellar door, left.

He did not go straight to Logan Airport.

He spent the morning and early afternoon in Harvard Square, drinking coffee, wandering shops, sketching faces of Susan on a legal pad, considering each, trying to perfect. In the afternoon, he drove out and visited Concord Bridge again. There was a man in monk's robes there, standing immobile with his hands on the bridge rail. Mark watched him and for at least fifteen minutes he did not turn. Finally he broke and moved, looking directly at Mark, saying "Hello." "Hello," Mark said, with a surprised smile. The monk went and stood fully motionless under a large bordering beech, and Mark watched him again. He looked amazingly healthy, like a swimmer or wrestler underneath the robes. Mark wondered about the perfection of his stillness and stance and about the powerful ropelike veins on his shaved head. About five o'clock, he left the man and drove back into the city. He rented an empty room and stood by the single window in it until well after nine, drawing Susan scrupulously on the unwashed glass, on years of dusty film. He thought he saw someone getting stabbed on the narrow and angled street below, but it was instant, and he could not tell. When he left, he went and drank wine and ate eggplant in an Italian grill. A woman with a bearded older man in one of the candled booths looked somewhat like Rachel or Heidi. He thought he tasted Susan in the oregano. His forehead bruise hurt and he decided to leave his tortoni. He went and paid his car-rental bill at the airport. His shuttle back to New York, unlike his strange unpeopled flight before, was almost full. He swept the near-midnight sky with a convention-bound delegation of Shriners from Ayer, Watertown, Concord: towns representing the Greater Boston area.

From his back seat in the limousine from the airport, Mark could see nothing of his driver. Mark guessed that he was a dark man with dark hair. The wheels made no sound. There were only the lit figures of the meter ticking, mounting their increase. There was no wind. Yet the car seemed bodiless, a moving frame of the night. There seemed as well to be the smell of the sea, perhaps from Rockport, perhaps from the room he had rented near the Boston wharves. Or maybe it was just the cemeteries, stretching oceanlike over the city beyond.

Mark asked to be let off a halfblock from Susan's apartment, at the corner. There was no sound, no answer, but the car stopped with his request and the fare tray folded back for him. He put his money in, saw it disappear, saw the tray fold out again with change. He left the change for whoever it was that had driven him and stepped out onto the street corner, breathing deep. He thought somehow that the city might have vanished, slipped away, but it was there; he could see and feel it. It moved around him totally appropriate to the hour. He could smell cantaloupe, crushed by truck tires earlier in the day somewhere on the street. And somewhere too, not very far away, someone must have been grinding coffee. A very tall, pantsuited girl, with what looked like a black leopard on a leash, passed him and headed north. He remembered Rachel, across from him at The Fin and Claw picking at her scallops, saying, "That's why you can't sustain anything." He remembered a lamp in Heidi's house.

He turned and began slowly—he might even have said weightlessly—toward Susan's. There were still children running up and down building steps. The TVs and radios from the surrounding tiers of rooms seemed almost to harmonize: news broadcasts, commentators all pitched at slight perfect intervals. He was hearing the war report in barbershop. And the children, climbing and circling around the stoops, were all firing guns. He pictured a 21-inch boxed quartet of Eric Sevareid, Walter Cronkite, Roger Mudd and Charles Kuralt, all in striped red coats and straw hats, singing the death count, "Mortar fi-i-re!" A whole note, held. He watched a child trip and fall just in front of his feet. He caught a sudden image of Susan's comments in the margins about strength: "*I have always looked for strength*," underlined.

The light in her building lobby glowed slightly, offwhite —a pale violet, perhaps green. And the simulated marble took on the motion of its designs and swirled. It made the rust-colored carpet seem to pulse, to throb softly like an organ, perhaps a heart. And within all of this, the rows of brass-plated mailboxes seemed to grow ominous. Behind each one, from where Mark stood strangely still and looked, there seemed to open up an ever-widening tunnel, leading to a cavern, leading . . . ? Mark remembered Susan's temples, where they seemed, almost, to indent. He remembered her tongue against his neck. He remembered the fishman, cleaver held high, on 125th Street. He remembered Susan's . . . S. Weiss's . . . *Susan's* calves on the back of his legs. He remembered her laugh. He remembered Rachel against his coat. He remembered Heidi, sleeping with her pillow, and her patched blunt bones. He remembered the other, earlier Heidi, standing once in the rain on the George Washington Bridge saying, "Something's gone." He shut his eyes.

The building guard, who had been swaying in his maroon uniform in a lobby chair where he slept, rose and moved toward Mark.

"Are you all right, sir?"

Mark didn't open his eyes. Why wasn't he just moving straight? Why wasn't he just crossing to the elevator and going up?

"Are you looking for someone?"

He pressed his lids tightly against his upper cheekbones. Susan was listening to mandolin music. He knew that.

"Sir?"

"I'm . . ." He unlocked his eyes. "I'll be fine," he said to the man. "I'll be fine." Then he turned and left. He stood outside the building motionless another minute, feeling the guard's eyes on his back, before he loosely began to drift back up the street, east to Broadway.

He started down. He stopped at a cigar stand and called Susan: "Hi."

"Are you back?"

Something large, spherical, slightly rank, started a slow, interfering rotation in his head. His bruise throbbed. "I'm sorry—what?"

"From Boston?"

"Oh . . ."

"Mark? . . ."

"No. Not quite back."

"Are you at Logan?"

He did not understand where his words began. "Yes."

"I want you *here*."

"Yes. I want . . . I want to be . . . there. I do."

"I've bought us some Riesling, and some incredible Camembert!"

"Wonderful." The spinning ball started up again, faster.

"Are you coming? I mean, right away? . . . Mark?"

". . . Yes. I think so."

"Do you have your ticket?"

"Yes."

"I'll wait up."

"Well . . ."

"I will. I *want* to. I'll listen to some Telemann and some Purcell. Trumpets. Perfect! Maybe I'll even get acquainted with Camus. . . . Am I teasing, Mark? Do you think I'm teasing?"

"I . . ."

"I may be a little silly when you get here. If I start in on the wine. But I promise . . . I promise, darling, I'll be good."

"Susan?"

"Yes?"

"Susan, do you know how perfect you are? Do you know how goddamned perfect?"

"Well . . ." Her voice had pleasure in it.

"Do you know what that does to me?"

". . . I don't know."

"And do you know what that . . ."

"What?"

". . . Nothing."

". . . I'll be here. . . . Will it be—what—about an hour and a half?"

". . . Yeah. I guess so."

"Everything go well?"

"What?"

"In Boston?"

"Pretty well. Yeah."

"Hurry."

"Yes."

"I love you."

"I . . ." His throat closed.

"I know. . . . I know. I hate airports too. . . . Soon."

"Yeah."

"Bye."

He hung up. The ball slowed its turning. His lips were almost withered, dry. He ran his tongue over them, swallowed, dropped another dime in and called Jan. An unfamiliar male voice answered.

"Is Jan there?"

"Right." The voice made no move in any way to give up the phone.

"Can I speak with her?"

"Right."

"Please."

"Who's calling?"

Mark hung up. He sat without any physical organization in the booth. He smelled sea again—*saw* it, sea awash with objects: pried-open crates, oilcans, plastic dolls. He tried again. This time it was Jan. Her voice was light, had a slight helium music.

"Who was that?"

"His name is Tank."

"Tank?"

"Tank. Can you understand me? I'm rather stoned. High-quality stuff. Where are you?"

"In a tobacco store."

"Will we ever be together again? Will you ever come back?"

Mark's jaw opened but seemed to lock. The opening only lubricated the spinning of the ball. "I don't . . . Probably not."

"I see."

"Where did Tank come from?"

"Excuse me?"

"Tank. Where did he come from?"

"Wherever Tanks come from." She laughed.

Mark found himself, once again, nearly crying. He started raking his free hand heavily through his hair. "Why are you stoned? Why do you need to *do* that? Jan! . . . I don't—!"

"You're the Phantom Sculptor, *aren't* you?"

"Yes."

"I *knew* it. . . . Oh! Oh, and Mark?"

"Yes?"

"I didn't die in the bed." She hung up.

Mark waited to see if she might not pick up the phone again, but the disconnect sounded, the sound drilling, making his eyebrows fuzz. He let his own receiver down. He stretched his head back, felt the cords of his neck pull tight and long. There were spider nests in each of the four upward corners of the booth. He dropped his head down again, shut his eyes, pressed his fingers hard against the lids. In his head, it seemed, the phone began to ring. Eyes shut, he groped for it and picked it up again. "Hello." "Hello." "Is Gloria there?" "Gloria?" "Yeah." "No." "O.K. Thanks." "G'bye." He hung up. He let his hand down, opened his eyes. Had the phone really rung? Had he answered it? Did someone really ask for Gloria? Goddamn it, Christ! Why wasn't he on West End Avenue with Susan?

He wandered down Broadway until it pressed out and became Times Square. He walked in curves. There were circles spreading, in to outside his head. He felt a centrifuge. He could sense small words starting at the exact center of his skull and whipping and whirling out, adding loops and syllables: "can," "canto," "cantata," "incantation," "incantatory," "incantatorium," flung out on and on, circling, spun finally against some rim; wherever concentrations of color and light were most intense. He found—with the syllables—his body thrown, swirled too. Car lights sweeping by pulled him repeatedly into the street. He'd find himself pressed against neon scribblings in store windows, head stretched up under still-ablaze marquees, trying to spin out his blood to some invisible hoop of filaments beyond.

Everything grew liquid, like wine. He kept hearing Susan, uptown, calling him. "Hurry! Hurry," she said, arranging the avocados on her window sill. He felt the reflections from the centers of hubcaps sucking him toward their rush. Had he sustained some sort of permanent injury from the Nova's air vent? He set a hand against his head. Had something been dislocated in the football game? The hand which he'd cut more than a week before with the chainsaw began, almost unbearably, to throb.

There was a parking meter beside him and he grabbed it tightly with both hands and squeezed. Nearly an hour dropped out and the red "Violation" flag went up. The centrifuge in and outside of him seemed to shrink again, to become contained. He took his hands from the meter and stood straight. It was silly. He would have coffee. He would taxi to Susan's. They would live out the journal of their life together and be very vulnerable and glad. No . . . no, not the *journal* of their life, their *life*; there was a difference; their *life*, live *that* out. Their *life*? Their *lives*? Which? Wasn't that what he and Jan—? He and Heidi—? He squeezed the meter again, strangled it until the red flag disappeared and nearly an hour and a half showed as increase.

There was a Howard Johnson's across the square and he walked there, taking tiny steps to be sure of steadiness and direction. He had, he supposed, underestimated the blow given his middle in the football game. Still, he kept well-based, grounded and straight. Before he entered the restaurant, he looked up, trying to find some sky, only to see himself way above the square, his shoulders glowing in an old Coppertone ad, half ripped down now that it was fall. He thought that his chest bones looked pared. He couldn't begin to understand the expression on his face. Had they touched it up? What had he been thinking about at the time? It seemed momentarily that all the lights in Times

Square were flashing, flashbulbs popping off all around to hold and capture him. He moved in.

Inside, there were cutout Mother Goose characters on every wall, every surface and plane; menus, mirrors, dividers. He hated the two colors he saw everywhere, aqua and orange, but he sat at the counter and ordered himself a cup of coffee black. On one side of him was a skeletally thin, fiftyish man with small knuckles and enormous rings. On the other was a woman in a gray goat-colored false fur. The man was pressing, perhaps drunk, trying very hard to banter. "How do you make it last?" he leaned right and shouted. Mark could almost feel the man's breath on his eyes.

"What?"

"How do you make it last?"

Mark leaned back, looked for another stool. There was none.

"Make what last?" The woman had blue scars on her face.

"How—? A *marriage*. How do you—?"

"I don't know." She turned and giggled at the girl beyond her.

Mark's coffee came. He picked his spoon up and felt some cartilage start to swell in his throat.

"Come on! How?"

Mark saw the man's jaw hanging beside him like a hook. Was someone screaming inside? He found a piece of bone in his cup. "Could I have another cup of coffee, please?"

"*Sure* you do."

"No."

"Come on. How do you—?"

"*Tell* us."

They were closing in, playing a net game. The Piemen on

the mirrors started throwing pie plates at Humpty Dumpty's shell.

"O.K. *I'll* ask, 'How do you make it last? How do you make a marriage last?' And *you* say, 'We don't know. How *do* you make a marriage last?' O.K.?"

"O.K."

Mother Hubbard's dog grabbed hold of her ankle and was refusing to let go. She was screaming, shrieking. There was blood. She was jabbing at him with Little Boy Blue's pitchfork.

"Could I have that coffee to go, please?" Mark almost shouted.

"What?"

"How do you make a marriage last?"

"*To go! To go!* Could I have that coffee, please, *to go?*"

"Sure. Christ, calm down."

"We don't know. How *do* you make a marriage last?"

"Make everyone else first!"

Everyone started to laugh: the girls, the waitress, Humpty Dumpty, Little Miss Muffet, her Spider, the Piemen, their Pies, the Clam Chowder, the Bar-B-Q Beef, the Fudge Ripple, the Banana Chip. Mark threw a dollar on the counter, grabbed his cardboard container and ran out. He ran for a halfblock before he slowed, stopped, leaned against a building and brought a free index finger to his forehead, touching his scab. He would take the coffee immediately to Susan's. They would drink it together. They would share it with their wine and cheese. He stuck his hand out for a cab.

The cab that finally stopped looked as if it had been tie-dyed. The driver was long-haired. He wore a choker and a Nehru jacket.

"Where to, man?"

"937 West End Avenue."

"Yeah, I can dig that." He started the meter up. But as they pulled from the curb, Mark, looking up, saw an enormous new billboard, obviously unfinished. It was made from logs or log facing, something like pecky cedar, only darker. In the upper left-hand corner there was the start of something like a thatched roof. Mark imagined an ad for something like The Tiki Hut, some Polynesian restaurant or chain. But, at the moment, except for the logs, it was almost blank. And there was scaffolding set up, all in front of them. Mark felt the weight of the sketch pad in his pocket. "I'll get out here!" he said.

"Here?"

"Here."

"But we've gone only forty feet, man."

"That's all right." Mark reached for his wallet.

"O.K. If you dig a forty-foot ride, it's all right with—"

"No! No. No, wait a minute! Take me to Grand Central! Grand Central Station!" He was excited.

The cabbie pulled over, turned around. "O.K., now . . ."

"Grand Central! I'm sure."

"Not the Statue of Liberty?"

"Grand Central."

"Not the Empire State?"

"No. Grand Central."

"You're not trying to rip me off or anything?"

"Grand Central."

"O.K., I can dig Grand Central if it's cool. Is it cool?"

"Sure. Right."

"Beautiful."

Mark drew an enormous breath. His heart was driving; his eyes were wide and absolutely clear. *How fantastic,* he thought. *How fantastic! When Susan saw that!*

The cabbie turned around and started singing: "We're going to Grand Central, Grand Central, Grand Central. We're going to Grand Central, aaand . . . we ain't goin' nowhere else." He pulled out and made the first corner east.

Mark unlocked his locker and drew out the green bag with its saw. He looked at the shoes underneath, more than a dozen pairs. He looked at the ties and the ten suits above. He glanced at the three other lockers, which he knew to be filled with shirts, sweaters, coats, underwear, socks, ties, ascots, vests, scarves, bottles of cologne, cufflinks, tiepins, watchbands. He shut the locker door slowly. There was something nice, unpretentious, anatomical, in the sound of its metal clacking and sliding into lock position. Mark took the four locker keys that he had lived by and with for almost seven years and threw them into a trashbin on his way out.

He jogged back to Times Square and found the place. The log billboard stood atop a corner building and he would have to get to the roof to approach. It seemed, as he explored around, that the sole access to the building, primarily an office building, was through a Chinese restaurant at the front, Ton Wah's, on the corner of Fifty-second Street, which was closed and locked. He walked down an alleyway at the building's side, passed an old man who was having a whore against the bitten bricks. All Mark could really see was her red hair and her one hand as she beckoned him over the unconscious and groaning man's shoulder. But he moved on.

At the back he found two doors, one locked fast and tight, the other only bolted inside with a chain. He threw himself hard into the door several times and the chain gave, as, he suspected, it had previously done several times. He slipped in, quietly shut the door behind him and stood. The staleness in the air was so strong it seemed like loud sound. He waited. He let the bag drop, a shroud sheath, from his saw. It made no sound as it hit the floor, and although Mark could not see it, he knew there rose up a timecloud of dust. He could smell two-hundred-year-old eggrolls, and char ding from the thirteenth century B.C.

He started to explore the dark, gradually to move front. Flecks of red and violet inside his vision peopled the dimness for a while and then real shapes occurred. There was a banister, a hall. Ahead he could see restaurant tables; to his right a door to the restaurant kitchen. Mark kept his right-hand fingers on the saw's starter cord the whole time. He crossed the restaurant, moved step by step into its lobby, then found the entry hall. There were stairs which rose from it and he started backing up them. Something in the shadows he had passed through had made him apprehensive and unsure. Each step he backed up had its own half-wheeze, half-whistle sound; it was like climbing the carcass of a calliope. Then, suddenly, he knew what it had been in the unlit restaurant below that had unnerved him.

There was a rustle, the chained ring of a metal collar, a great deep-throated growl, the sound of toenails on linoleum and then a lunge. A huge black shepherd caught Mark on the ankle and tore, ripped at him savagely. Mark pulled and started the saw. There was a snort and yipe and whining retreat. It had caught the dog on the snout, perhaps, nothing very serious. The beast stayed below, alternating savage salivating growls with meek whines. Mark backed hurriedly up the stairs. At the top was a door. He reached behind himself, grabbed the knob, opened it, backed through and shut it, closing the space. He turned off the saw, heard the dog bounding up the stairs, lunging at the door, ripping against its woodgrain with his claws. Mark hurried the six flights to the roof.

When he stood at last on the building top, at the foot of the scaffolding, he felt, in a strange way, amazed. All the spiraling lights, the wine-like lights, stopped their motion, stayed, held their image, held a city-beauty still and motionless for him for a moment to see, invest, catch completely. It was the arrest of something fine, the capture of it. For perhaps three minutes, despite the bleeding tooth cuts on his right ankle, New York City was a kind of art, was the best night-Manhattan it could expect to be. There were lights beyond lights, buildings beyond buildings, rivers beyond rivers, edges beyond edges, lives beyond lives. And there was no substitute for that. Only the best worked any more and was redemptive. Crystals worked, capsules, distillates, stopped intensities, life without scars of motion, question marks rising straight and exclamatory, proud perfect unwithdrawn statements in the margins: only the best could ever work, only the best—he found himself nodding in agreement with the best, the best after-midnight Manhattan—things had to be the best or it was all wasted and mad: two-dimensional as a razorblade ad. You had to live a Camus journal or an O'Neill play.

So he began, hand over hand, the chainsaw slung over his left shoulder, starting up the scaffold of thick pipes. The city became a transistor radio, a meek box broadcasting sound, scratching tin music distances away. Mark looked behind him once, dizzied, but resumed his climb. He could see that the darkwood surface, the simulated logfronting now before him, would be easy to work on. The billboard lights flashing on and off all around the square made the pipes he moved up and through seem in motion, seem somewhat liquid and plastic.

Mark undid the buckle of his pants belt, then fastened himself, relocking it, to a pipe. He faced his canvas. He wondered if he was high enough; he would rather work down than up; *no*; no, though it would be easier to work down, it would clearly be *better* to work up, ascend. He would start where he was with Susan Weiss's chin. When he finished—when he drew the final line, made the final rounding, in however much time it took him—he would finish with the crown of her head. He loosed the chainsaw, fastened its strap as well to his belt, steadied himself against the scaffolding pipes, gave the starter cord two or three sharp pulls until it buzzed fiercely on and then began.

Give her a strong chin, Mark thought. "I have always looked for strength," she had written, and she had it and he would show it to her; he would give her that. He touched the spinning sawblade to the wood surfacing lightly, gently, and the dark pulverized and cut pieces flew away with the cuts like viscous dust into the hazy mid-New York night air. He moved his arms slowly, slowly shaping, drawing, making lines, turning them where he should. People in the square below began to look up at the sound, began to see the dark billboard take on brief line and shape.

Mark moved his belt along the pipe, first left, then right, getting the chin, focusing it, defining it as he thought it should and must be done. When he had done all he could reach, he unfastened his buckle again and climbed up again another four or five feet. Here he reclamped himself, reclamped and restarted the saw. He continued the chin. He gave it rise. He caught the slight, unbalanced cleft in it. He started in on the lips.

Should she smile? She *did*. She smiled and laughed. Often —with him. But is that what should be set down? Is that what should exist, remain, stand for her, be shown? Was that her meaning? What . . . what had it *first* been? Before he had seen her, how did he see her; how had she been that first afternoon in the Strand when he'd first looked into the margins of that book? He shut his eyes to see her. His head seemed to tip first to one side, then the other. It was . . . it was . . . not a face, not a face which *told*, which telegraphed, which *sent*. It requested, *required*. It awaited watching. It held out a question, an expectation, and waited to see if the watcher, the viewer, the witness would, *could* possibly meet the expectation. It put the burden of being on *you*. On *me*, Mark thought. You—*I*—had to live up to what that face *hoped* for. And that was *it*. That was how it must be. He started once more to carve, draw. The lips must be just so slightly apart, waiting, hoping, seeing, not resolving. And the rest will be very much in the brow and eyes. Mark had never drawn her quite that way on the pad earlier, but he knew the sketches there had just been preparation for what he was realizing now. People were doing more than glancing up now, below. They were gathering in groups, standing still, studying. Mark's cuts descended to them with the sound and vision of dispersing vanishing swarms of light white insects.

He moved left. He moved right. He moved left, right and center again, retouching. He unhitched himself and moved up. Now there were cheeks to do. Now there was that strange crease between her upper lip and nose. And the nose as well, trying to do that. Mark had no awareness of the cars converging on the Times Square area, a number of which spun red or blue blinkers on their roofs. He had no ear for the sirens which they spun out as well. He could only hear his own blade. And he could hear Susan speaking to him, from the Camus: "Why not 'exceptional'?" about herself; and from the journal of their own short life together: "What I notice most about myself at such moments —is that I breathe." There was too, under the singing drive of the saw, the music of thousands of eave and loft pigeons who, Susan had said, in their journal, most owned the city. And when the first floodlight swung and crossed and struck against the billboard from the street below, it seemed no different from the bulbs of ads, his own suntan ad included, around him everywhere.

Crowds swelled below. It was nearly like New Year's Eve. Thousands stood, many of them blocking the traffic in the streets, watching the puppetlike figure high above them complete the nose, unhitch himself, climb yet higher to begin work on the eyes, reattach himself again. And there was a unison gasp when they saw him reach again for the chainsaw, pull its cord to start it, accidentally drop the saw, have the weight of it, strapped to his belt, pull him from the pipes so that his feet dangled and he had no footing. But the belt held and they all saw him scramble back up, climb into position, pull at the cord once again, start it up and begin to add lines to the growing carved drawing of Susan's face, a drawing which stood now, from chin to lower eyes, nearly fifteen feet.

He did not hear the cars with the two-way radios arrive. He was not aware that the falling sawdust, which seemed to glitter and give off sparks, was now caught in the sweep and swing of positioned white and blue floods. Both his arms ached. Water almost spilled from his skin. He looked intense and malleable in the long sways of light. From certain angles, it looked as if he *himself* were changing shape—had perhaps strapped himself to a lathe; or set his own wax figure up against the direct, hot police light. His arms grew, stretched. His neck took on a fine tautness. The center line of his back became, at once, more delicate and strong. His eyes, had anyone below been able to see them, deepened in color, took on more aquatic clarity. It was even in the smell and taste of his tears.

He continued to move: left, right, back again, more center, up a bit, down, touching up, adding, shaping. Each of her eyes was nearly bigger than his entire frame. He created, stared, then suddenly, surprisingly, was an image in *her* eye, was being *watched* by *her*, felt all her expectation there, hoping: her need to be completed, retouched, rounded perfectly. "Making": so that's what it all finally meant! He was *making* her. He was a man making his woman. Fantastic! *How do you make it? How do you make it last? Make all the others first.* No! No, the man in Howard Johnson's had been wrong: "Make her best!" Yes! "Make her best!" And now he was giving her touches of hair: left, right. Another touch again on the eye, the brow, a line of lash, down to catch something neglected on the bridge of her nose.

Words broadcast now through the air, words which he barely heard. He could sense question marks rising up like curled balloons through the air, but thought they were his own and didn't really hear the words, words like "Authorization?" "Identification?" If they reached him at all, they were only cut into syllables—"ri," "za"—and then into letters and then only small strokes and lines by his saw, all vertical, all leaving a residue of, if anything, only lift. He unhitched his belt. He needed more height. There was just the brow and crown of the head and hair to finish off. Then Susan would be best. She would reign best. She would make everyone in the city sad and strong at the same time. She would make tie salesmen, subway conductors, snipers, pancake-house waitresses, pretzel vendors—*all* vulnerable. He rose up, found footing, refastened his belt and began the brow. Shoulders and back strained and bent, ignorant of bullhorns and warnings, he carved on.

Fire equipment arrived, ambulances. Sirens uncoiled like berserk wire, snarling, converging in and above the square. Pickpockets wound the crowd for easy looting. Whores sold quick, standing dryhumps for five dollars. Pushers with shoeshine boxes vended soft drugs. One segment of the crowd began to chant, "Jump." More lights swung onto Mark, holding him in a ragged iris. One more last barking through a bullhorn rumbled up, was trimmed into lines and syllables. Mark didn't hear, didn't know. He worked only to finish. Each line, he knew, must be select, be rightly placed, be the most deft. He moved left along a pipe, catching a slight left-hand upswing in her brow. One gunshot spit itself out.

It was impossible to tell whether the shot came from a police officer or not, but with its sound, with its initial clear report, others followed from all points. It was a free-for-all, almost as if an entire population had been in wait. From all points, from unidentifiable sources, an incredible volley of shooting bloomed, bullets passing sawdust, in an explosively lit midair.

Mark heard the fire, concentrated more his selections, moved left to right to make them. He felt a sharp bite in his upper back and then, almost simultaneously, at the right side of his neck. Almost everything, for an instant, seemed to go red, turn ablaze. Yet he moved, arms aching, spreading himself across his work, adding, touching—crown, hair. Then, in a violent rush, he could hold center, hold his focus, no more. His head spun out. His vision uncoiled. The worst elements of the centrifuge took over. He swayed. He experienced chills.

There were, though, a few thankful residues of control.

He undid the saw and let it drop. There were screams and scatterings below, but the firings did not stop. They continued peppering the air. He undid his belt and began to fumble his way down the pipes. Small fragments of hard metal rang off the metal piping, setting up an overlap of ringing—an alarm system beyond anger; one gone mad. He misstepped and fell and caught himself around pipes with his wickedly sore underarms until, almost impossibly, he dropped back onto the roof. His eyes blurred and stung. He felt as if the roof pebbles had been plastered into them.

There was a whine in Mark's head, a sound like wind moaning through branches. He got up. He moved to the door beyond which stairs led down. He opened it: more sounds, something like pebbles, surf. He started down. Then he heard the black shepherd snarling at others who were trying to get up. There was a very loud shot. All the moaning, all the wind-whining dwindled to a slip of sound, tiny, a scrap of paper, its edge barely catching the wind. Someone had killed the dog, and Mark could hear them, hear a lot of them all beginning to clatter up.

He went to the roof again and looked around. His vision had scratches on it, scratches and chips. There were still crowds, swarms, below; and he could see them clustered, a square full of humming berries far beneath. If he jumped, he wondered, would anyone catch him? Would Susan be there—with pillows? Would Rachel—with a net of hair? He moved back from the edge to shut them out, then across toward adjoining rooflines. He staggered. He heard drumbeats growing on stairs. His shoulder felt as if it had a half-inch metal rod jammed through it. What if Heidi had found him under Rachel's bed, he wondered suddenly, would she have given him blood? But that made no sense. The footbeats grew. Mark looked across to the next roof. It wasn't that far. It was a reasonable span. Or maybe if he thought about it hard enough, mind over matter, he could simply make himself light, float up out of reach. Out of *shot?* His eyebrows seemed to burst, sprout suddenly, thick as jungle fern. They clawed his eyes. He strained beyond them, struggled, tried violently to see through.

And he saw . . . what? A man? Yes. Another man. There was another man on the next roof and he was—was he?—yes again: signaling. The man had a too large suit on and he was signaling, waving his arms. The man kept—without speaking, without sound—kept gathering his arms in, gathering them in, as a signal, again and again. Had he seen the drawing? Had he been below? Did he know about Susan? About their margins and journal? The whites of the man's eyes seemed remarkably large, silver white, almost metallic. His arms circled, circled again and pulled—no word, no sound, no explanation, just the draw, his gathering. Mark heard voices now, joining the drums, only a flight or two below. If he were simply shot or apprehended on the roof, what would Susan write about that in her margins? How would it fit within her comments about strength? *Waiting for arrest on a Times Square rooftop denies the strength of flight;* Mark saw it written in Susan's, in S. Weiss's, hand-writing in the western margins of the sky. He began a slow trot starting about thirty feet from the roof's edge. He gathered pace. He hit one foot off the edge of the roof—and flew.

The air between the two buildings felt cool. It felt watery and chlorinated like a pool. Mark saw the man, the gatherer, arms out, through swimming goggles, and he wrenched himself: swam, stroked his arms, scissored his feet and moved through the night-pool of resistant air *to* him. And the man grew. His bones remained thin. His anatomy held in dark clusters. But his height and the metallic whitesilver of his eyes rushed to enlarge.

He was grabbed. The man's amazingly strong arms and hands *had* him and pulled him back onto the other roof. There were short, dark chimney shapes, like large checkers, everywhere. And small moving shapes. Mark thought he heard grinding teeth. Still the man said no word, only took hold of his sleeve, led him through a door, down four flights of unlit stairs, through another door, into a bed and tabled room, where he opened a closet door and led Mark in. The man put a finger to his lips, shone his two eyes at Mark as if they were beams of inspecting light, then closed the door.

Mark stood alone in the small, dark closet. Why had he come? Why had he let the man lead him, or assumed him a friend? A smell like wood dust, like chainsawed cedar, deepened around him. Mark imagined himself holding a woman's shoe. He began to smell citrus fruit, felt the shoe change into orange peels in his hand. He heard Susan's pen, saw her script, smiled. He thought he felt her dark hair, heard her sleeping sounds somewhere—where? Beside? Above? Material, clothes of some sort, hung lightly around him. They felt like loose, ragged cocoons, like garments of cheesecloth. He had the sensation of the closet having loosed itself; of it, sometime after the man's closing of the door, having begun slowly to drift up, free from all studs and nails. It seemed somewhere past the room now, a sleepy balloon dozing up a shaft, never bumping the walls until, gaining speed, it had left the building and now rose through the New York night air. He imagined the eyes of the man below beaming two parallel lines of light up. Were they what buoyed him, what supported him in this case?

For the first time, he considered the sudden back and

neck pain that had loosed him from his scaffold work. It had felt like a sudden jab, a pointed branch, a hard stick. Something had passed through just under his skin. Something had penetrated him; in, then out. He had been shot. He was wounded. He placed his right hand on his lower neck where the ache stayed on. It was sticky, viscous; some blood still leaked, but much had already begun to congeal. He touched himself with his other hand on his upper back. His suit was damp there, sticky and diffused. It was hard to tell about his equilibrium or vision there in the dark.

He listened. He could hear nothing outside, not even the sound of bedsprings turned upon. His sensation of motion, though, intensified; the closet took on an awful velocity. He felt it whisk past the branches of trees, thud against large aerial birds, mangle clouds. It began to orbit the earth. In a matter of hurried seconds, he became—and he wondered how Susan would record this in her margins—became successively: probe, relay station, obsolete piece of hardware.

"Hardware." He thought about the word for a moment. He took it apart, divided it, set the syllables at right angles to each other, examined fragments of it: "draw," "are," "hard." The pieces of cheesecloth hanging around him felt shredded. "Shredded pieces of hardware." What was "shredded hardware"? What did that mean? What was his mind doing with him, anyway? Where had the word "hardware" first come up? Who'd said it first? Who? He was the only one! Where? . . . And who was he?

Who was he? He should know that. A person should know who he was. Wait a minute; wait a minute; he knew who he was; any person should know that; just wait a minute. But who? Something. Something about . . . lines, a saw. Something about the ocean and a pier. Maine. Was he in Maine? Was he a lumberjack living in Maine and this was his dream? It felt very much like that. O.K. O.K., if that was true, if that was true, then what was his name?

The door opened. There was an aqueous sense of gray. A hand took hold of him, led him across a space. Very softly, the hand pushed him down, was joined by another hand moving him into position, taking off his jacket and shirt, laying him out. Mark couldn't really see anything, just general shape-invaded gray. There were sounds of sheeting being ripped. He smelled vinegar. It smelled like the basement of somebody's house. It smelled like a burnt-out fuse. Or like a toilet-bowl cleaner. Or certain stretches of shore. Mark felt the approach of heat, nearly scalding on his back and neck. His head burst red, then violet, then white. There was an explosion of flowers, blooms like jonquils tickling the inside of his mind. "Mark!" That was his name! Then he knew very specifically, or didn't know with equal specificity, where he was. How much time had elapsed?

Without words, the man finished dressing his wounds, put something like a dry shirt on his back, led him again to the door, down three more flights and to the building's front door. Mark felt the man pat him on his good shoulder, saw the door open for him. "Thanks," he said. The word made his head turn again; it was the first word he had said in over three hours. The man patted him, took strong, manly hold of his upper left arm.

Beyond the archway, Mark could see only darkly blocked color and shape. Something had happened to his eyes. There were no lines in his vision any more, just color texture and shape. He had a rough sense of space, but none of distance. The bullet must have hit a nerve, struck or pared or sliced some sort of central nerve which determined

lines in his sight. Perhaps it was just temporary; perhaps as
the wounds on his back and neck healed, his sight would
restore too. He felt the dark man's hand applying pressure
to him, moving him decisively through the door and out.
Mark felt for the hand, took and shook it, then felt his way,
step by step, down to the sidewalk and the street.

There were mostly only drifters, junkies and the poor
dying old in the area now. A sense of stale rankness pressed
out from the hearts of the square's short hotels. Mark
headed east. Within two blocks, almost a dozen dogs converged and sniffed at him, as if they understood that he
needed some animal sight as a lead. Still he could not see
lines. He followed green circles, green lighted shapes, crossing what he concluded to be streets. If there was much
sound of traffic at all, it was only haunted and far. Mark
had no idea what time it was, only that it must be some hour
at the far edges of both day and night.

Yet, despite his fumbling sense of time, his groping sense
of seeing anything like a line, his head felt extraordinarily
good. The centrifuge that had existed in it for hours—or
was it days, a year?—was completely gone. He could feel
the rim of his skull, the perimetrical casing, sure and strong:
hardboned, almost metallic, alloyed, concrete-reinforced in
its strength. Yet it was not heavy. It was free, mobile,
flexible. He could tilt it left or right and feel it, know that
it was there, understand the direction that it inclined in. He
thought that it must shine for others on the street like
buffed chrome, buffed chrome with fiercely strong mirrors
inside.

"Do you need help?"

The voice belonged to a man. Mark judged the man to
be about forty. He could see the man's general shape and
sort of charcoal-brown color, about his own size and build.

"I don't think so." His voice sounded as if it had scraps of tinfoil in it.

"Can you see?"

"Partly."

"You came fairly close to that car."

"It came fairly close to me." The tinfoil scraps discharged with his words.

"O.K." The shape began to drift away, fade.

"*Oh!*"

"What?"

"How close to the river am I? I thought I could smell . . ."

"Pretty close. About two blocks. Stop when you get to it. Don't walk in."

Mark laughed. There was an amazing pleasure in meeting a stranger with a sense of humor at this point of outland time and territory. "No. Thanks. I won't. *Oh*—and is there a telephone booth where I'm headed? In that direction. Toward the river?"

"There's a place—not in the next block—but in the block after that. It's an all-night place. Coffee—short-order. I think there's a phone in there."

"Thanks."

"So long."

"So long."

Mark walked the next block, waited for the green disk of light, the tiny emeraldish moon, to appear, crossed and moved slowly along the next. The river was clear to him now, direct and sharp. He could smell its motion. He could smell the wind on it, turning it, churning the offal, eddying it in angered patterns, almost spitting its own drifting crust. Yet, in the motion and agitation which he could smell, Mark could also sense a hard pride. The river after all. And it seemed never to forget that. And as dank and acrid as its surface was forced by the neglect of others to be, it could not lose the smell of river; *that's* what it was first; that's what it was in its depth, its currents and its motion. It was River, River which fed into a body which, despite the clutter and slime of its estuaries, was and would be for a great time the Sea.

Mark found the faded lights, then the glass fronting, then finally the door to the twenty-four-hour sandwich shop. "Do you have a telephone?"

"You blind?" The voice belonged to a white shape that Mark could just barely make out. It sounded as if it came from a tape recorder behind a closed door.

"Well . . . yes, partly."

"Oh. Sorry. Against the wall. The right wall. No. To your left. To your left. In front of you. There."

"Thanks."

"Sure. Can I set you up anything while you're calling?"

"Yes. Coffee, please."

"Sure enough."

Mark reached for his wallet, which he suddenly realized was in a dark-man's room with his jacket, and his Camus in a building somewhere off Times Square. He did still have some change in the pockets of his pants. He found what felt like a dime. "Is this a dime?" he asked the white shape.

"A penny."

He felt around again. "This?"

"Yeah."

He dropped the dime in and dialed Susan's number, having to feel and count the proper digit each time.

"Mark?"

"Yes."

"Are you in New York?"

"Yes."

"Are you all right?"

"I think so."

"God, they announced a shuttle crash from Boston an hour and a half ago. I was sure. I was so sure. Oh, Jesus-God! I've smashed every piece of china and glass that I have, that I owned. I was so sure. Everything breakable I broke. Just broke and broke and broke and broke until there just wasn't anything left to break. I thought . . . I thought, Well, God, my life is rubble now. Now it's rubble, isn't it? And so, and so, and so I just might as well make that, make it clear. Break! Break! Everyone complained. People called. The super came up. The police came. They almost hauled me off. Oh, Jesus, you're safe."

"I'm sorry."

"Are you near?"

"Am I—?"

"Near?"

"Well . . ."

"Are you coming right up?"

"I'm sorry . . ."

"No. That's all *right* now."

"No—that I caused you pain."

"It's only because I love you."

"I know. I know; I love you."

"*Do* you?"

"Yes."

"God, I didn't think anyone ever would."

"Thousands must have."

"Hardly."

"Yes: 'heartily.' "

"No. I said, 'hardly.' "

"I'll keep my version."

"Oh—you're safe."

"Yes. Pretty much."

"Oh, Mark!"

"Can you recycle all that stuff?"

"All my refuse, you mean?"

"Yeah."

"Sure. You just get here—and it'll be recycled. Good as new. *I'm* recycled."

"Are you?"

"Yes. Come!"

"Susan? Listen, I love you."

"Oh, I know!"

"I mean, in a very extraordinary way."

"Thank you."

"A very—well, *perfect* way."

"You're beautiful!"

"No, *you. You* are. That's the point."

"Hurry."

"I won't . . ."

"Won't what?"

"Have it broken. Erased. Crossed out."

"No."

"That would be wrong."

"I know."

"It's so . . ."

"It *is*. Yes."

"So goddamn, goddamn right." Mark was weeping.

"Then hurry."

"But, but to hurry . . ."

"What?"

"I'm . . ."

"What?"

"Susan, it's the best. It's the best. We're the best. We're the best 'us' we can ever be right now."

"I now, darling, please . . ."

"Well, then . . ."

"What?"

"I did something."

"What?"

"Tonight I did a very fine thing."

"What was it?"

"In the *Times* . . ."

"The where? The *Times*?"

"In the *Times* tomorrow—look. Or if not tomorrow the next day. Better still . . . better still, tomorrow take some time and go over to Times Square. Go there and look up!"

"If you take me."

"The *Times* or Times Square. Look up. Look."

"What did you—?"

"You'll . . . you'll just be very, very proud. You'll feel timeless. You'll feel strong."

"Darling, hurry . . ."

"Look."

He hung up. He stood at the phone for several minutes running his left hand around the nicked box of it. Though he could not really see through them, his eyes smarted. His lips and cheeks felt beaten and swollen. His shoulders ached. He lived by deep breaths, holding them nearly impossible lengths, finally letting them out.

"Say, listen; this coffee's cooling."

"Thanks," Mark said in the wrong direction, turned and felt his way to the counter. He could smell the coffee, bad, but coffee; he could sense the heatwaves rising up, oscillating the air above it.

"Your woman?" the dim-voiced, now closer white shape asked.

"Pardon?" Mark had one fist wrapped around a sugar shaker.

"On the phone. Your woman?"

"Oh. Yes. Yes, my woman. Yes." He released his fist. With a finger he felt the polygonal glass.

"Anything else?" the shape asked him.

"I think I'm fine," Mark said.

He could feel his blood circling horizontally through his temples and vertically up through his crown and neck—like pictures of atoms he had seen. From a fissure somewhere in the shop, he could smell the river, sense the river of one name joining the river of another and that uniting with a third, and all of them moving around an island called Manhattan. He sensed the wind as well, through whatever same small crack, looping down from the sky on a counterclockwise design, passing along the streets, then sweeping up into an unknown height of sky—only to be recycled, and recycled then again. He took a sip of his coffee and began, with quite incredible precision, to repeat from memory, starting on the inside cover, repeat the margins of their book.

The following New Year's, it was difficult to move in Times Square, hard to turn. There was a great deal of light but no wind, a great many city birds but all under eaves. Shortly before midnight, a fire broke out in a roast-chestnut cart. People screamed. Someone mistakenly poured brandy on the flames. A woman's leopard coat nearly caught. Two college students sprayed the fire out with quarts of beer. The vendor dumped the cart over on its side in the street, and someone urinated on the coals. At midnight the ball fell. People cheered and went home, the fur collars on their coats smelling like distilled smoke.

Out from this, at the eastern river edge of the mid-Seventies, Mark Eliot sat once more drinking coffee. His sight was essentially unchanged. He was getting along on residuals from his ads, sleeping nights in a small square room where he could smell the wind all the way from Avenue A. He looked either older or younger; it was really impossible to say, to determine anything in him but change. He drank his coffee slowly. He was not aware of the hour. He imagined Susan Weiss cutting dates, making patterns on the kitchen table with the stones. He saw her filling now the margins of someone like Chekhov, maybe Tolstoy. He re-memorized the journals of their life together—he and S. Weiss's—adding margins to his margins to his margins to their margins, feeling an almost total satisfaction as it all grew and moved out. A frail woman in her late thirties at the far end of the counter stared, magnetized by Mark, drawn. She was a woman who worked at the print shop at the Metropolitan Museum of Art and she saw him as an almost perfect Edward Hopper. When he left, she followed him toward the river.

A Note on the Type

This book was set on the Linotype in Janson, a recutting made direct from type cast from matrices long thought to have been made by the Dutchman Anton Janson, who was a practicing type founder in Leipzig during the years 1668–87. However, it has been conclusively demonstrated that these types are actually the work of Nicholas Kis (1650–1702), a Hungarian, who most probably learned his trade from the master Dutch type founder Dirk Voskens. The type is an excellent example of the influential and sturdy Dutch types that prevailed in England up to the time William Caslon developed his own incomparable designs from them.

Composed, printed and bound by
The Haddon Craftsmen, Scranton, Pa.

Typography and binding design by Andrea Clark